The Ripple Kingdom

Gigi D.G.

First Second
New York

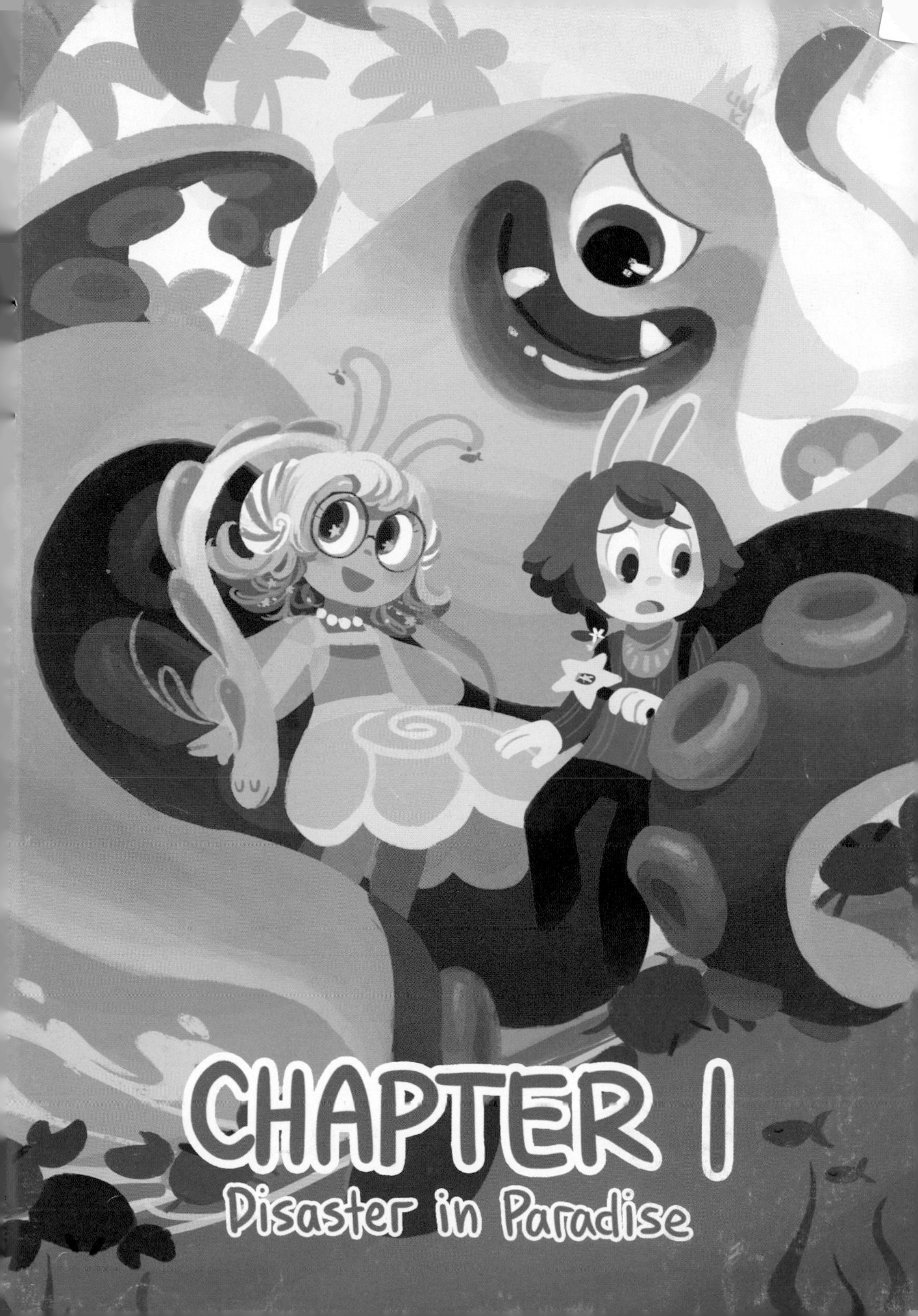
CHAPTER 1
Disaster in Paradise

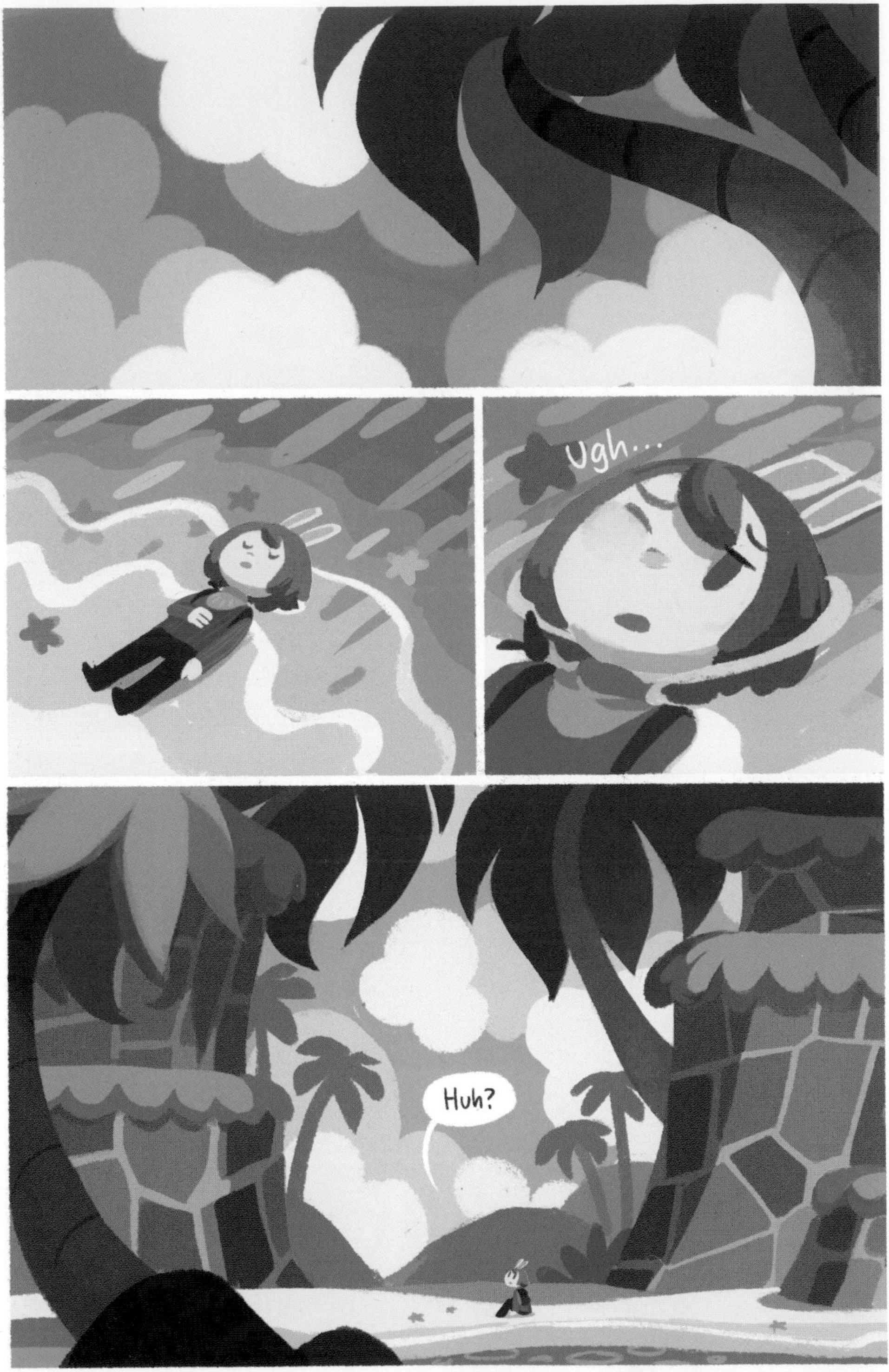
Ugh...
Huh?

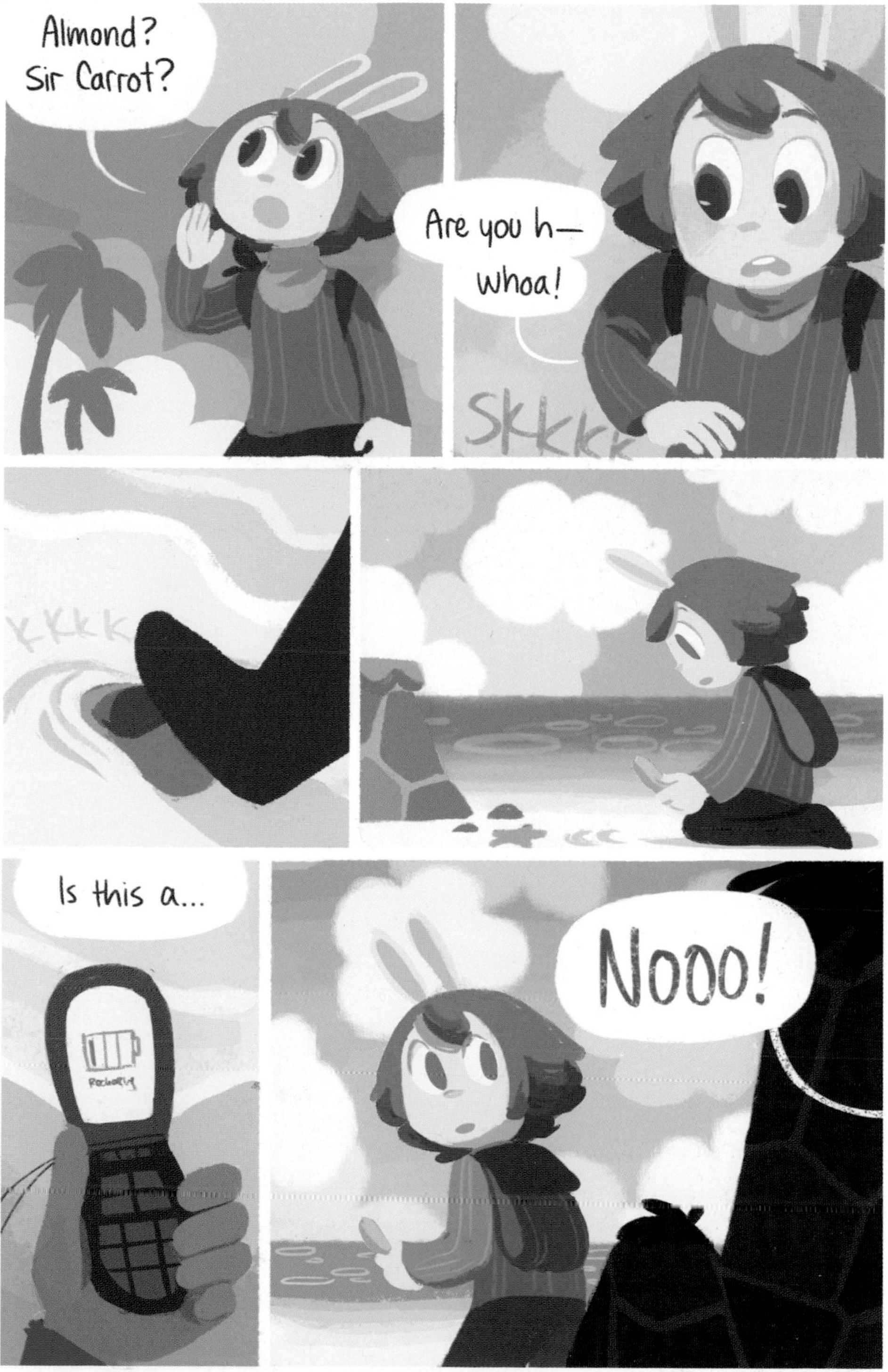
Almond? Sir Carrot?
Are you h—
whoa!
SKKKK
KKKK
Is this a...
Nooo!

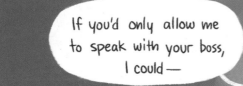

4

But I'm —

And you know what happens to kids what don't got reservations?

They get a clippin', see?

Yeah! A clippin'!

Yeah!

A clippin'!

Yeah!

Yeah!

Yeah!

clip

clip snip

clip

clip

clack

snip

EEEK! Nooo, don't! I just got this dress!

clack

clip

clip

clip

clack

clip

clack

clip

Someone — anyone, HELP!!

Hey!

You should, um...

You should stop that!

What's **your** problem, kid?

well i just

um

Tongue-tied, eh?
Clip him, boys!

Uh-oh!

scuttle scuttle scuttle scuttle scuttle scuttle scuttle

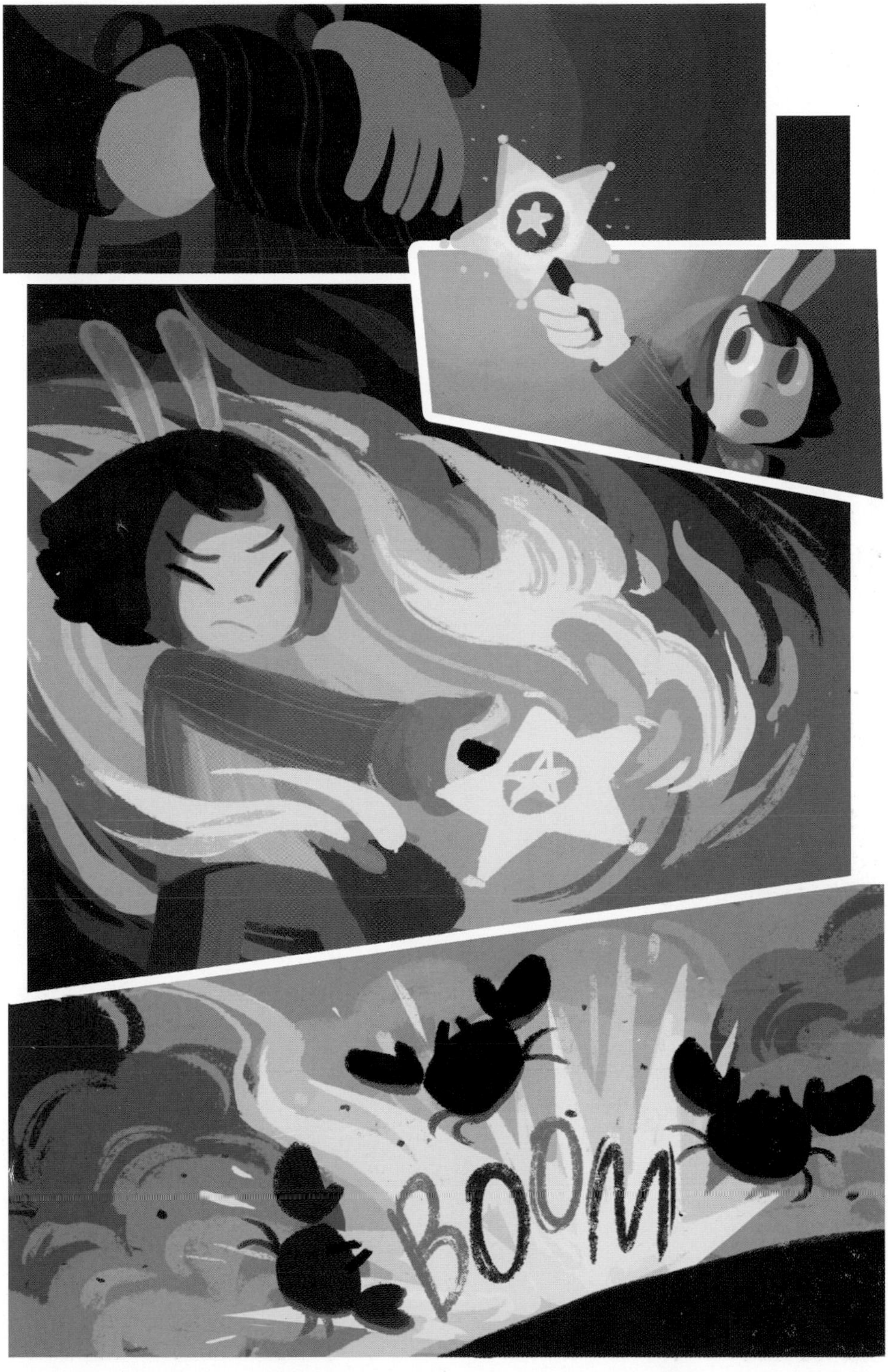
BOOM

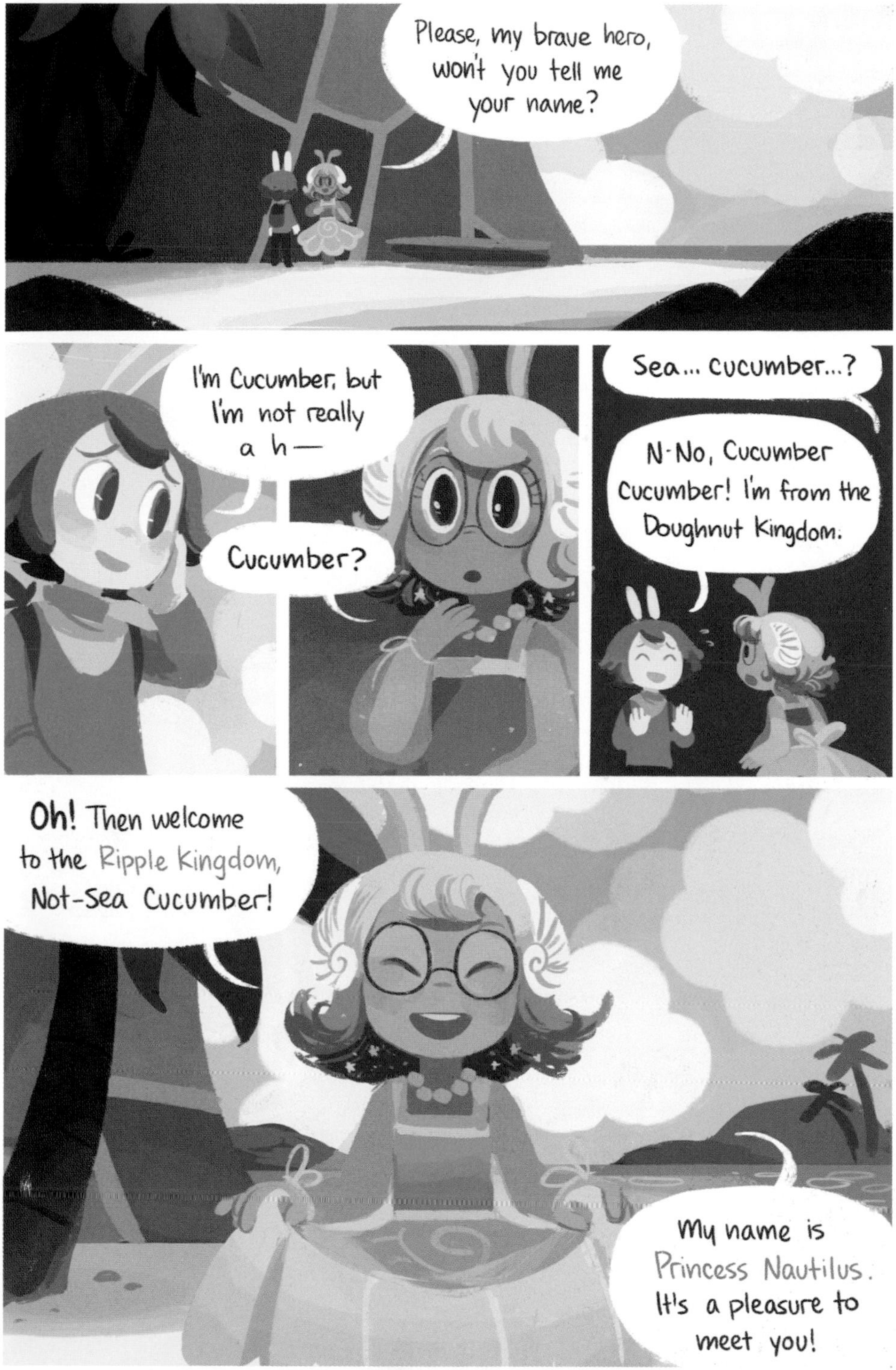
Please, my brave hero, won't you tell me your name?
I'm Cucumber, but I'm not really a h—
Cucumber?
Sea... cucumber...?
N-No, Cucumber Cucumber! I'm from the Doughnut Kingdom.
Oh! Then welcome to the Ripple Kingdom, Not-Sea Cucumber!
My name is Princess Nautilus. It's a pleasure to meet you!

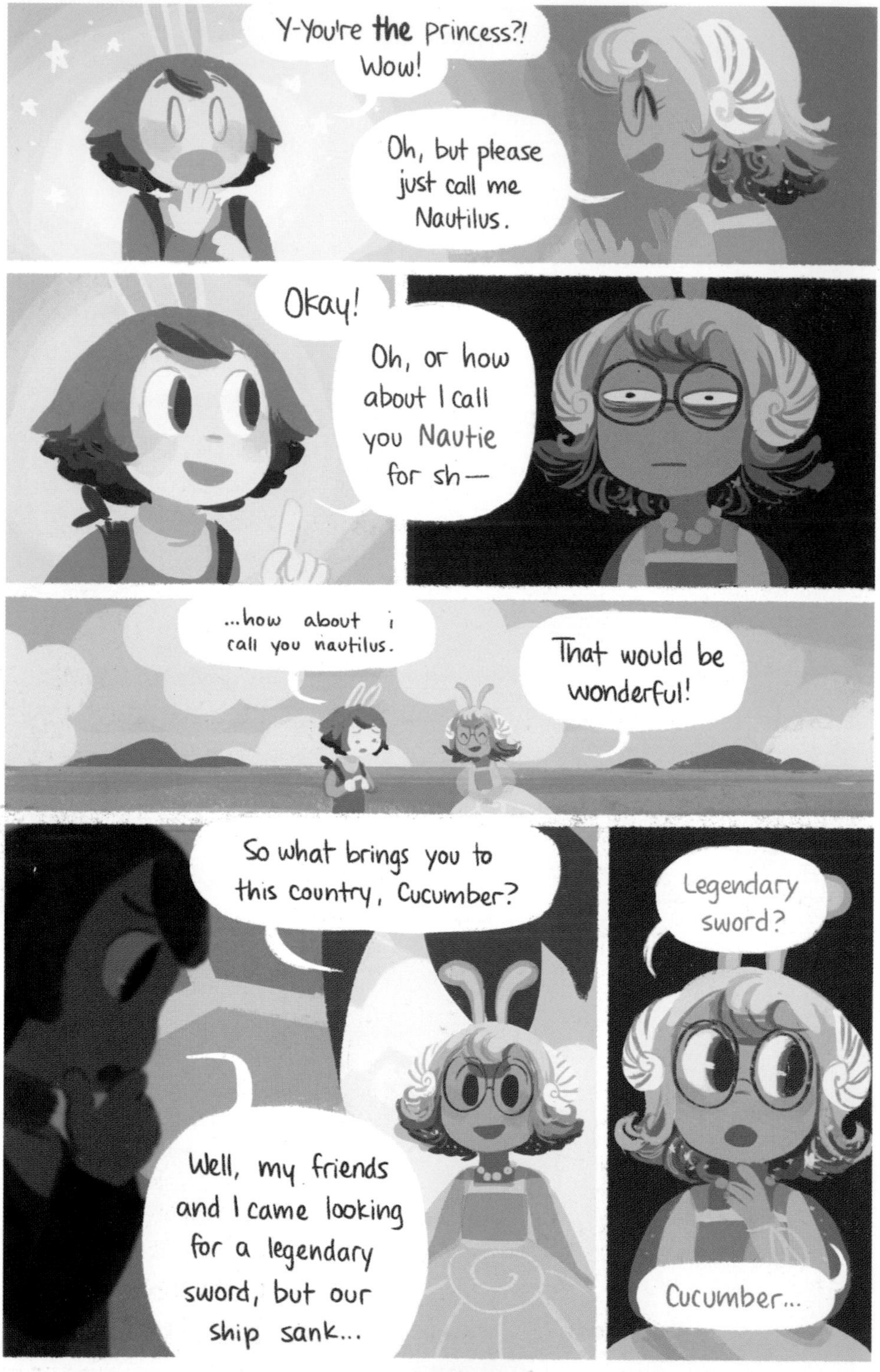

Y-You're **the** princess?! Wow!
Oh, but please just call me Nautilus.
Okay!
Oh, or how about I call you Nautie for sh—
...how about i call you nautilus.
That would be wonderful!
So what brings you to this country, Cucumber?
Well, my friends and I came looking for a legendary sword, but our ship sank...
Legendary sword?
Cucumber...

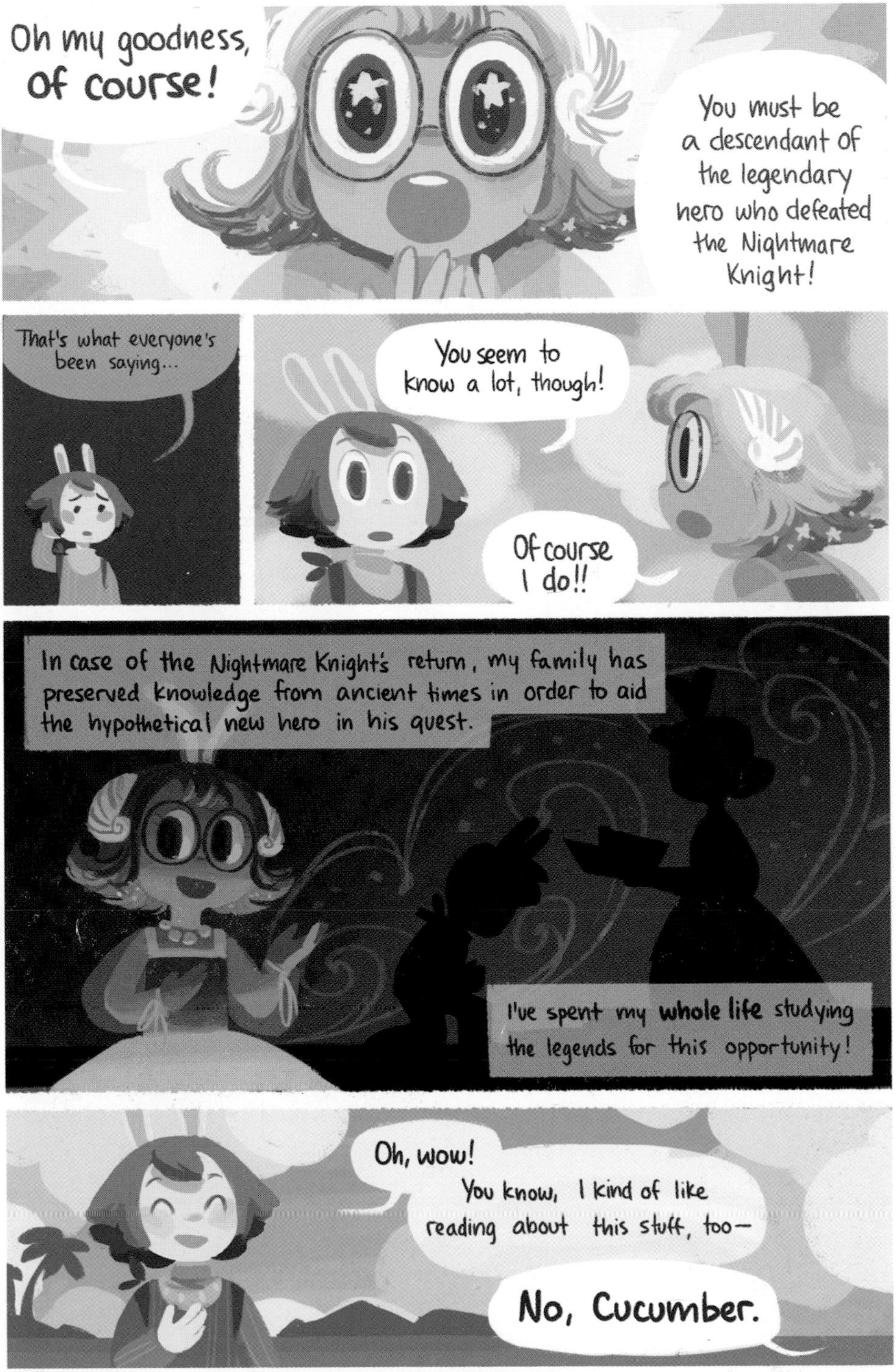
Oh my goodness, **of course!**
You must be a descendant of the legendary hero who defeated the Nightmare Knight!
That's what everyone's been saying...
You seem to know a lot, though!
Of course I do!!
In case of the Nightmare Knight's return, my family has preserved knowledge from ancient times in order to aid the hypothetical new hero in his quest.
I've spent my **whole life** studying the legends for this opportunity!
Oh, wow!
You know, I kind of like reading about this stuff, too—
No, Cucumber.

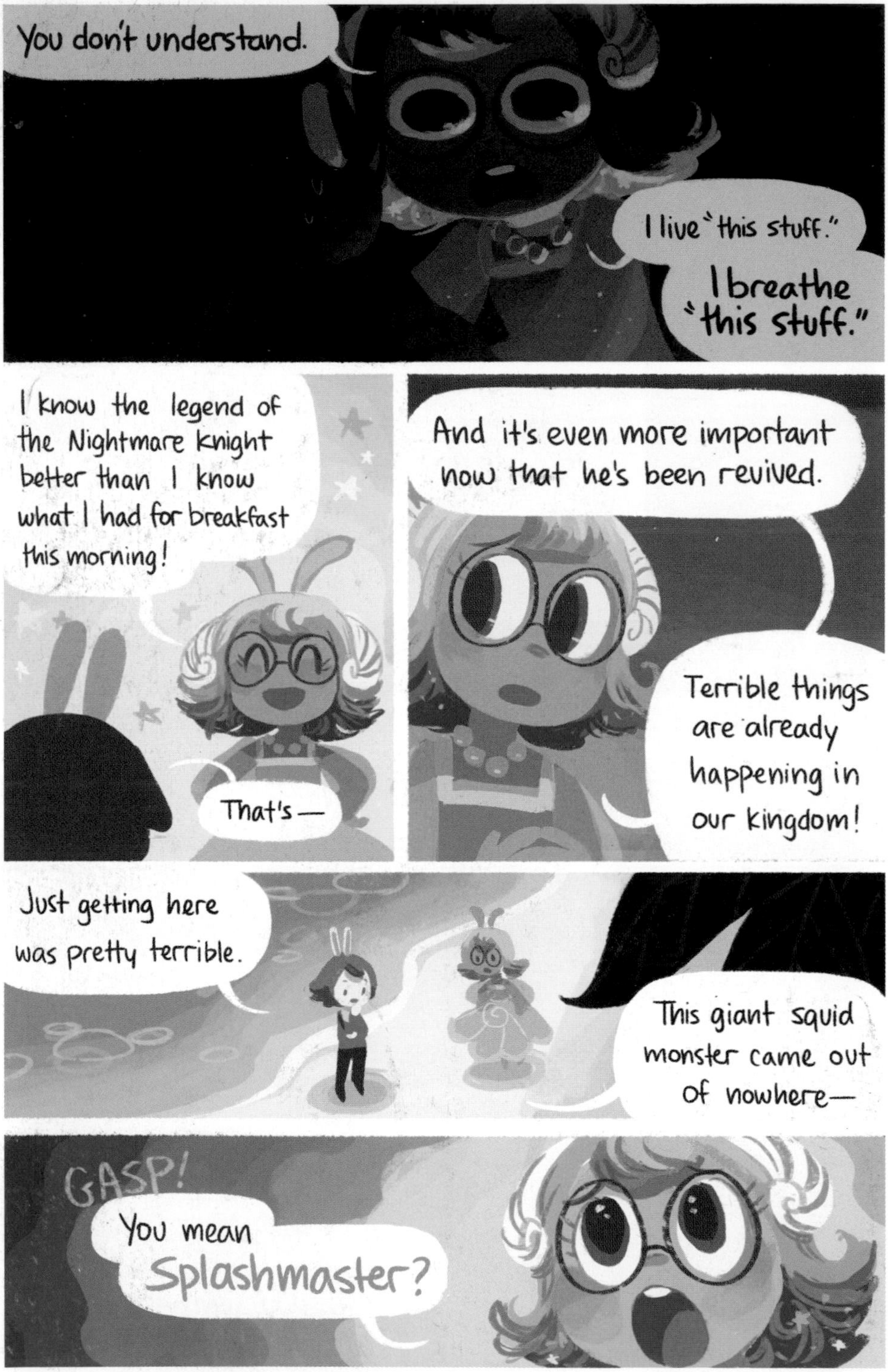
You don't understand.
I live "this stuff."
I breathe "this stuff."
I know the legend of the Nightmare Knight better than I know what I had for breakfast this morning!
That's—
And it's even more important now that he's been revived.
Terrible things are already happening in our kingdom!
Just getting here was pretty terrible.
This giant squid monster came out of nowhere—
GASP!
You mean Splashmaster?

Huh?

That's that horrible thing's name!

He's one of the Disaster Masters!

...Huh?

Y... You mean nobody's told you yet?!

ehehe ehe ehehehehehehe hehehe

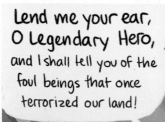

Lend me your ear, O Legendary Hero, and I shall tell you of the foul beings that once terrorized our land!

For such is my second-greatest duty as princess of the Ripple kingdom!

What's the first—

Shh! All things in due time, Hero! My gosh!!

I'm sorry!

ahem

Many, many years ago...

The seven kingdoms of Dreamside lived in peace and harmony.

But one day, the Nightmare Knight appeared to shatter that peace.

With his great and terrible power...

he cast our world into an age of darkness that threatened to last forever.

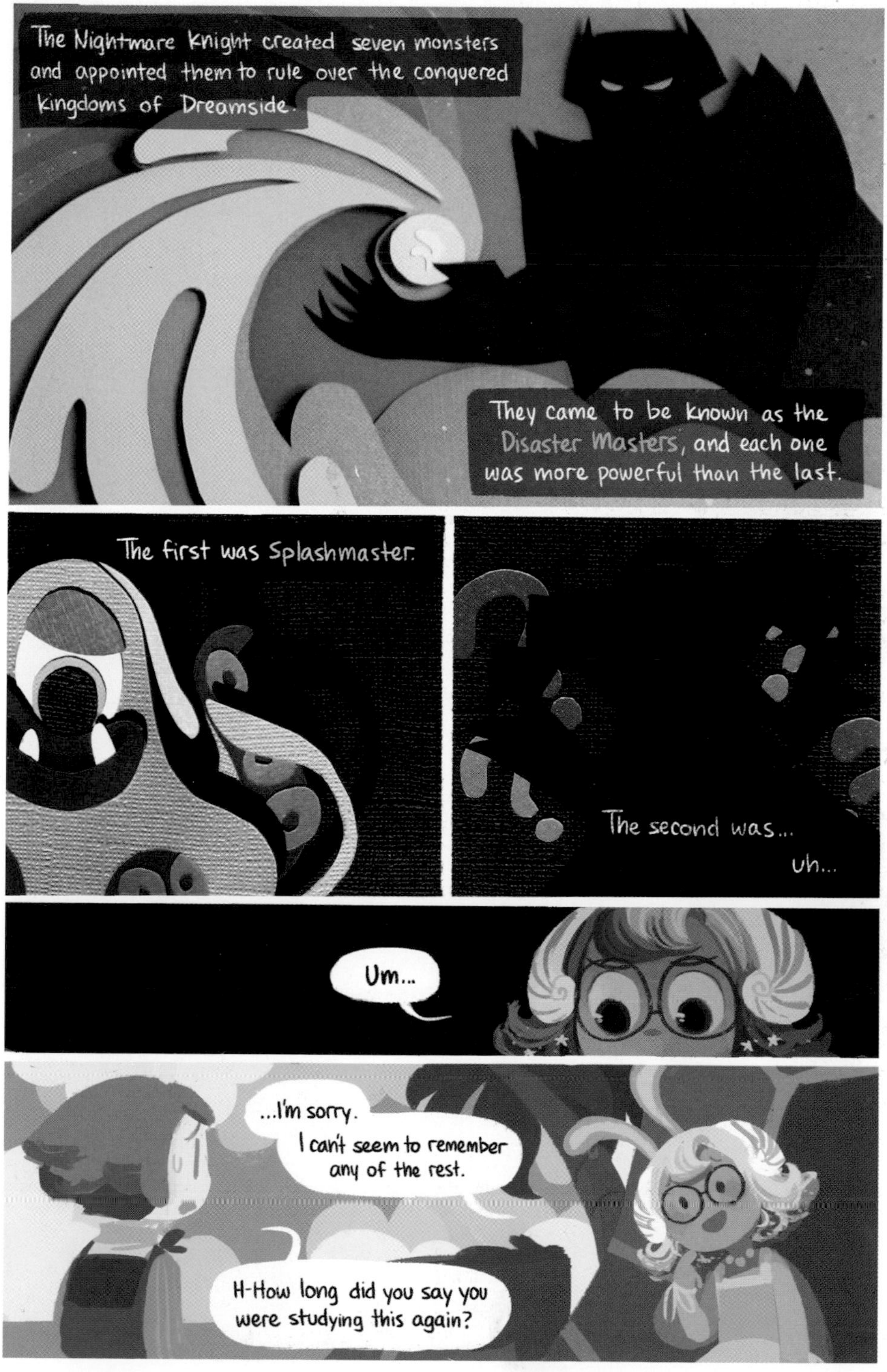
The Nightmare Knight created seven monsters and appointed them to rule over the conquered kingdoms of Dreamside.
They came to be known as the Disaster Masters, and each one was more powerful than the last.
The first was Splashmaster.
The second was...
uh...
Um...
...I'm sorry.
I can't seem to remember any of the rest.
H-How long did you say you were studying this again?

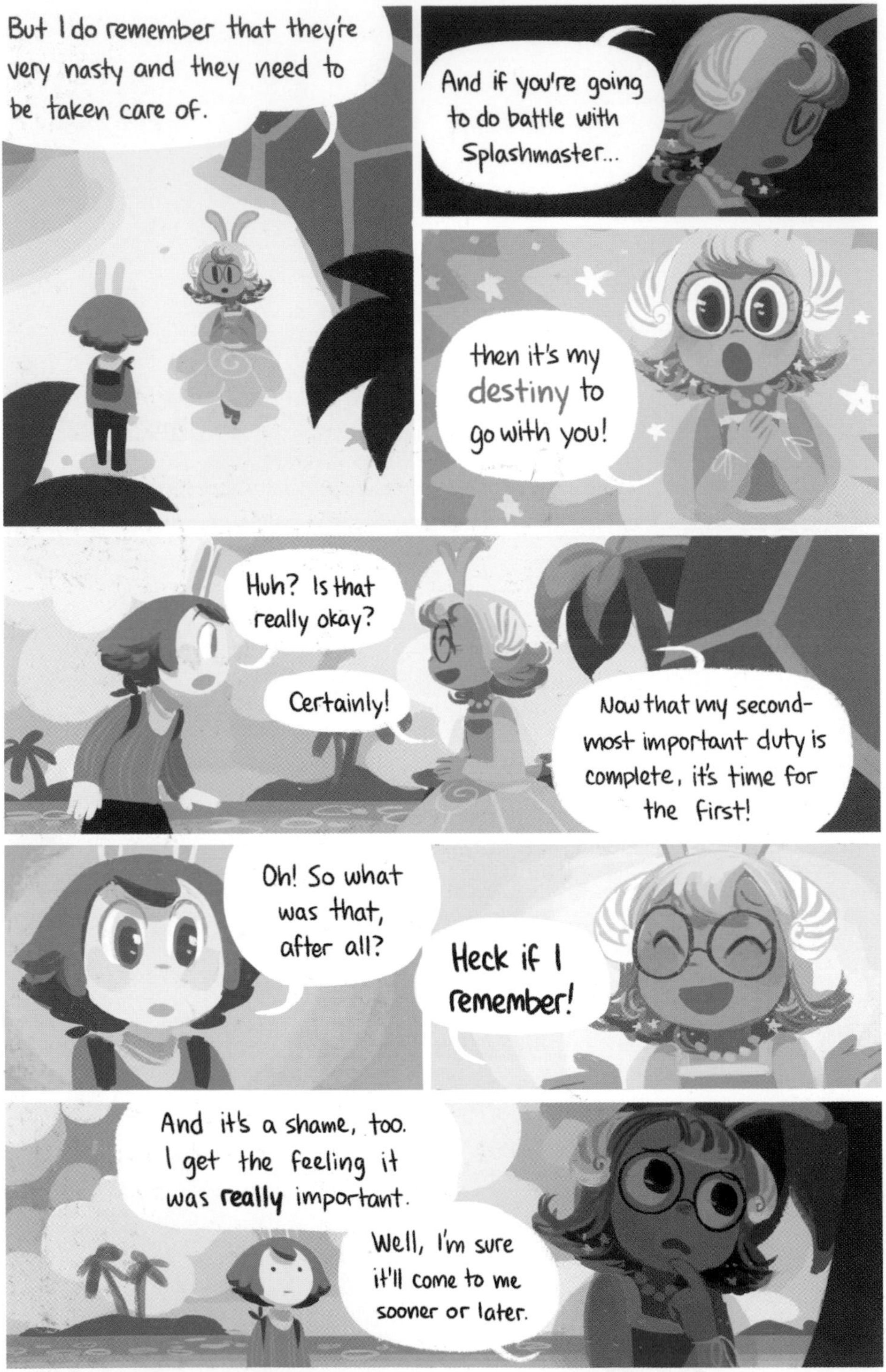
But I do remember that they're very nasty and they need to be taken care of.
And if you're going to do battle with Splashmaster...
then it's my destiny to go with you!
Huh? Is that really okay?
Certainly!
Now that my second-most important duty is complete, it's time for the first!
Oh! So what was that, after all?
Heck if I remember!
And it's a shame, too. I get the feeling it was **really** important.
Well, I'm sure it'll come to me sooner or later.

Oh, but first!

I hate to ask for your help again so soon, but there's something I'm looking for.

What's that?

I'm sure you've noticed, but this area is home to the Crabsters.

Just that way is the Crabster Resort.

The owner is a friend of mine, and I know he'll be able to help me get back home...

but the guards you saw earlier don't believe I'm really the princess, so they won't let me in.

Luckily, I've been trained in the royal art of summoning.

but when I washed ashore here, I lost my Royal Instrument of Summoning, and I can't seem to find it anywhere.

Oh, that's too bad.

If I can just call my familiar, that **should** be all the proof I need...

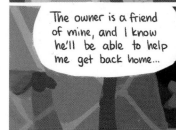

Well, I don't know anything about your summoning thing...

...but I did find this cell phone.

Maybe we can use it to call for hel—

GASP

That's it!!

My Royal Instrument of Summoning!

Th-This? But it's a cell pho—

YOINK

It's not a **cell phone**, Cucumber.

It's a **Royal Instrument of Summoning** that's been passed down through my **family** for **generations**.

i'm sorry.

21

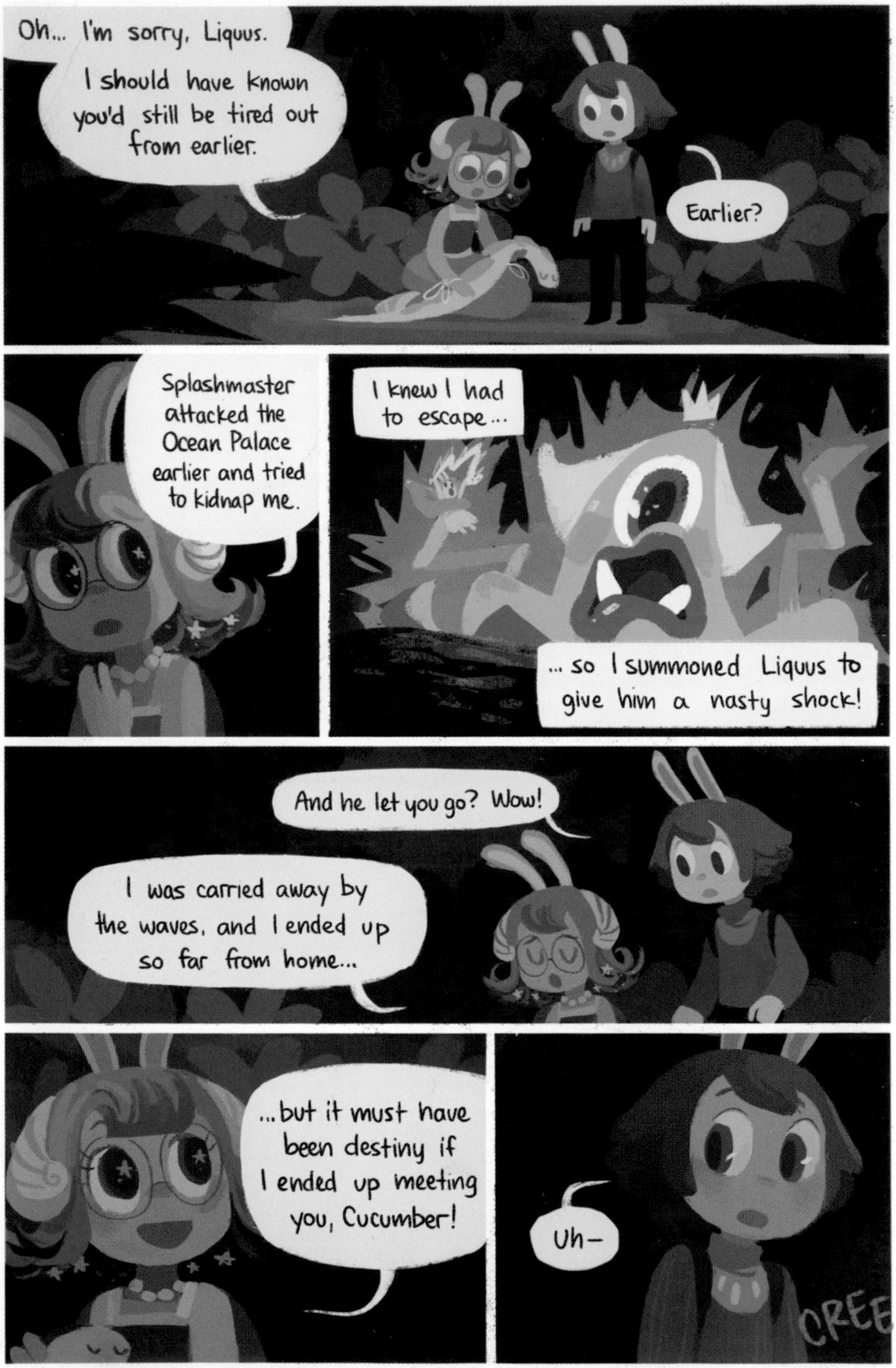
Oh... I'm sorry, Liquus.
I should have known you'd still be tired out from earlier.
Earlier?
Splashmaster attacked the Ocean Palace earlier and tried to kidnap me.
I knew I had to escape...
... so I summoned Liquus to give him a nasty shock!
And he let you go? Wow!
I was carried away by the waves, and I ended up so far from home...
...but it must have been destiny if I ended up meeting you, Cucumber!
Uh–
CREE

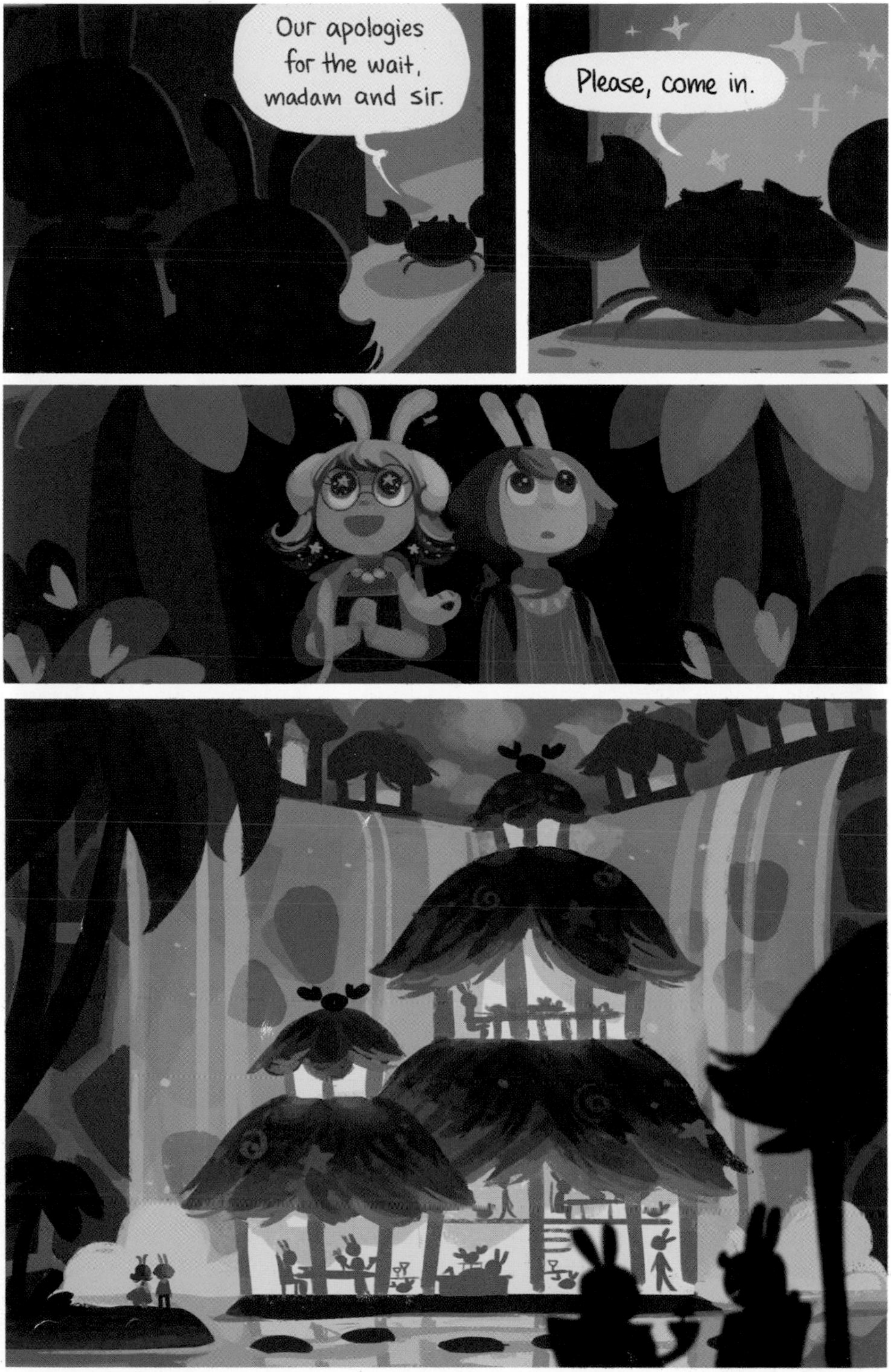
Our apologies for the wait, madam and sir.
Please, come in.

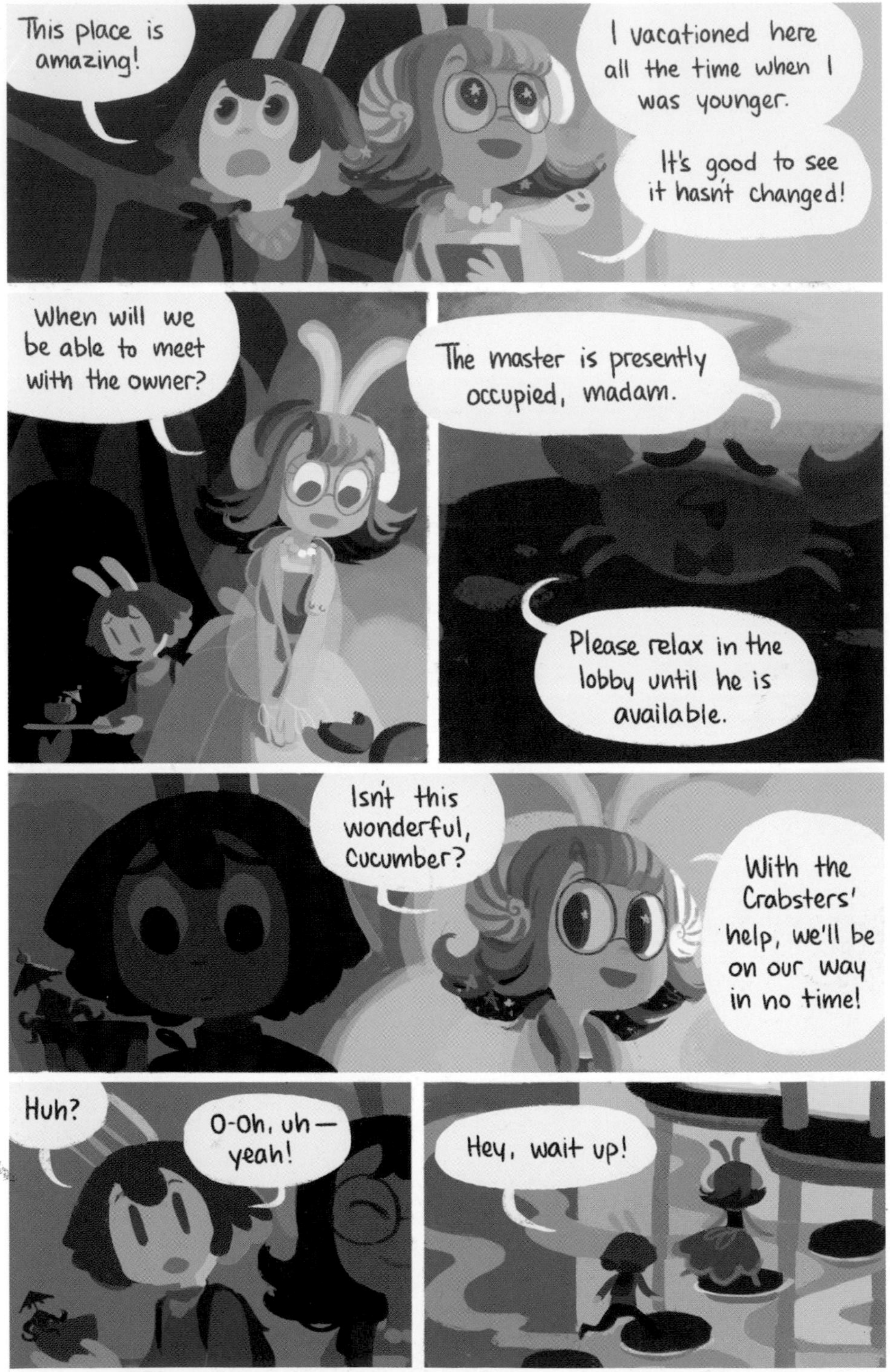
This place is amazing!
I vacationed here all the time when I was younger.
It's good to see it hasn't changed!
When will we be able to meet with the owner?
The master is presently occupied, madam.
Please relax in the lobby until he is available.
Isn't this wonderful, Cucumber?
With the Crabsters' help, we'll be on our way in no time!
Huh?
O-Oh, uh— yeah!
Hey, wait up!

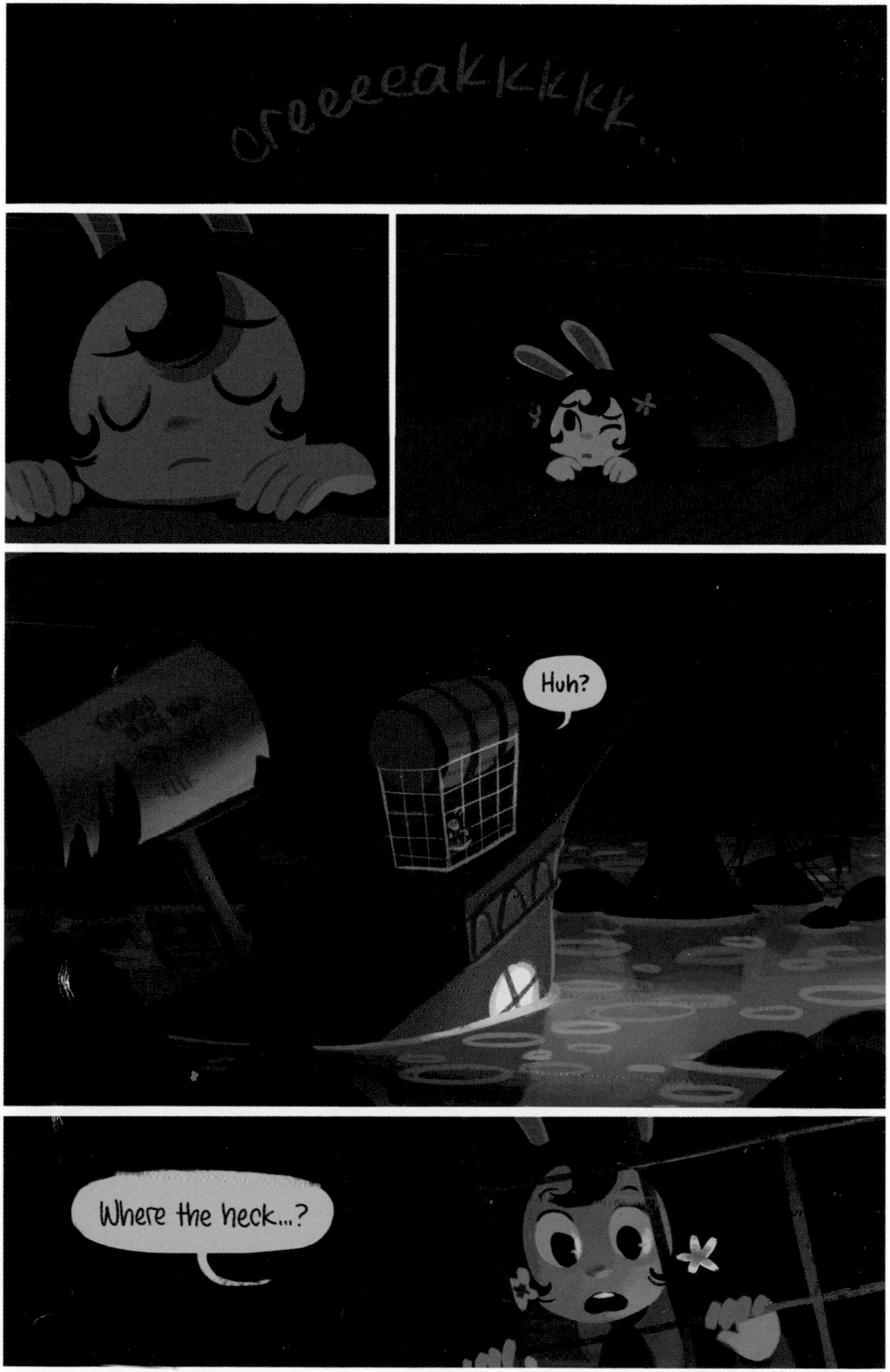
creeeeakkkkk...
Huh?
Where the heck...?

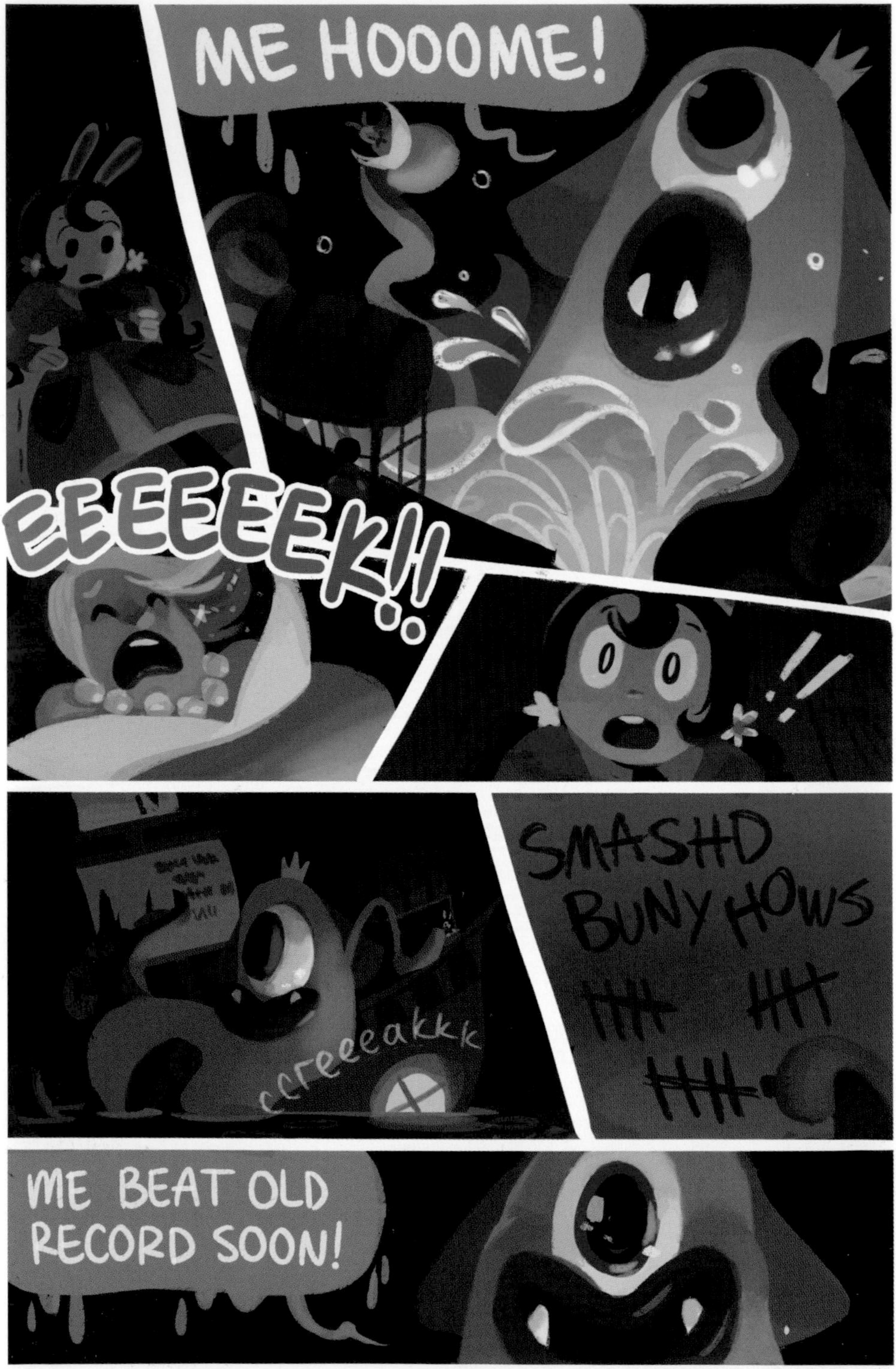
ME HOOOME!
EEEEEEK!!
!!
ccreeeakkk
SMASHD BUNY HOWS
ME BEAT OLD RECORD SOON!

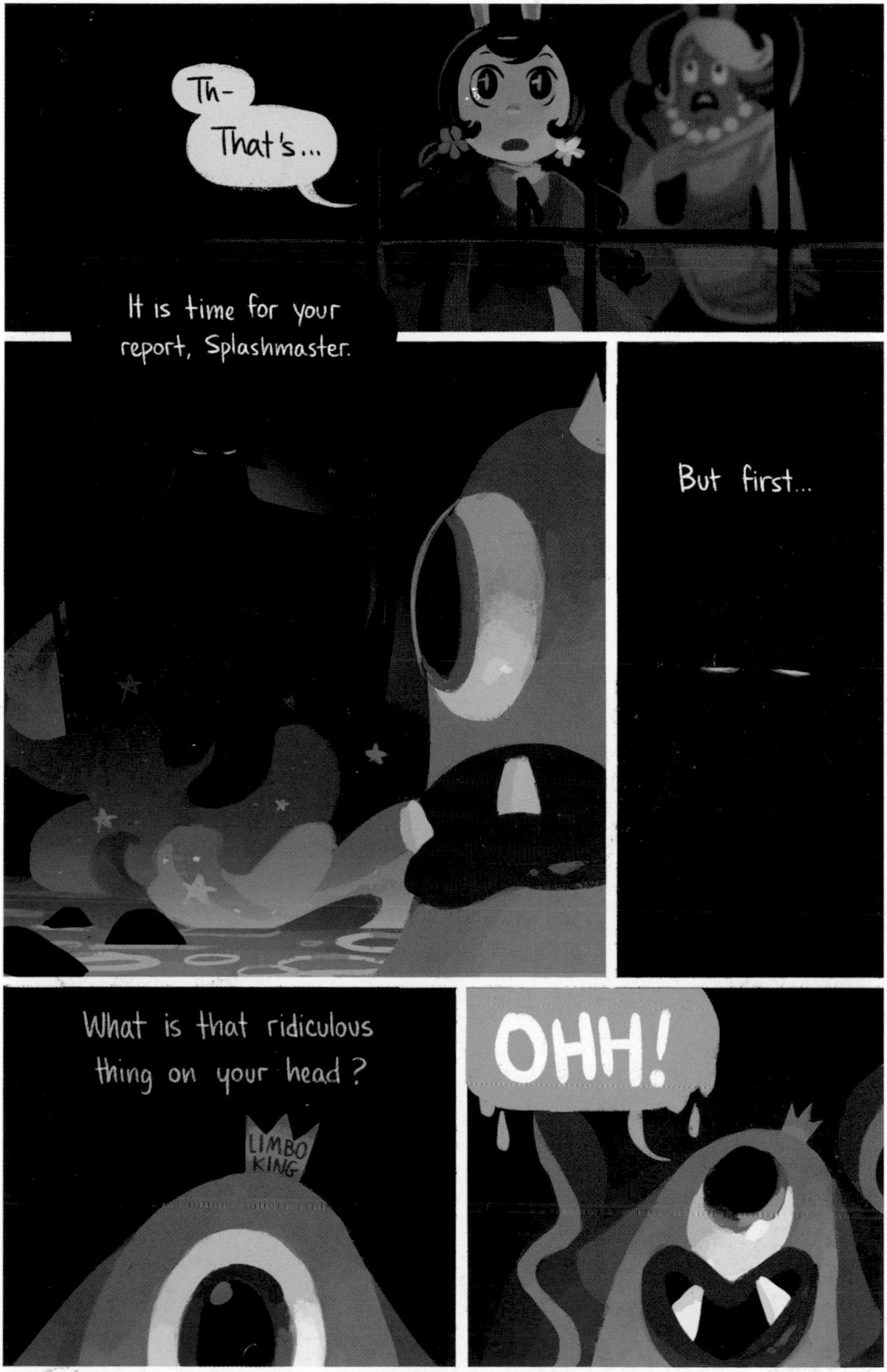

Th-
That's...
It is time for your report, Splashmaster.
But first...
What is that ridiculous thing on your head?
LIMBO KING
OHH!

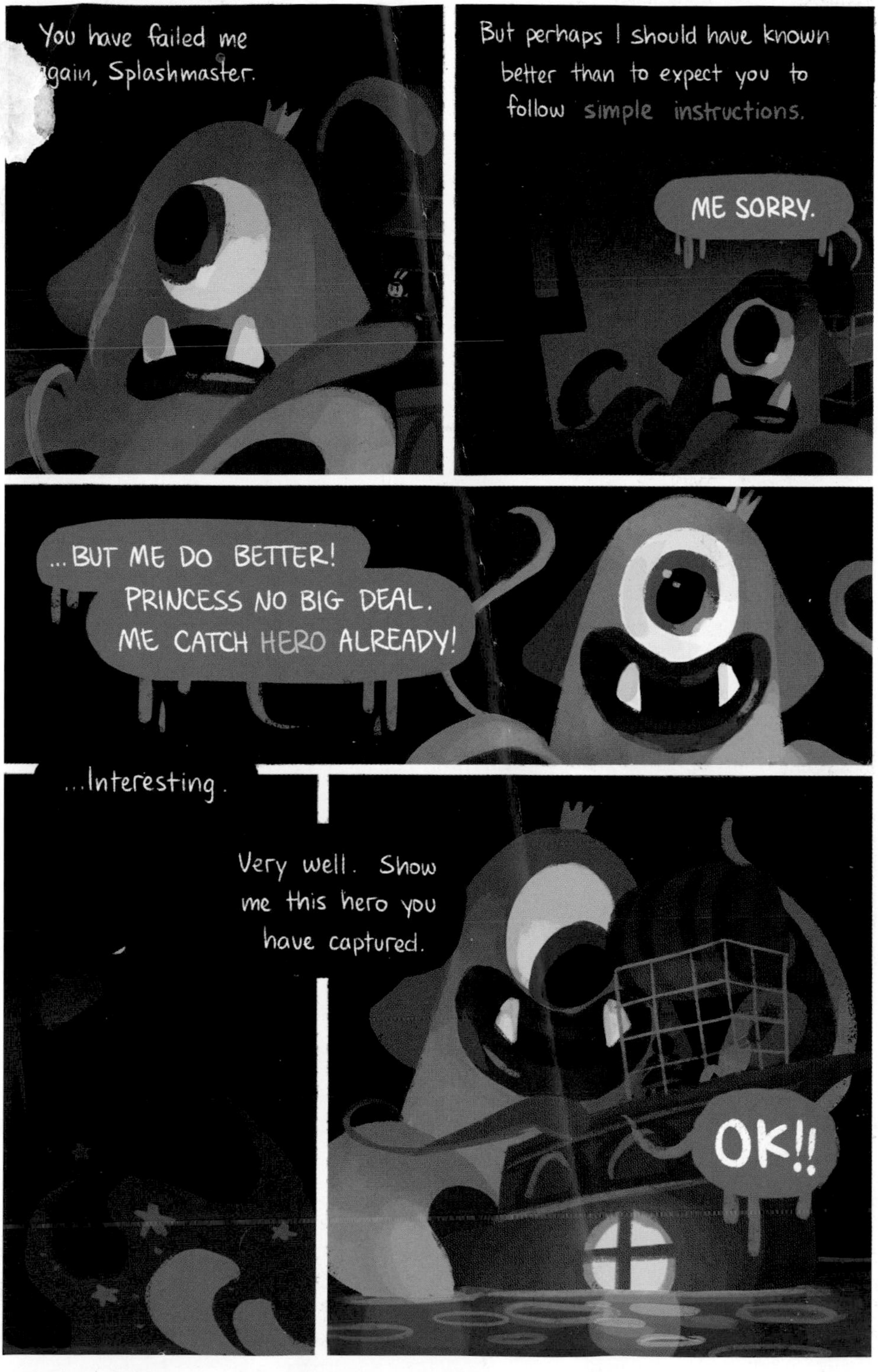
You have failed me again, Splashmaster.
But perhaps I should have known better than to expect you to follow simple instructions.
ME SORRY.
...BUT ME DO BETTER!
PRINCESS NO BIG DEAL. ME CATCH HERO ALREADY!
...Interesting.
Very well. Show me this hero you have captured.
OK!!

Gross!

UGH!!

This girl?

Is the hero not a
young boy by the name
of Cucumber?

That's my big brother.
Not like **he's** much
of a hero, anyway!

I see.

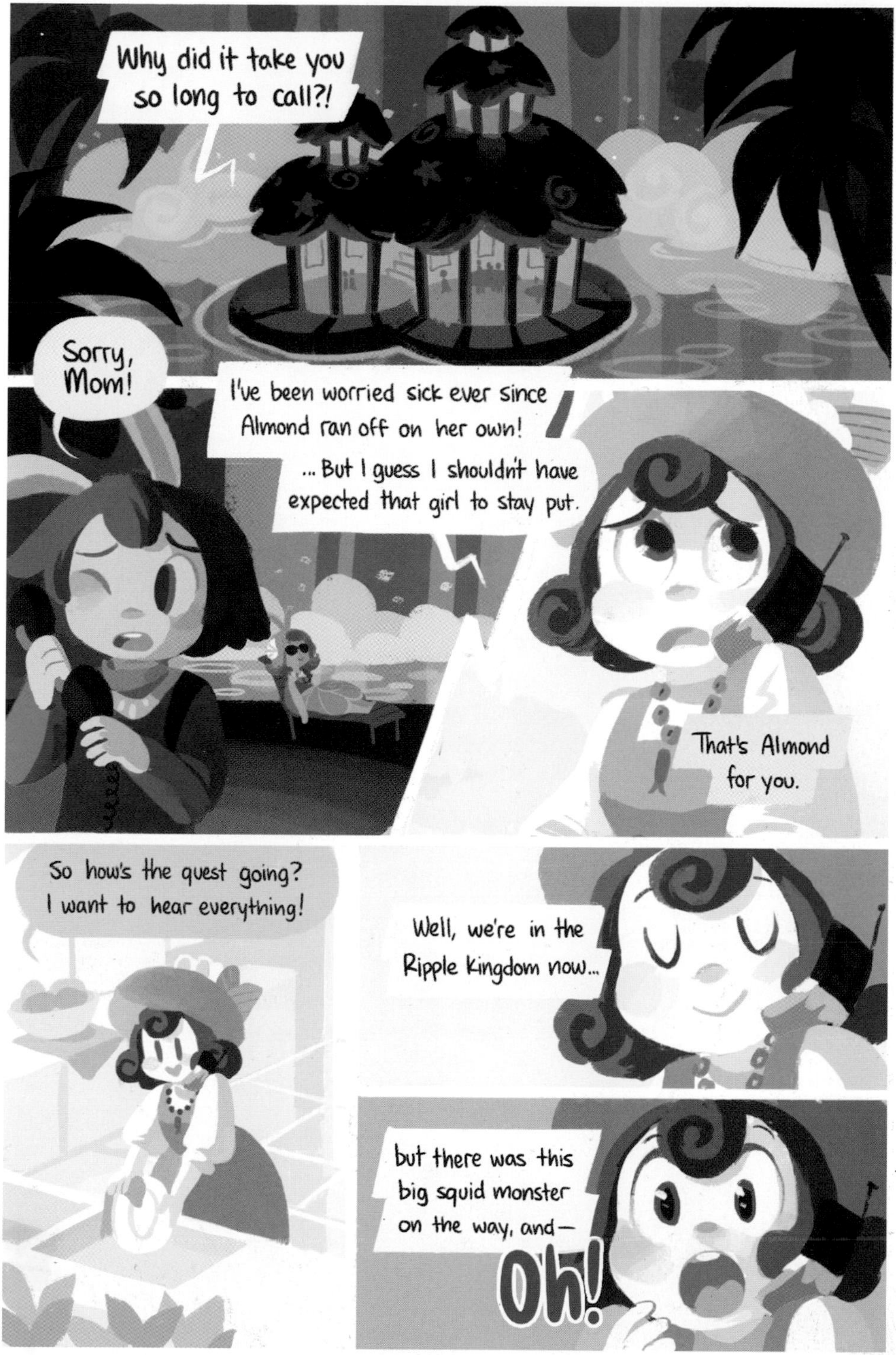
Why did it take you so long to call?!
Sorry, Mom!
I've been worried sick ever since Almond ran off on her own!
...But I guess I shouldn't have expected that girl to stay put.
That's Almond for you.
So how's the quest going? I want to hear everything!
Well, we're in the Ripple Kingdom now...
but there was this big squid monster on the way, and—
Oh!

Don't tell me all the scary details, sweetheart! You know how worried I am!

Okay, I guess...

But you seemed so excited about this before.

Oh, you know how parents are, dear.

Sometimes we just rush our kids out the door because it's so hard to say goodbye!

I... think you're the only parent who does that, Mom.

It was all very spur of the moment, honey. I'm sure even your father is up all night worrying about you two!

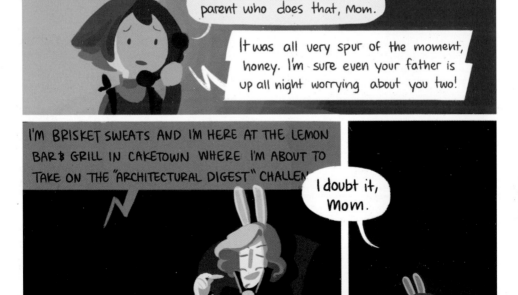

I'M BRISKET SWEATS AND I'M HERE AT THE LEMON BAR & GRILL IN CAKETOWN WHERE I'M ABOUT TO TAKE ON THE "ARCHITECTURAL DIGEST" CHALLEN

I doubt it, Mom.

CHIPS

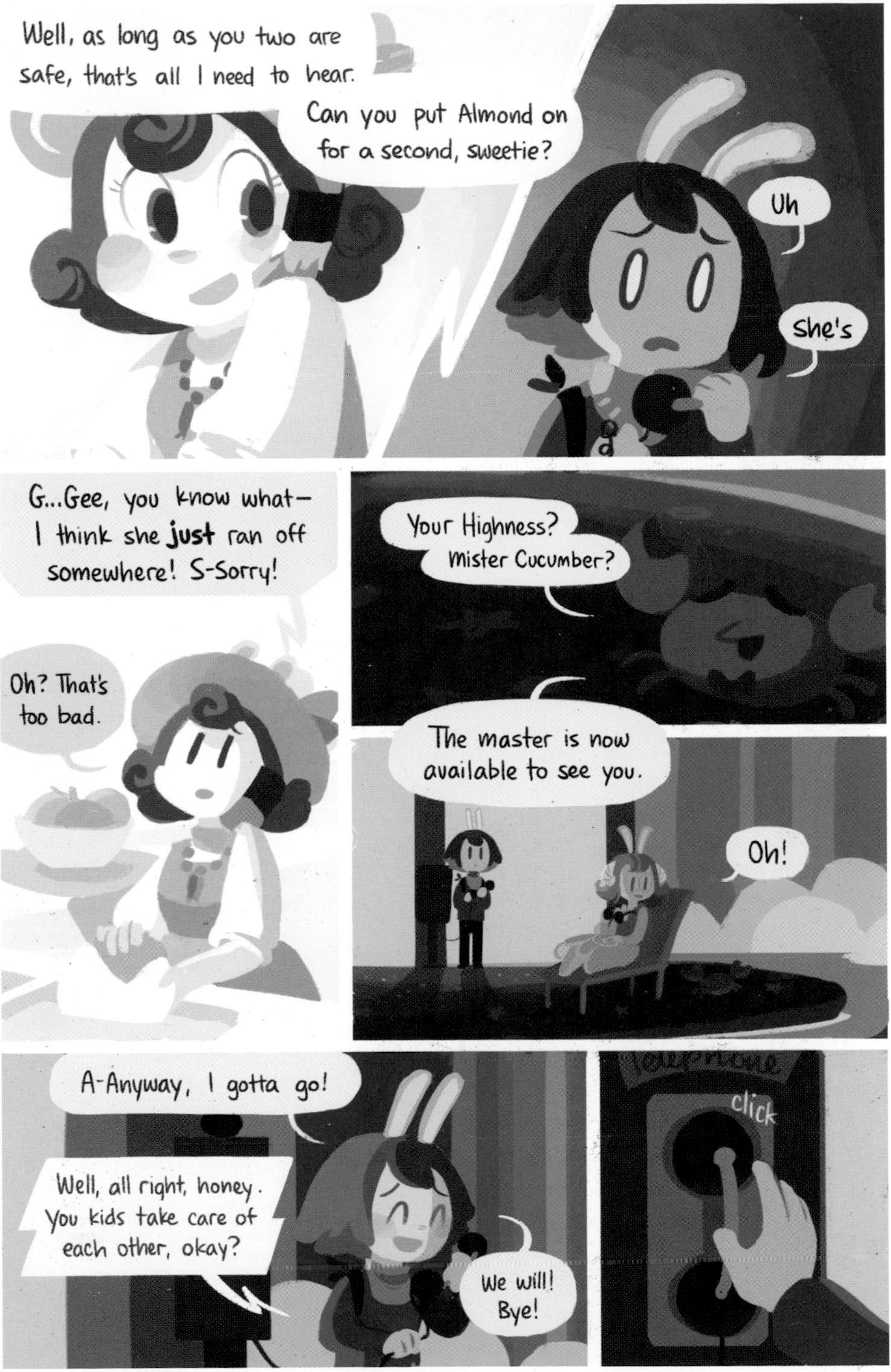
Well, as long as you two are safe, that's all I need to hear.
Can you put Almond on for a second, sweetie?
Uh
She's
G...Gee, you know what— I think she **just** ran off somewhere! S-Sorry!
Oh? That's too bad.
Your Highness? Mister Cucumber?
The master is now available to see you.
Oh!
A-Anyway, I gotta go!
Well, all right, honey. You kids take care of each other, okay?
We will! Bye!
Telephone
click

You know...

I still don't get why we couldn't just use your ph— Royal Instrument for that.

Cucumber, please. **Listen** to yourself.

This way, please...

Sir, there are guests here to see you.

Guests?

What'd I tell ye about bringin' in uninvited guests?!

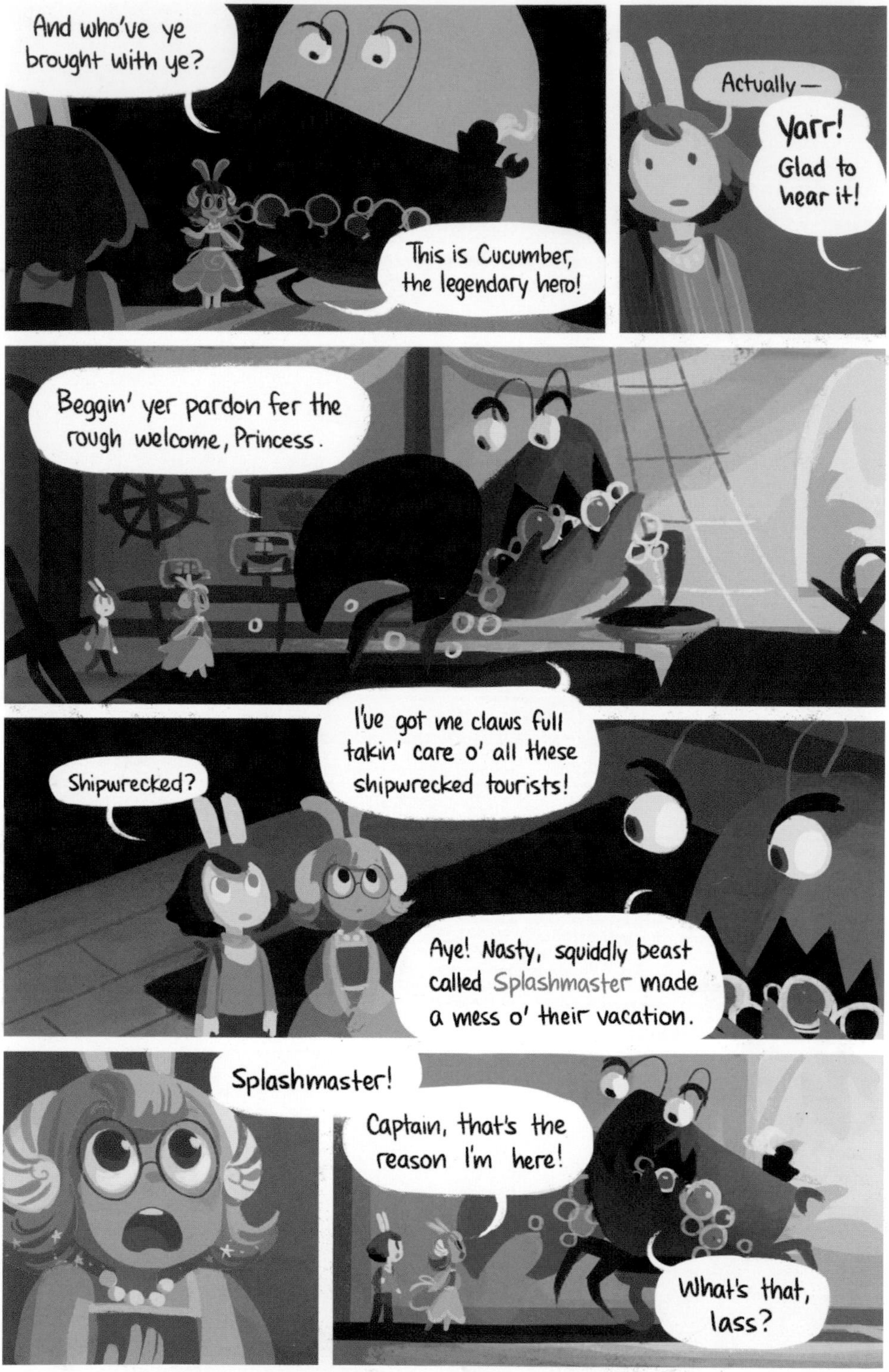
And who've ye brought with ye?
This is Cucumber, the legendary hero!
Actually—
Yarr! Glad to hear it!
Beggin' yer pardon fer the rough welcome, Princess.
I've got me claws full takin' care o' all these shipwrecked tourists!
Shipwrecked?
Aye! Nasty, squiddly beast called Splashmaster made a mess o' their vacation.
Splashmaster!
Captain, that's the reason I'm here!
What's that, lass?

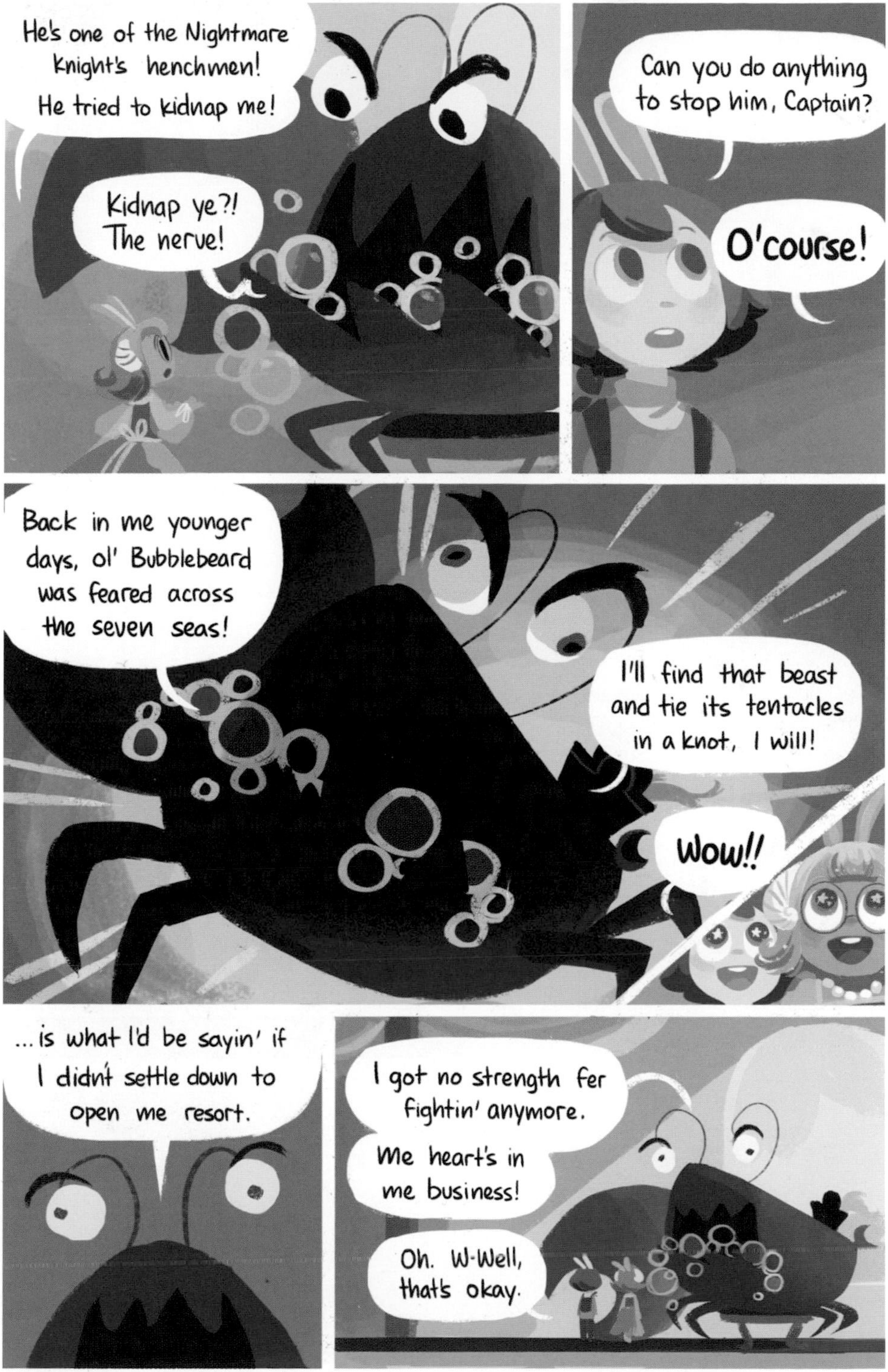
He's one of the Nightmare Knight's henchmen!
He tried to kidnap me!
Kidnap ye?! The nerve!
Can you do anything to stop him, Captain?
O'course!
Back in me younger days, ol' Bubblebeard was feared across the seven seas!
I'll find that beast and tie its tentacles in a knot, I will!
Wow!!
...is what I'd be sayin' if I didn't settle down to open me resort.
I got no strength fer fightin' anymore.
Me heart's in me business!
Oh. W-Well, that's okay.

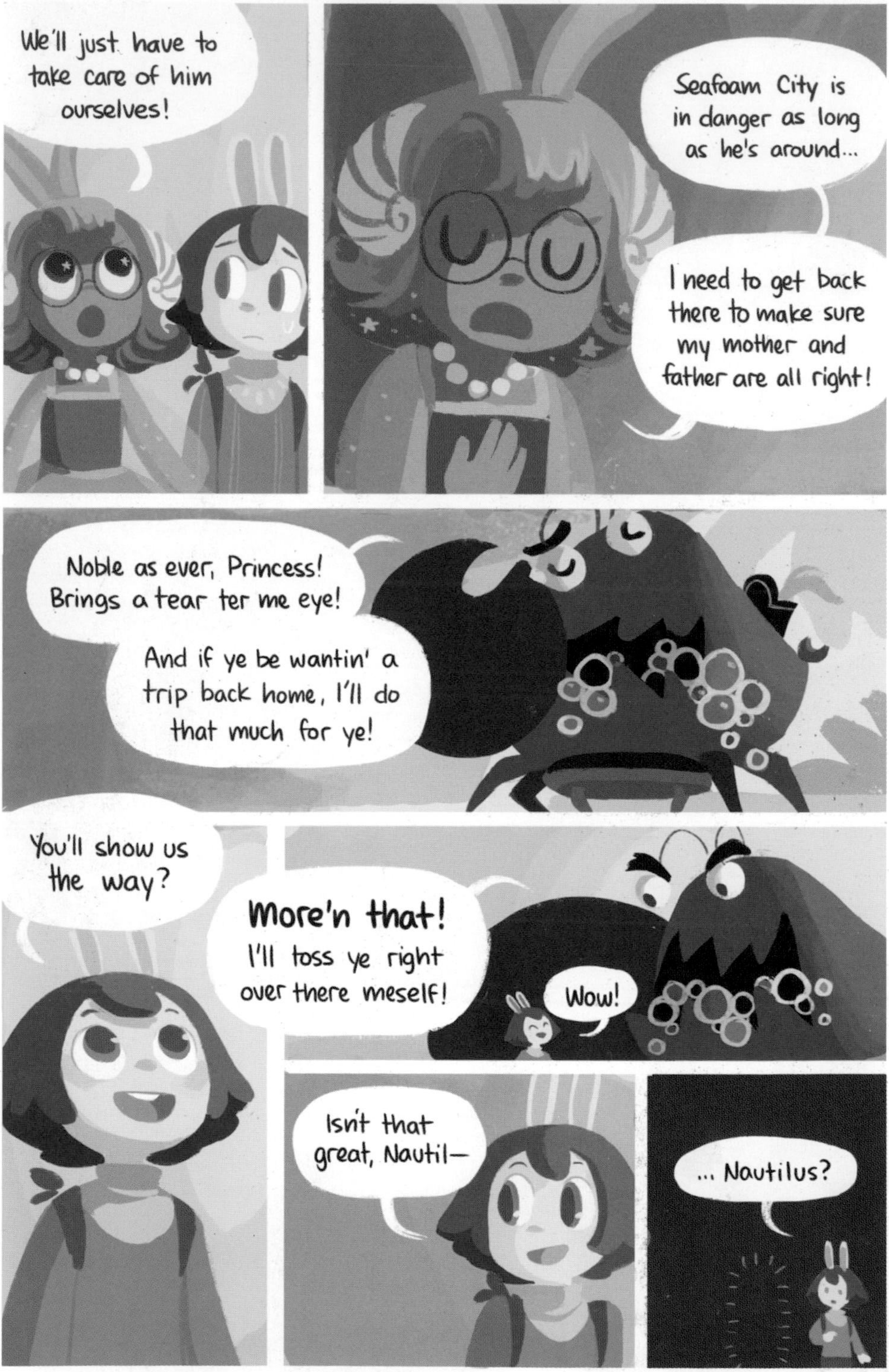
We'll just have to take care of him ourselves!
Seafoam City is in danger as long as he's around...
I need to get back there to make sure my mother and father are all right!
Noble as ever, Princess! Brings a tear ter me eye!
And if ye be wantin' a trip back home, I'll do that much for ye!
You'll show us the way?
More'n that! I'll toss ye right over there meself!
Wow!
Isn't that great, Nautil—
... Nautilus?

Nautilus!

43rd ANNUAL
LIMBO-THON

How low! Can you go!

Oh yeah! We've got a new limbo king here, everybody!

Or should I say... limbo queen!

Let's hear it for her!

Woo!

yeah!

Thank you! Thank you, my loyal limbo subjects!

We'd normally have a big crown trophy to give our champ, but, uh...

We kinda lost it when the ship sank. Sorry!

Oh! What a pity.

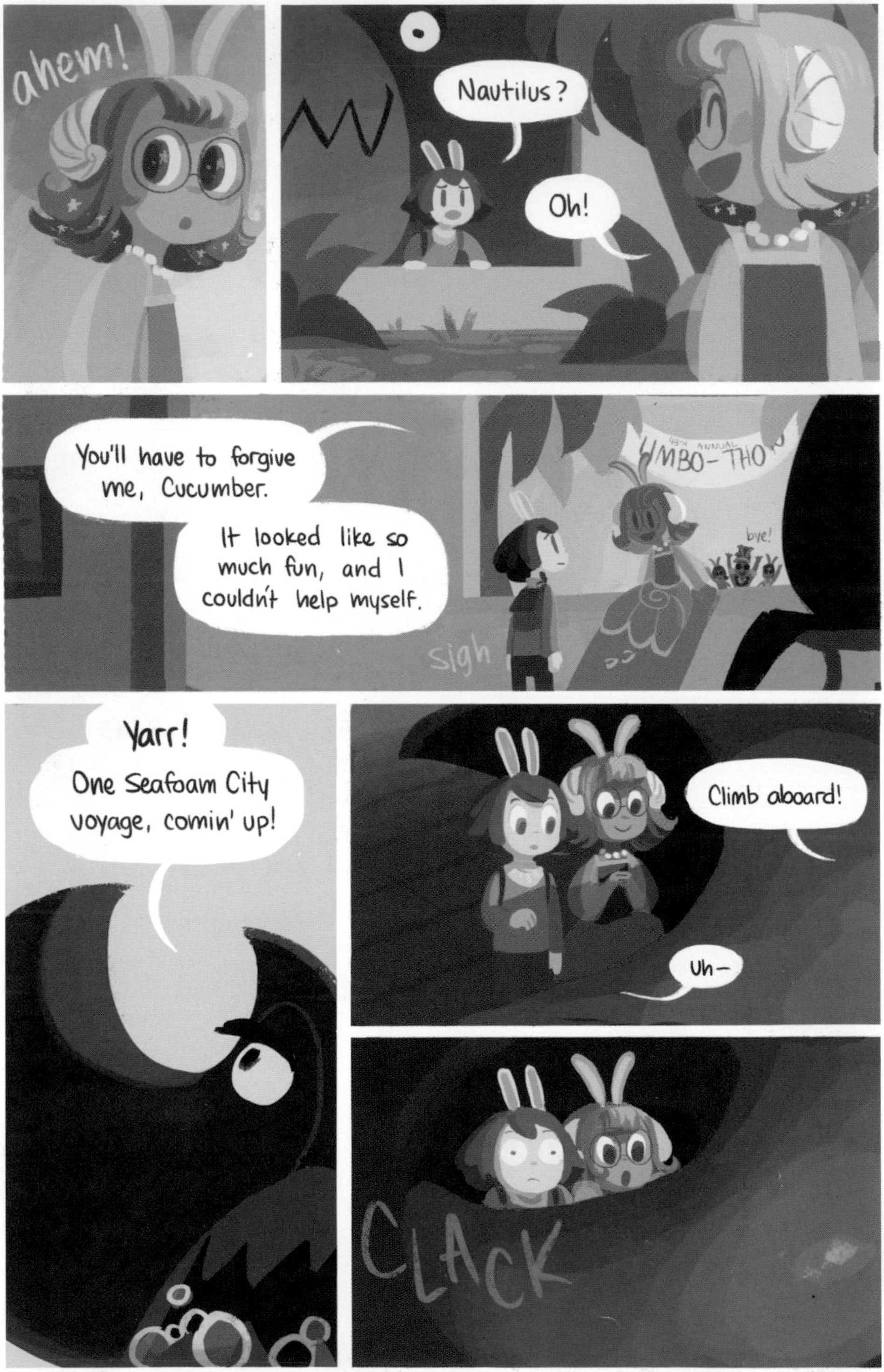
ahem!
Nautilus?
Oh!
You'll have to forgive me, Cucumber.
It looked like so much fun, and I couldn't help myself.
48th ANNUAL
UMBO-THO
bye!
sigh
Yarr!
One Seafoam City voyage, comin' up!
Climb aboard!
Uh–
CLACK

Are ye ready, kids?

Aye aye, Captain!

I can't heeear youuuu

Aye aye, Captain!

OHHHHHHHH

Uh, wait!

When you said you'd "toss us over," you didn't **literally** —

AAAAAAAAAA

BOMBS AWAY!

ding!

Yer welcooome!

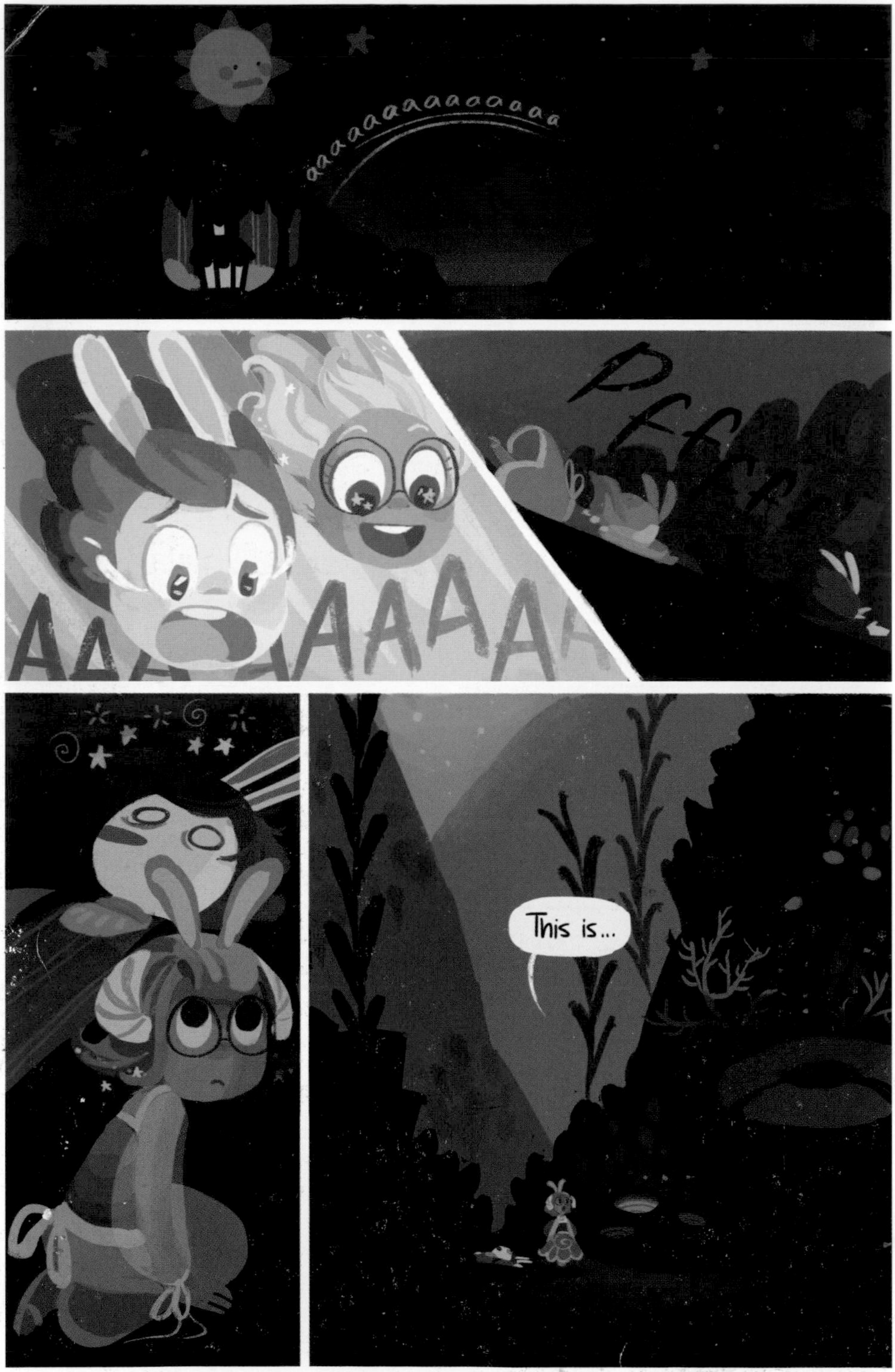
aaaaaaaaaaaaaaaaaa
AAAAAAAAA
This is...

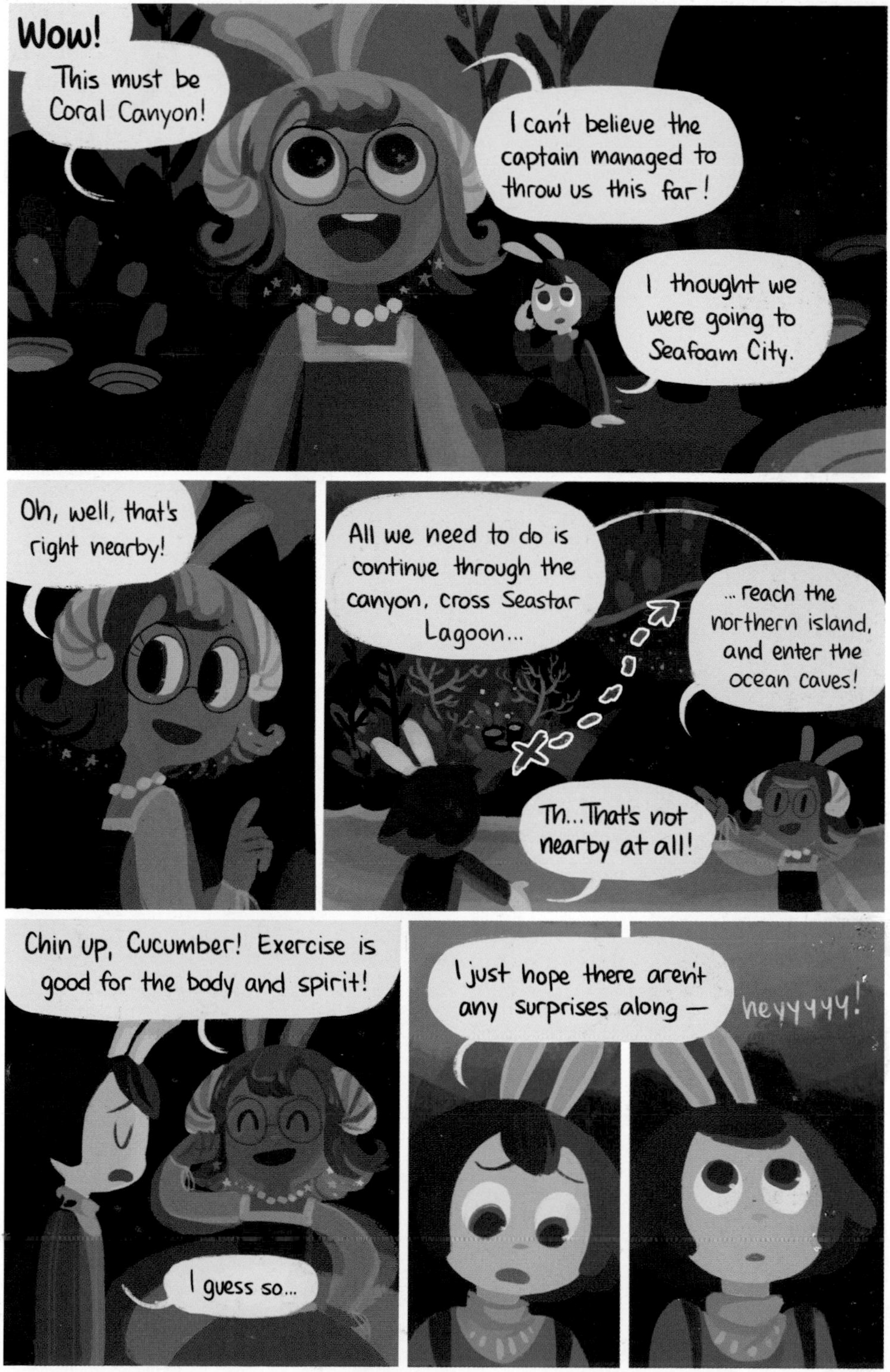

Wow!
This must be Coral Canyon!
I can't believe the captain managed to throw us this far!
I thought we were going to Seafoam City.
Oh, well, that's right nearby!
All we need to do is continue through the canyon, cross Seastar Lagoon...
... reach the northern island, and enter the ocean caves!
Th...That's not nearby at all!
Chin up, Cucumber! Exercise is good for the body and spirit!
I guess so...
I just hope there aren't any surprises along —
heyyyyy!

You're Cucumber, aren't you? The legendary hero?

...

I guess?

Great! My name is Chardonnay, and I serve the Dream Oracle.

There's something very important I need to tell you!

A servant of the Dream Oracle herself?!

How amazing!

I can only imagine what it's like to work for her!

scritch scritch scritch

S-So, um, what did you come to tell us?

Oh!

51

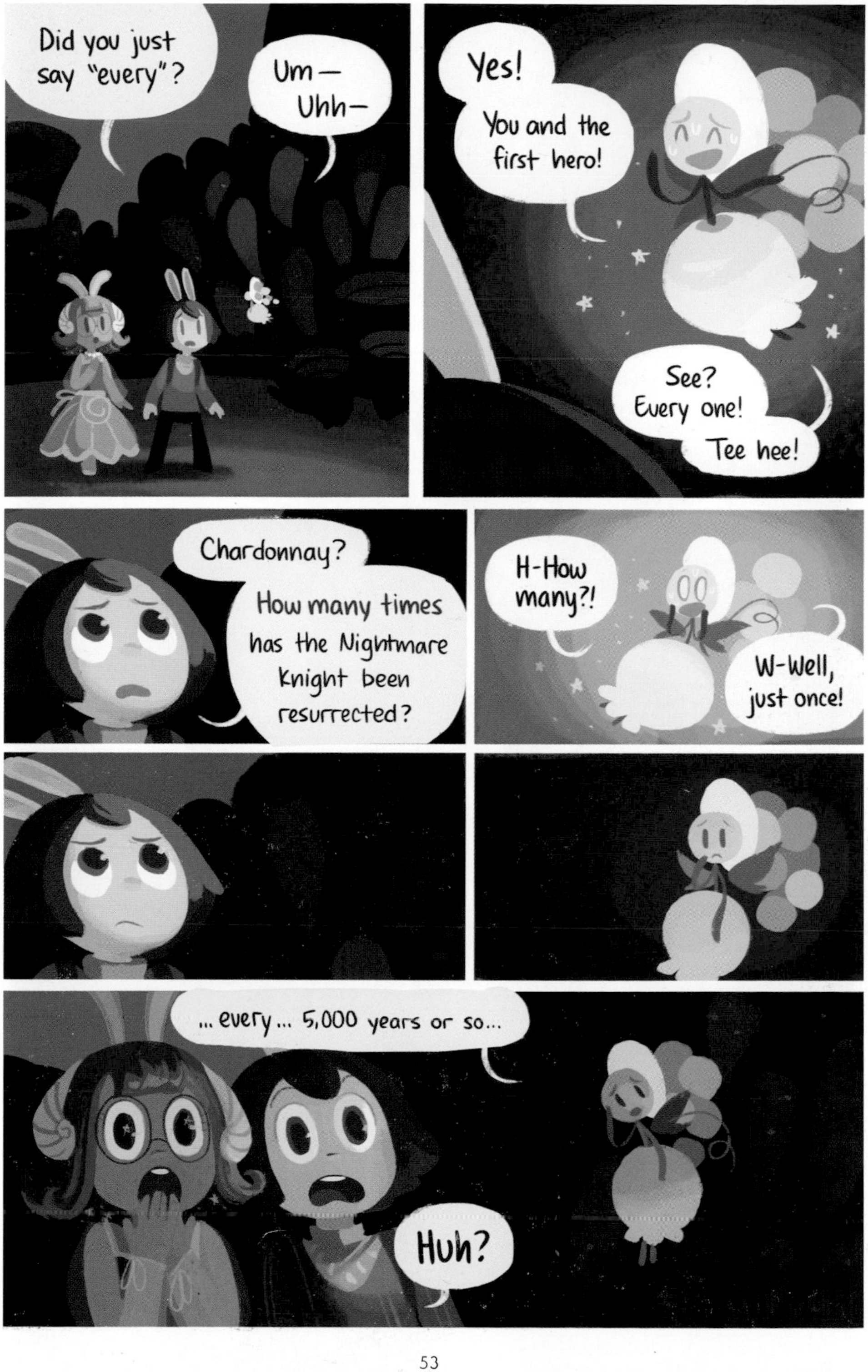
Did you just say "every"?
Um— Uhh—
Yes!
You and the first hero!
See? Every one!
Tee hee!
Chardonnay?
How many times has the Nightmare Knight been resurrected?
H-How many?!
W-Well, just once!
... every... 5,000 years or so...
Huh?

55

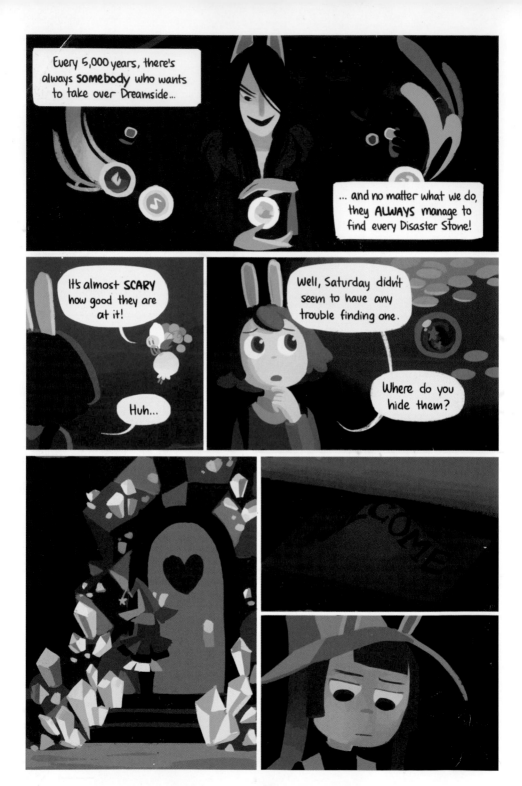

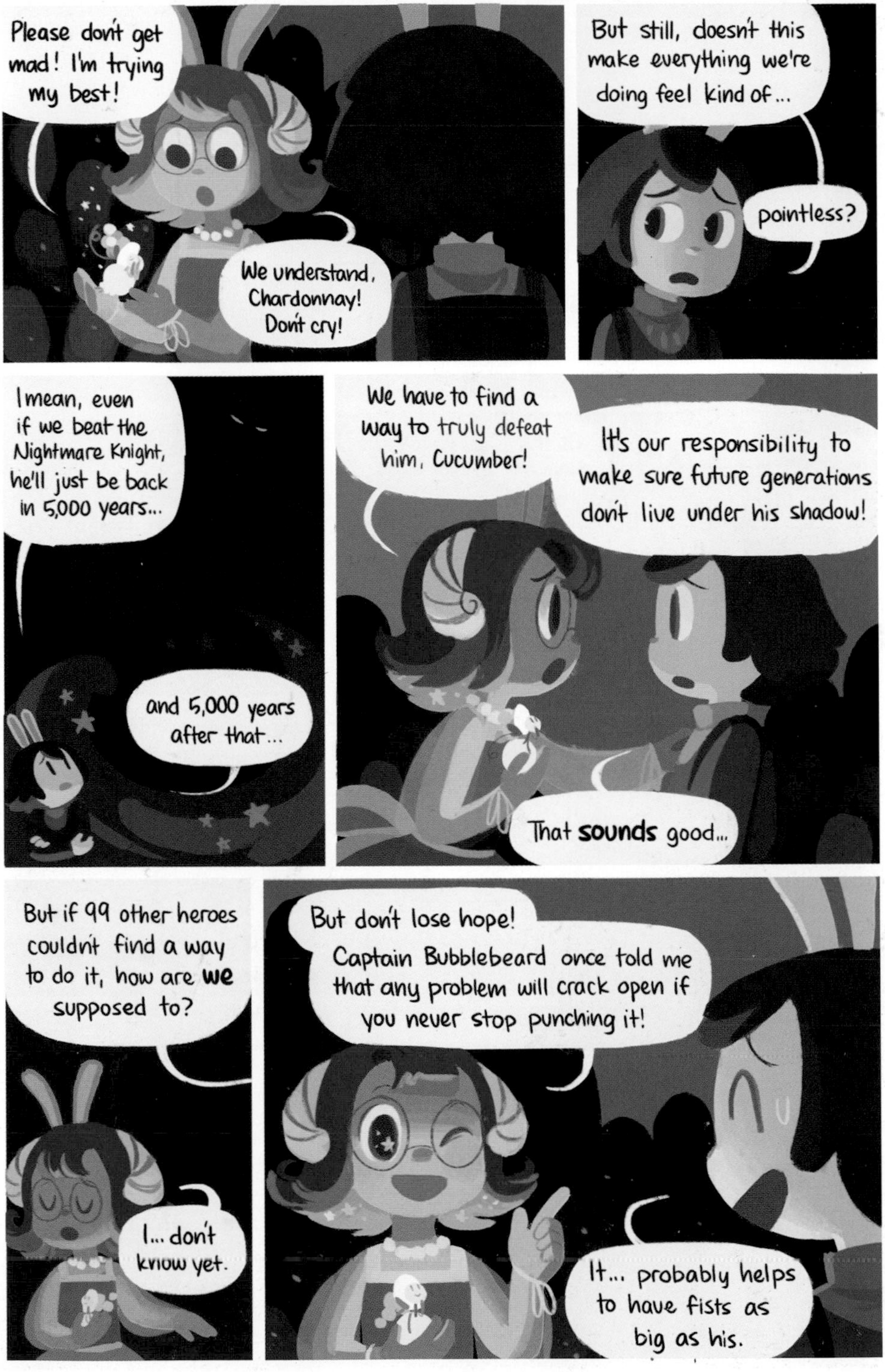
Please don't get mad! I'm trying my best!
We understand, Chardonnay! Don't cry!
But still, doesn't this make everything we're doing feel kind of...
pointless?
I mean, even if we beat the Nightmare Knight, he'll just be back in 5,000 years...
and 5,000 years after that...
We have to find a way to truly defeat him, Cucumber!
It's our responsibility to make sure future generations don't live under his shadow!
That **sounds** good...
But if 99 other heroes couldn't find a way to do it, how are **we** supposed to?
I... don't know yet.
But don't lose hope!
Captain Bubblebeard once told me that any problem will crack open if you never stop punching it!
It... probably helps to have fists as big as his.

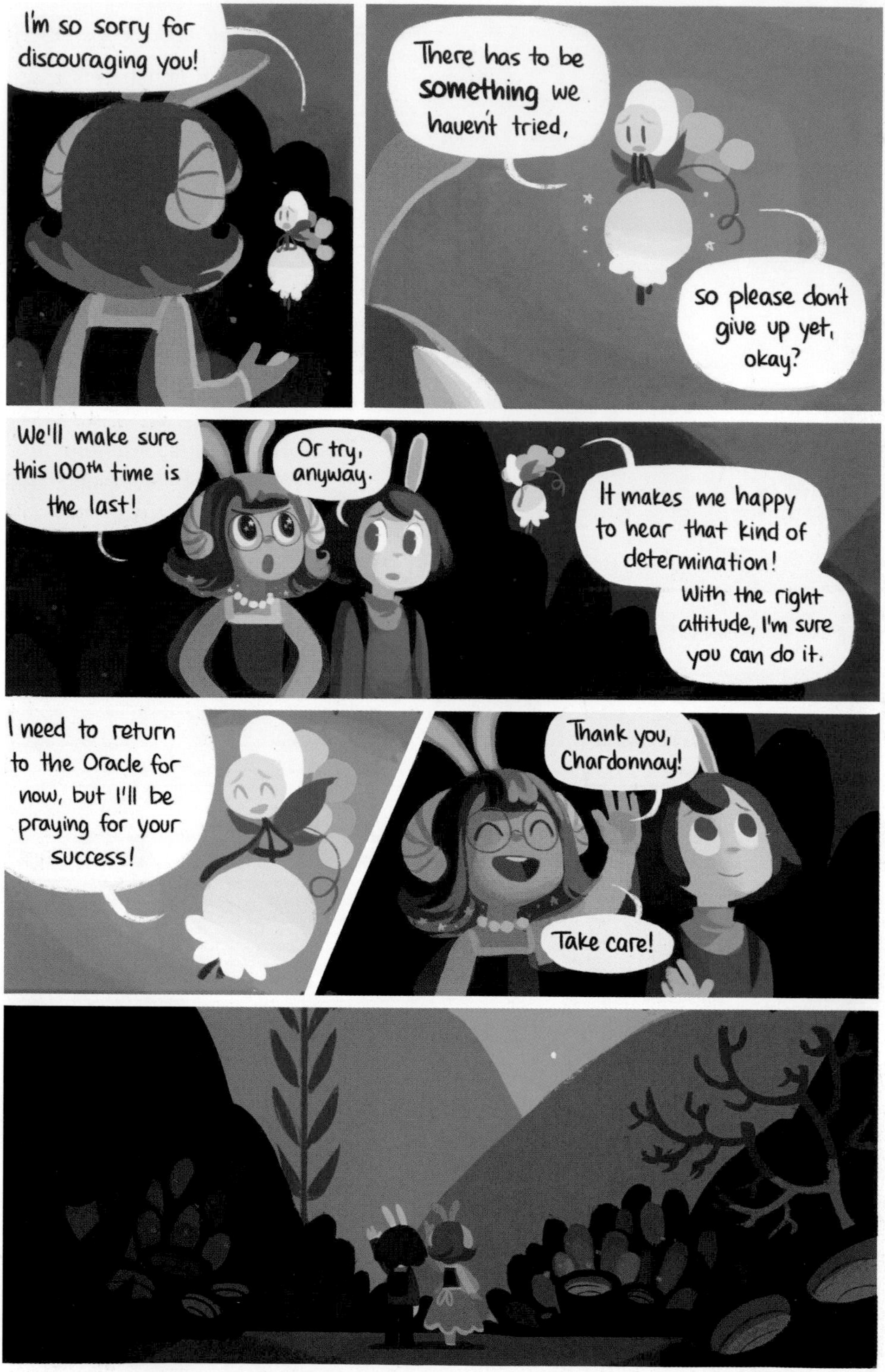
I'm so sorry for discouraging you!
There has to be **something** we haven't tried,
so please don't give up yet, okay?
We'll make sure this 100th time is the last!
Or try, anyway.
It makes me happy to hear that kind of determination!
With the right attitude, I'm sure you can do it.
I need to return to the Oracle for now, but I'll be praying for your success!
Thank you, Chardonnay!
Take care!

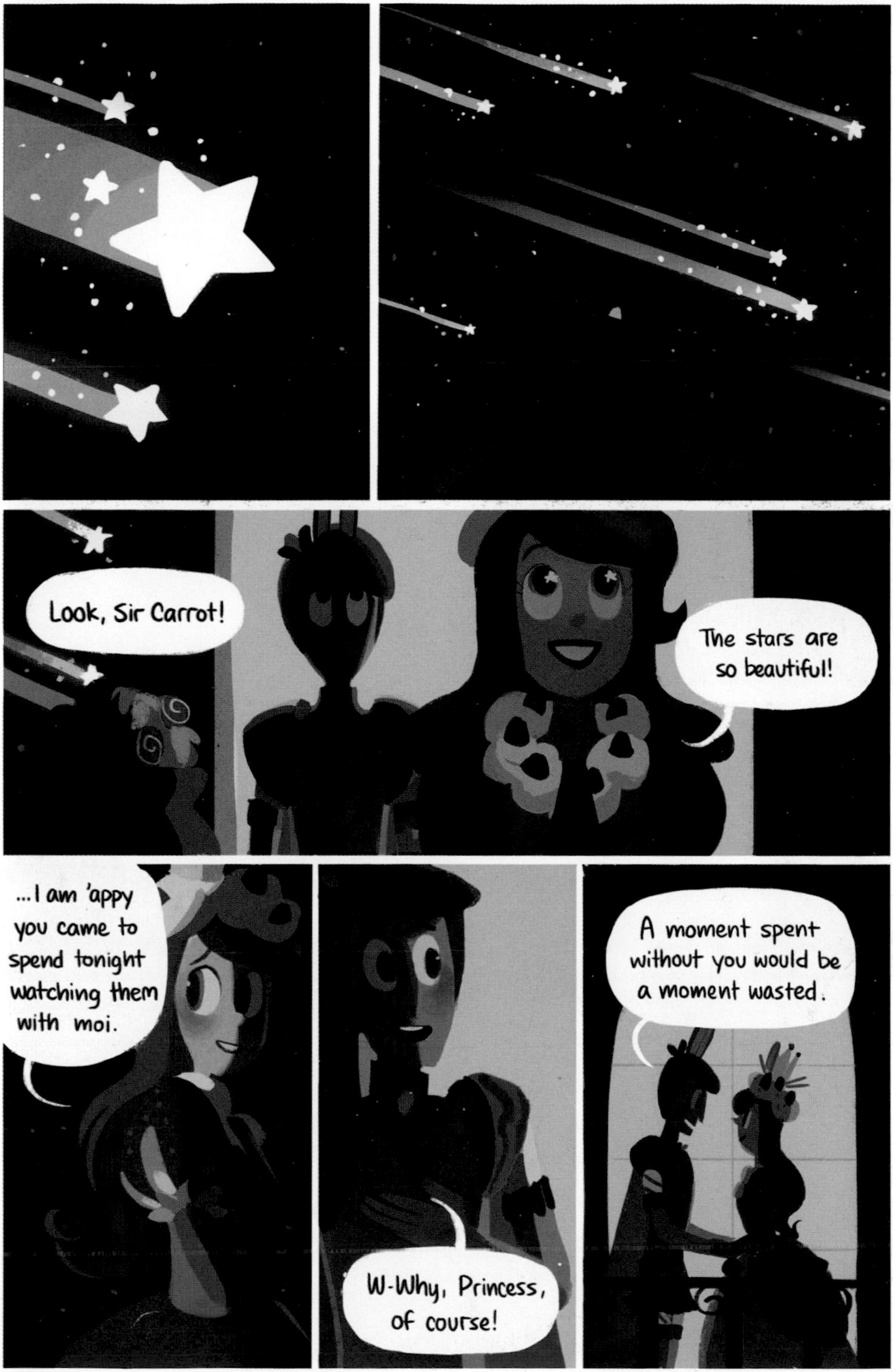
Look, Sir Carrot!
The stars are so beautiful!
...I am 'appy you came to spend tonight watching them with moi.
W-Why, Princess, of course!
A moment spent without you would be a moment wasted.

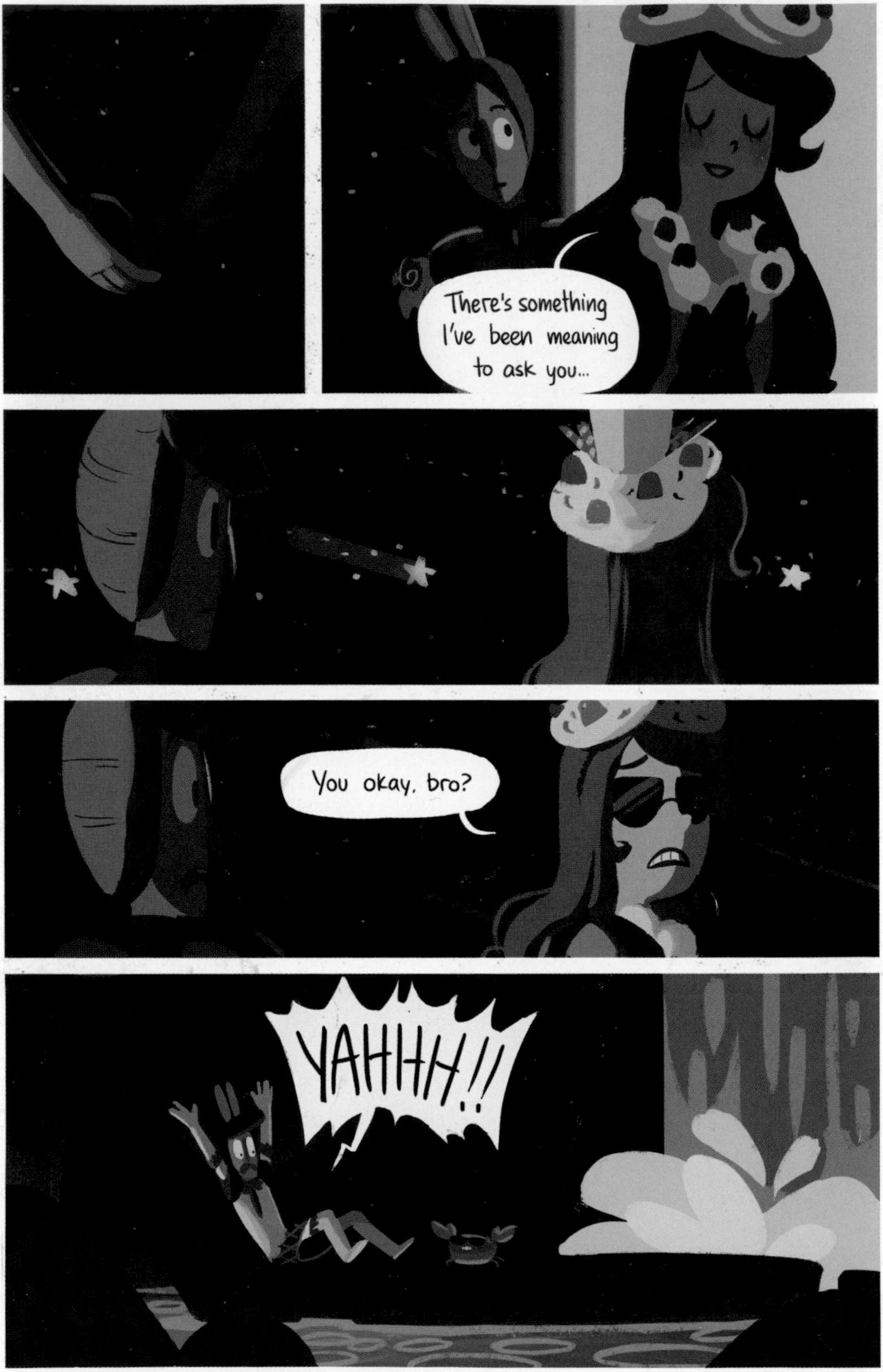
There's something I've been meaning to ask you...
You okay, bro?
YAHHH!!

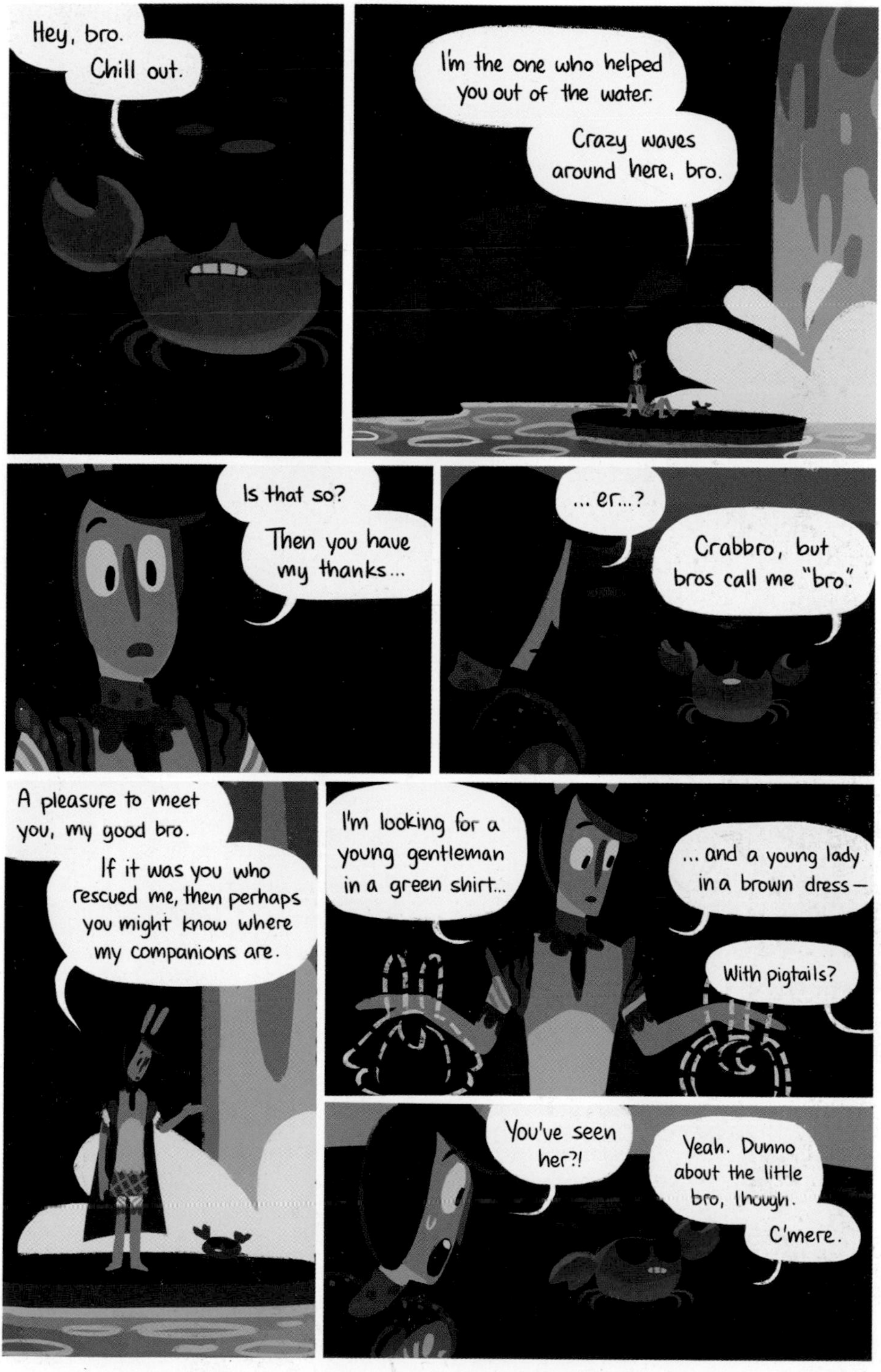
Hey, bro.
Chill out.
I'm the one who helped you out of the water.
Crazy waves around here, bro.
Is that so?
Then you have my thanks...
... er...?
Crabbro, but bros call me "bro".
A pleasure to meet you, my good bro.
If it was you who rescued me, then perhaps you might know where my companions are.
I'm looking for a young gentleman in a green shirt...
... and a young lady in a brown dress—
With pigtails?
You've seen her?!
Yeah. Dunno about the little bro, though.
C'mere.

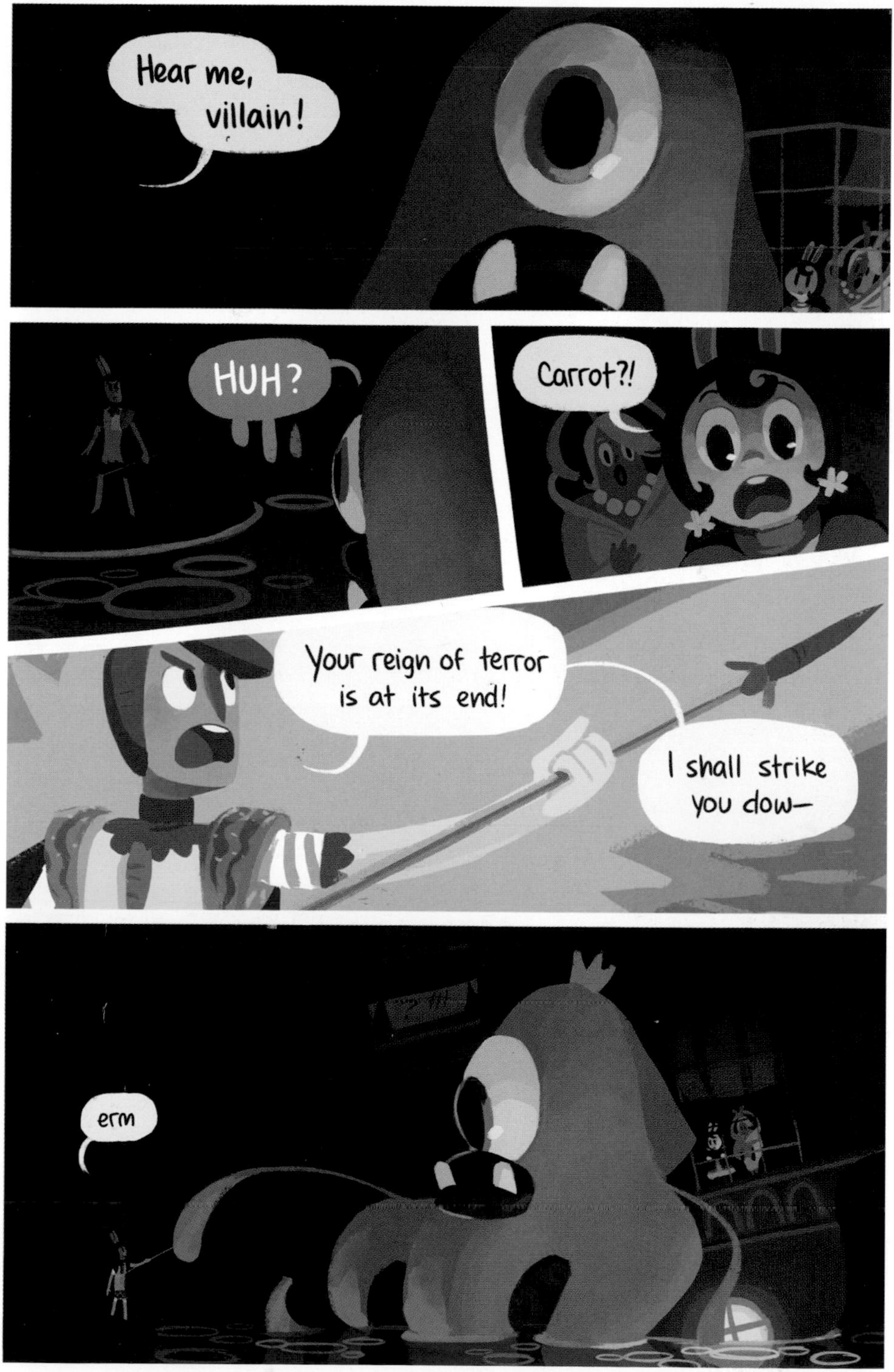
Hear me, villain!
HUH?
Carrot?!
Your reign of terror is at its end!
I shall strike you dow—
erm

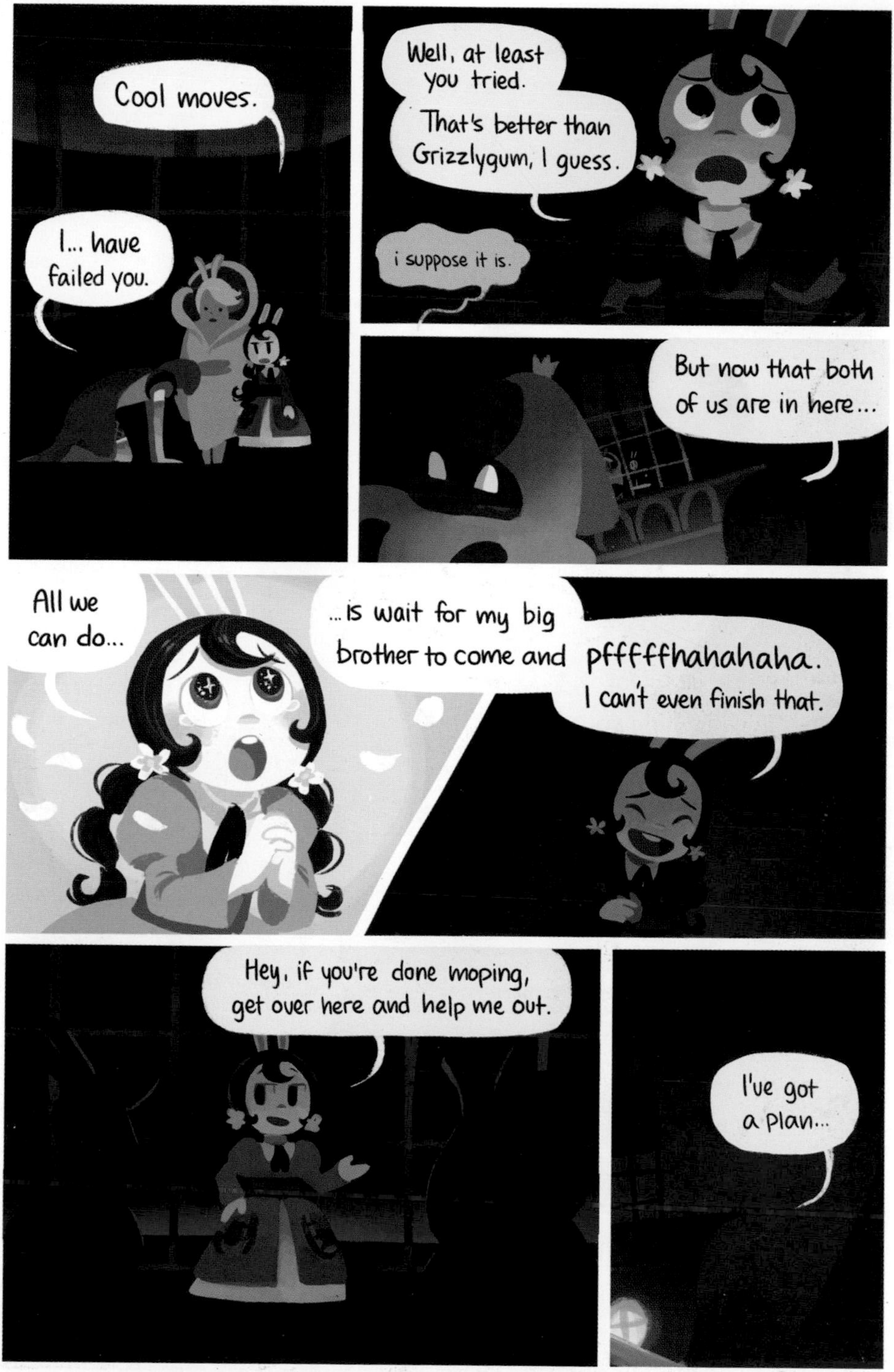
Cool moves.
I... have failed you.
Well, at least you tried.
That's better than Grizzlygum, I guess.
i suppose it is.
But now that both of us are in here...
All we can do...
...is wait for my big brother to come and
pfffffhahahaha.
I can't even finish that.
Hey, if you're done moping, get over here and help me out.
I've got a plan...

You aren't still depressed because of the Nightmare Knight, are you?

A little.

It's weird to know we're up against an enemy we can't really brrglrf

No negative talk, Cucumber.

We said we would find a way, remember?

yesh

I jusht wish we had a clue where Shaturday went with the Dream Shord.

That'd give ush shomething to shtart with, at leasht...

Poof

OW!

What in
tarnation-?!

Saturday?!

Wow!

The legend
IS true!

What legend?

It's said that
if you make
a wish on a
Shooting star
reflected in
these waters,
it'll come true!

We didn't see it,
but a star must
have passed by
right when you
made that
absentminded
wish just now!

Huh?!

If I'd known that,
I would have made
a **good one!**

I WISH ALMOND WERE HERE
I WISH I COULD GO HOME
I WISH I WERE IN SCHOOL

Urgh...

Hey now!

Yer that kid from the Doughnut Kingdom, ain't ya!

The name is Cucumber!

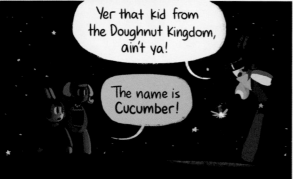

Tell a gal who cares!

Where'n the heck am I, anyway?

Seastar Lagoon!

I, uh... I brought you here, I guess!

Now how in Dreamside'd ya do that?

W-Wish power, I guess?

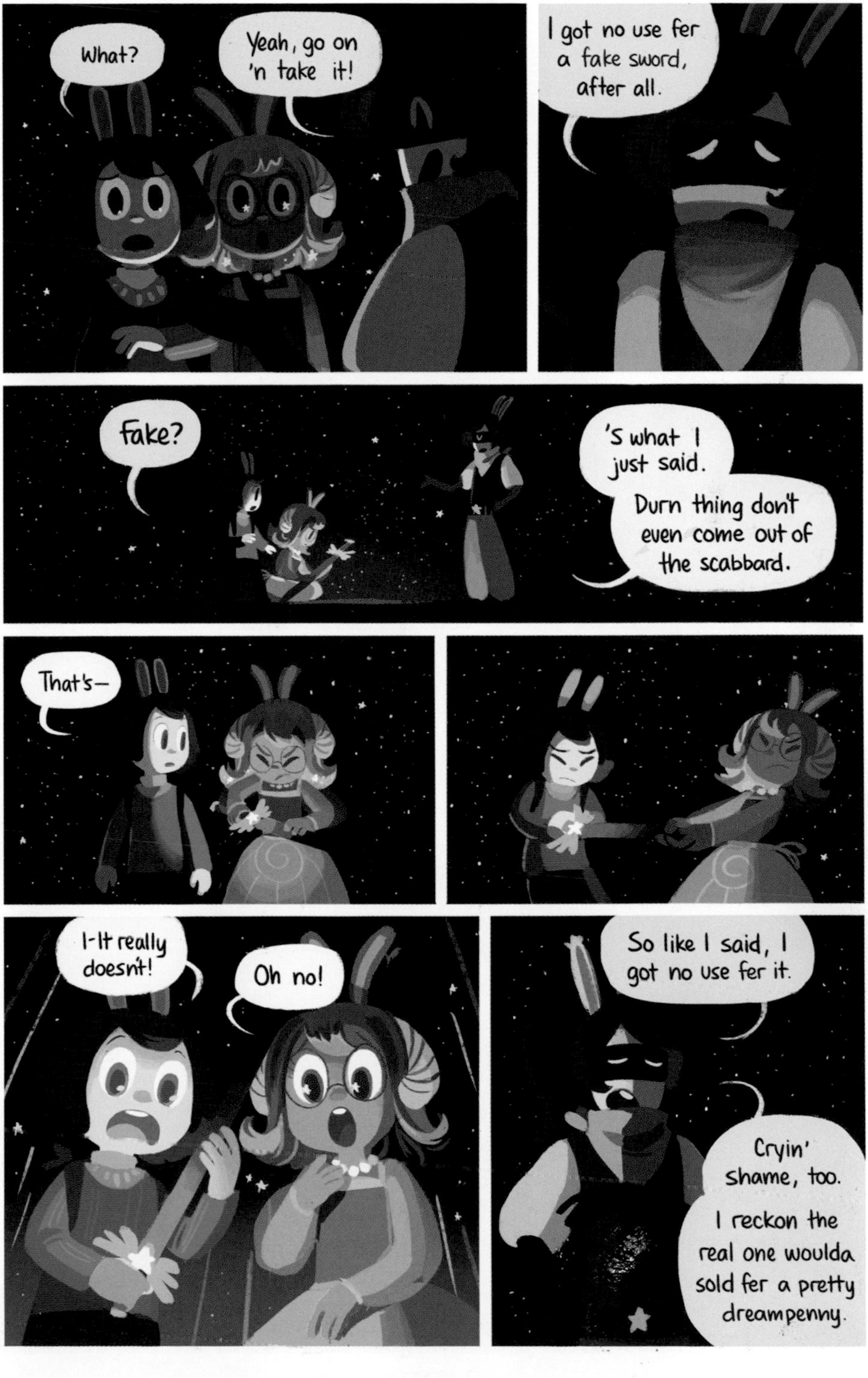
What?
Yeah, go on 'n take it!
I got no use fer a fake sword, after all.
Fake?
'S what I just said.
Durn thing don't even come out of the scabbard.
That's—
I-It really doesn't!
Oh no!
So like I said, I got no use fer it.
Cryin' shame, too.
I reckon the real one woulda sold fer a pretty dreampenny.

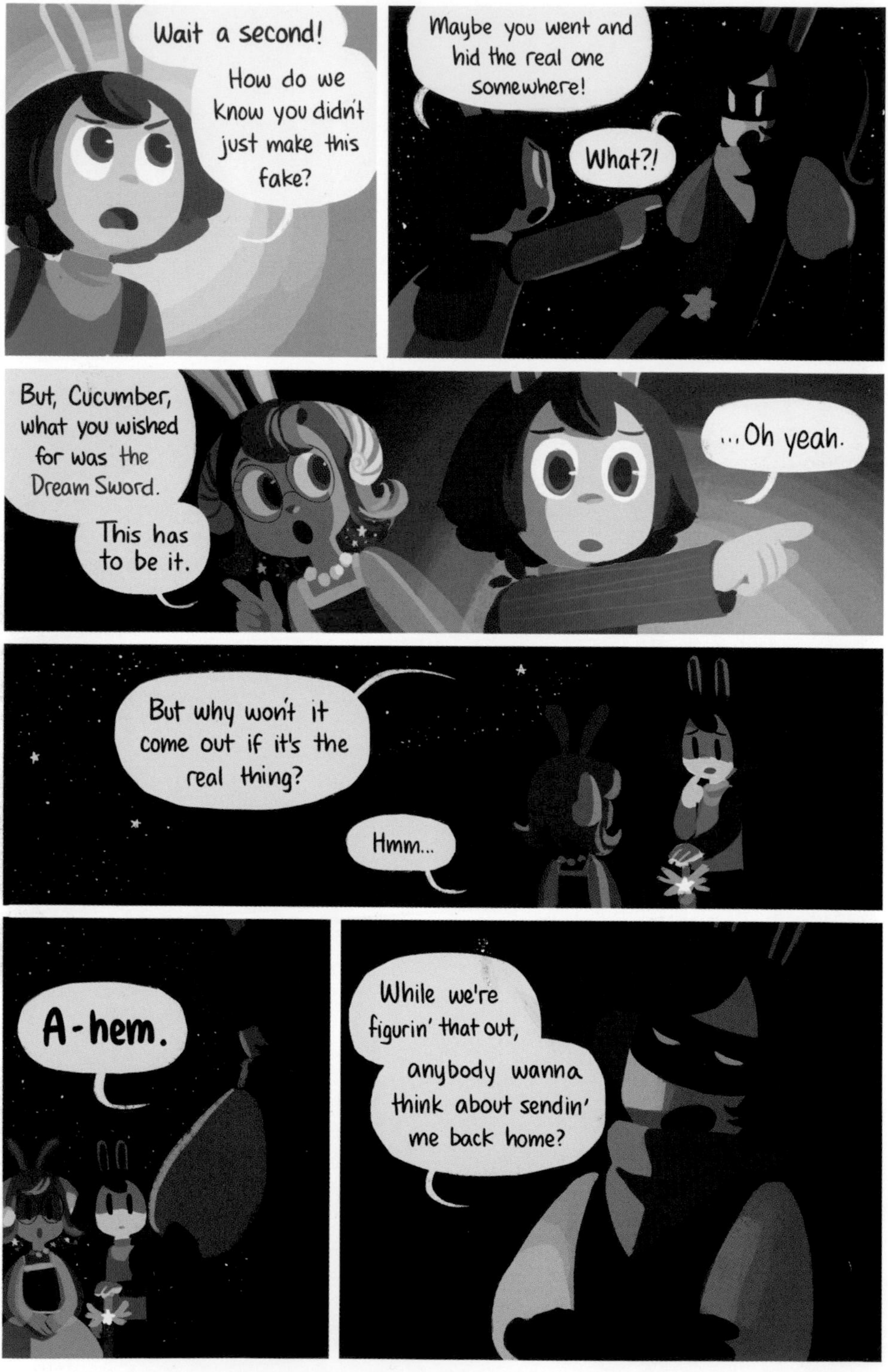
Wait a second!
How do we know you didn't just make this fake?
Maybe you went and hid the real one somewhere!
What?!
But, Cucumber, what you wished for was the Dream Sword.
This has to be it.
...Oh yeah.
But why won't it come out if it's the real thing?
Hmm...
A-hem.
While we're figurin' that out,
anybody wanna think about sendin' me back home?

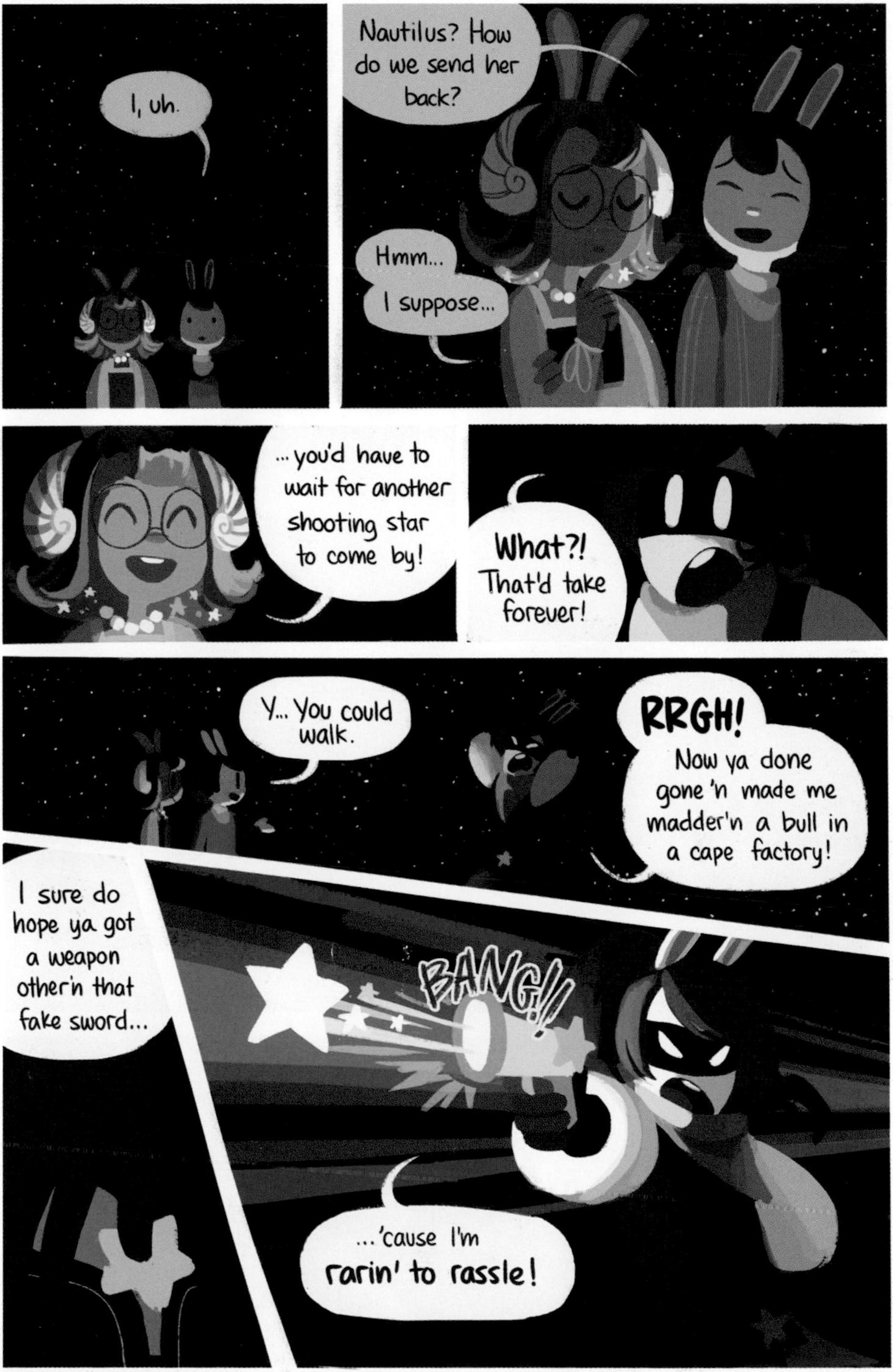
I, uh.
Nautilus? How do we send her back?
Hmm...
I suppose...
...you'd have to wait for another shooting star to come by!
What?! That'd take forever!
Y... You could walk.
RRGH!
Now ya done gone 'n made me madder'n a bull in a cape factory!
I sure do hope ya got a weapon other'n that fake sword...
BANG!!
...'cause I'm rarin' to rassle!

76

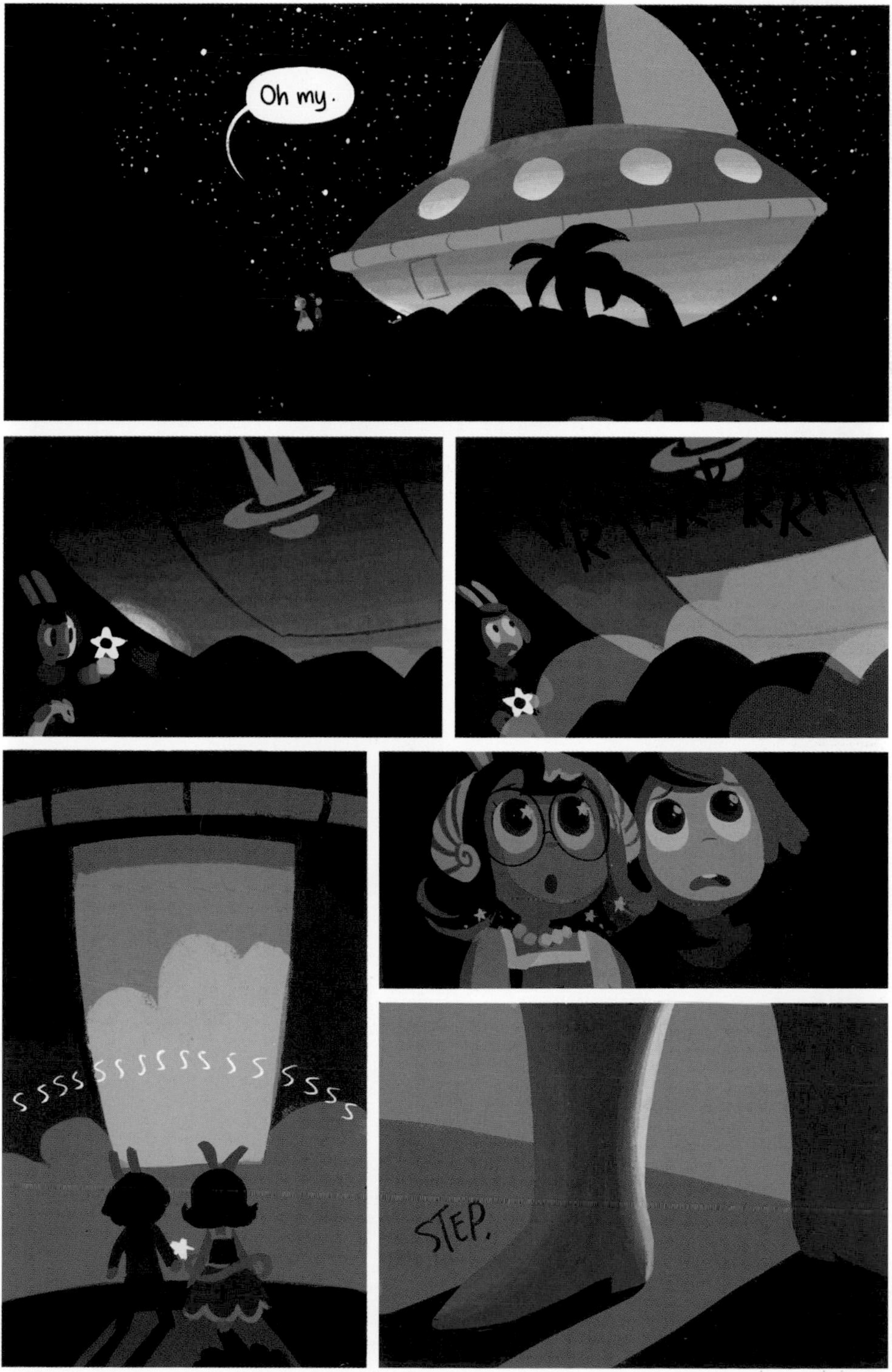
Oh my.
STEP.

A planet under attack!

Its citizens in peril!

A lone cry of distress **swallowed** whole by the darkness of space...

But **WHO** will answer it?!

WHO will come forth to defend the defenseless?!

WHO but...

hup!

Commander Caboodle, Champion of Justice!

Justice Log, Entry 5707.

After his sudden crash landing on a distant planet, the Champion of Justice makes contact with two strange alien creatures.

BUT WAIT! Could they be Dreamsiders? Judging by those adorable, floppy ears, all signs point to an intergalactic **yes!**

Greetings, rabbit children!

I am Commander Caboodle (Champion of Justice), and I come in peace.

Greetings, Commander! I am Princess Nautilus.

Um, and I'm Cucumber.

A hearty **hello** of **justice** to you...

...Princess Nautilus and Cucumber!

I'm here in search of a dangerous space criminal, and I've got to find my way to a place called...

..."Cake-Town Cast-Le," ASAP.

Caketown Castle?

Oh, this is the Ripple Kingdom!

You'll need to head east to get to where you're going.

Way east...

What?! **Curses!**

And I was **sure** I'd calibrated my navigator perfectly!

OK

Accidents will happen!

They will! **AND DID!**

hup!

Thanks for the tip, honorary champions!

And now... justice awaits!

KA - CHUNK

Caboodle...

AWAYYYYYYY

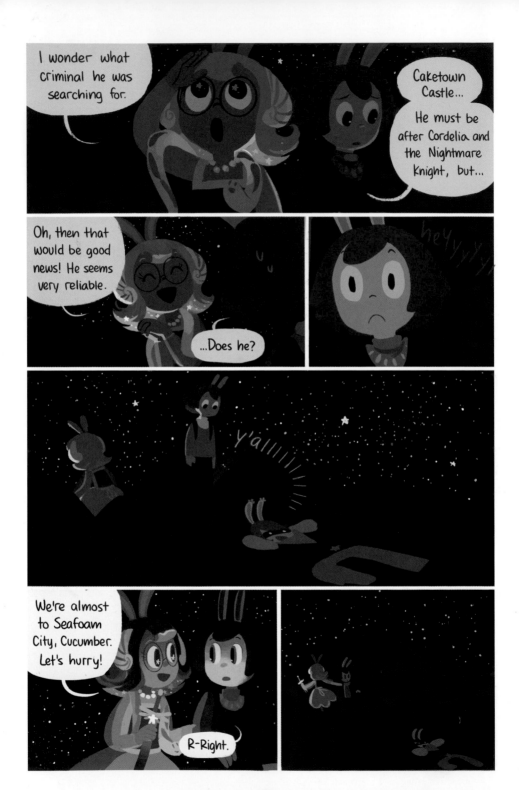

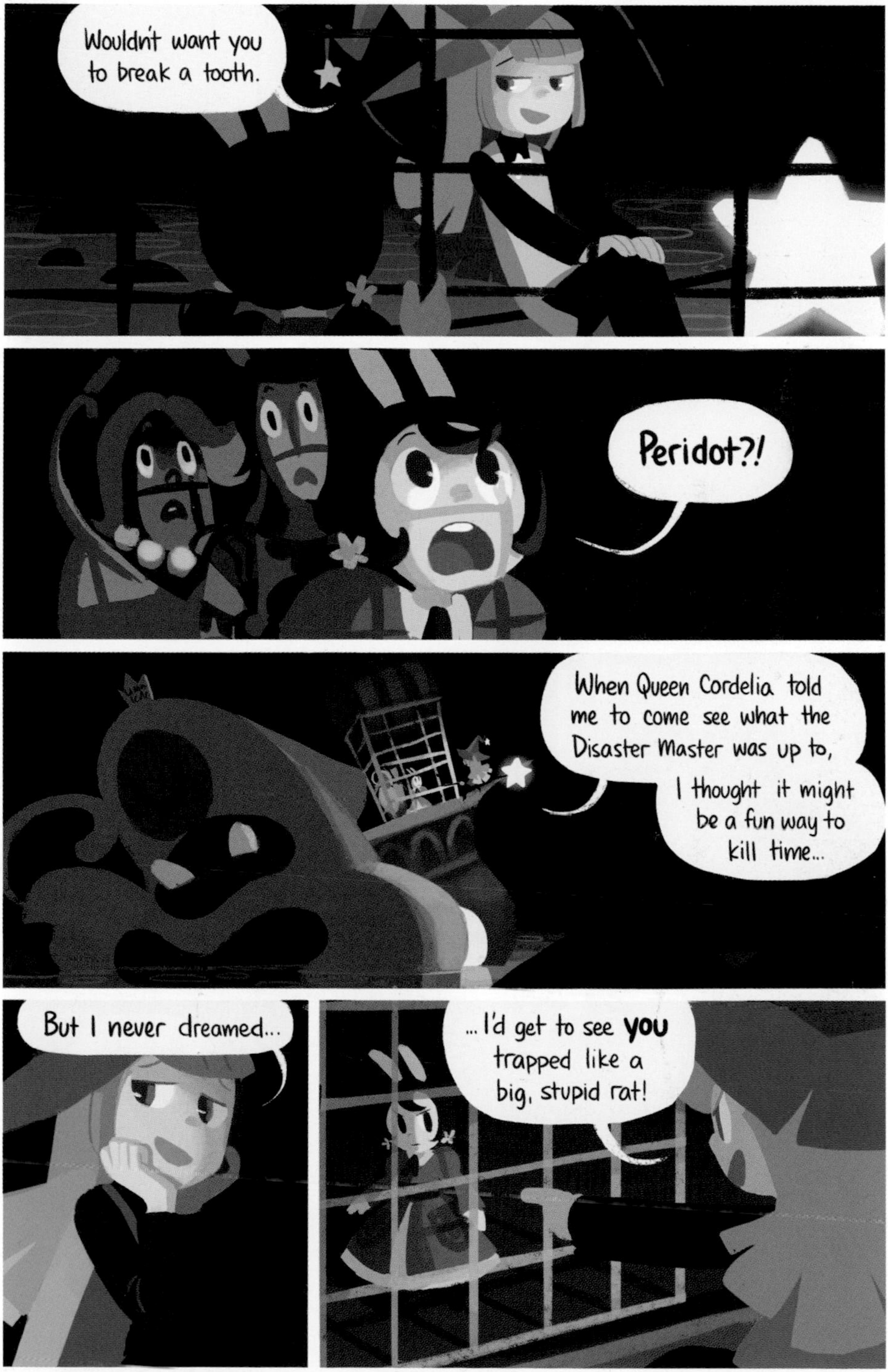
Wouldn't want you to break a tooth.
Peridot?!
When Queen Cordelia told me to come see what the Disaster Master was up to,
I thought it might be a fun way to kill time...
But I never dreamed...
...I'd get to see **YOU** trapped like a big, stupid rat!

86

GUH?

TINY BUNNY GIRL!

ME SMASH!

Huh?!

SPLASH!!

EEEEK!
What are you **doing,** stupid?!

I'm on **YOUR SIDE!!**

OH. ME SORRY.

Ugh!

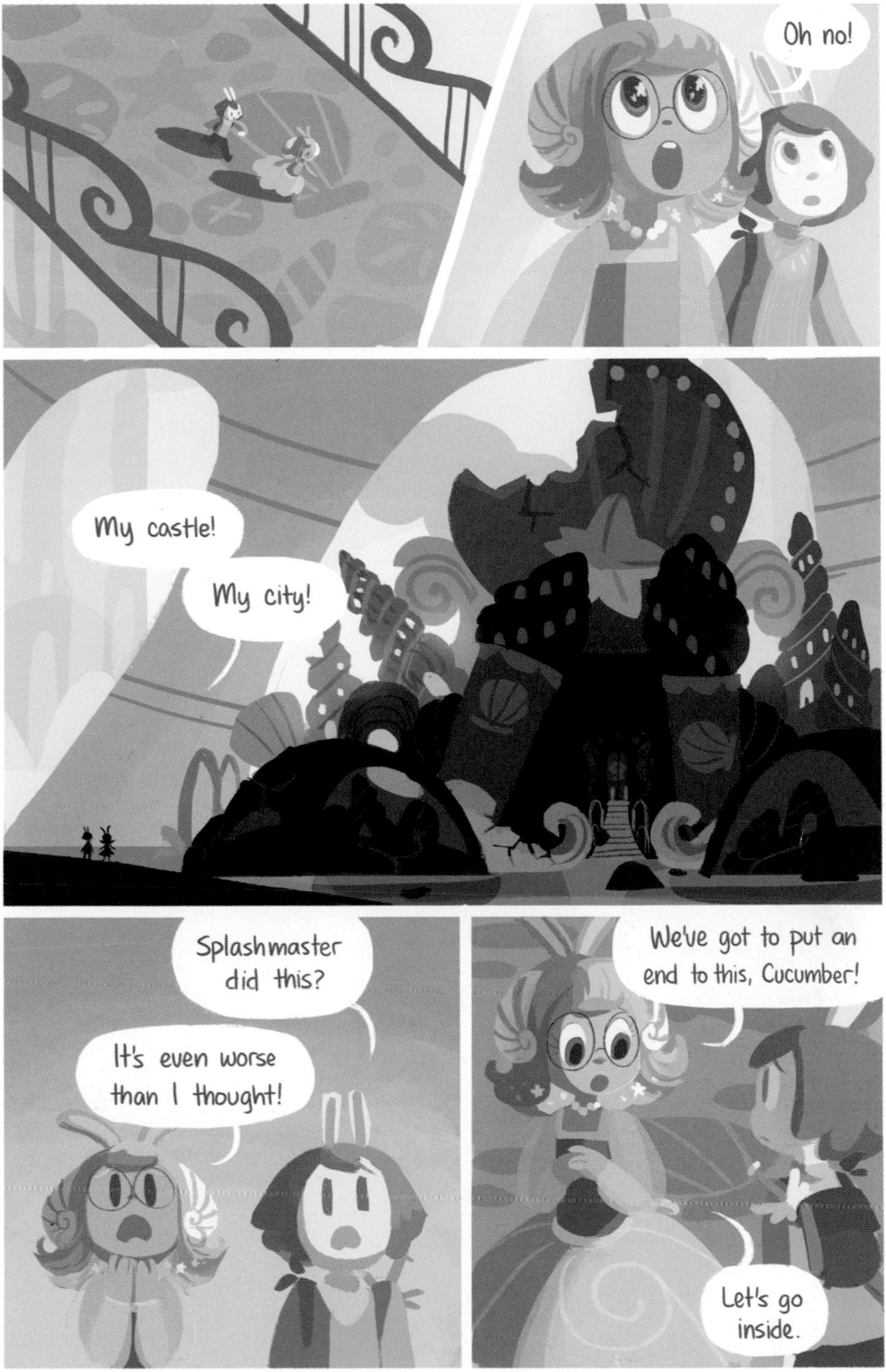
Oh no!
My castle!
My city!
Splashmaster did this?
It's even worse than I thought!
We've got to put an end to this, Cucumber!
Let's go inside.

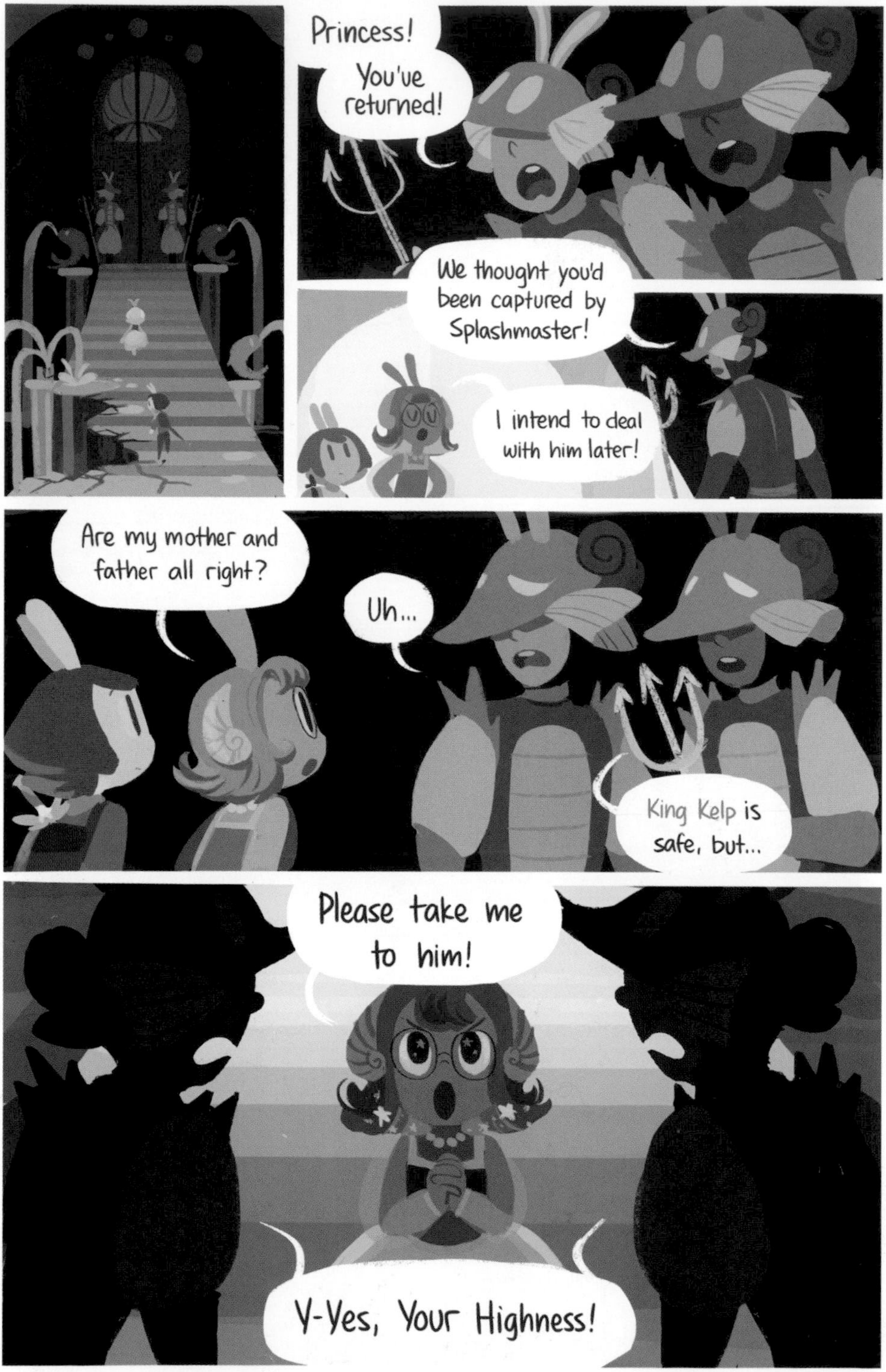

Princess!
You've returned!
We thought you'd been captured by Splashmaster!
I intend to deal with him later!
Are my mother and father all right?
Uh...
King Kelp is safe, but...
Please take me to him!
Y-Yes, Your Highness!

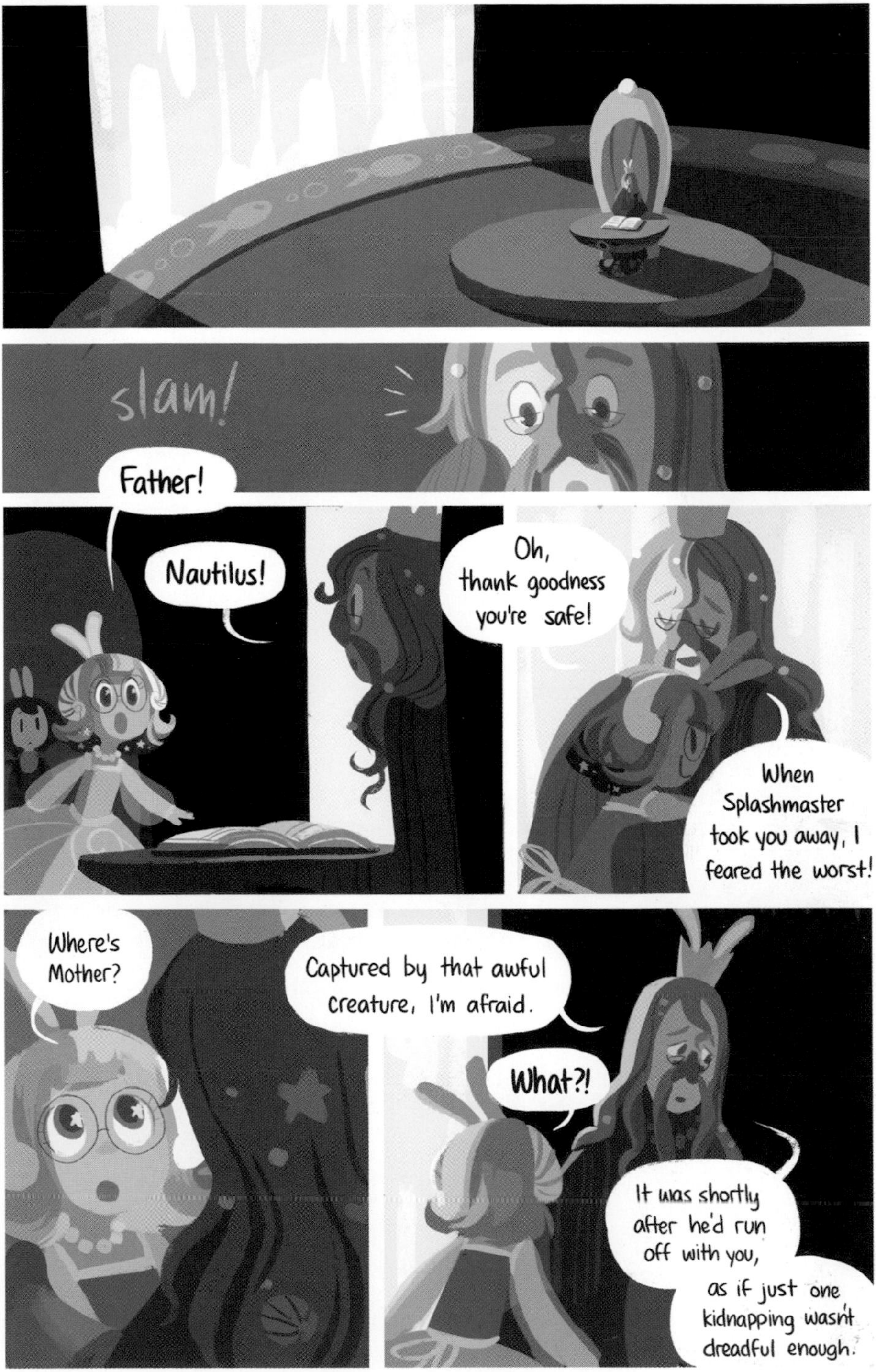
slam!
Father!
Nautilus!
Oh, thank goodness you're safe!
When Splashmaster took you away, I feared the worst!
Where's Mother?
Captured by that awful creature, I'm afraid.
What?!
It was shortly after he'd run off with you,
as if just one kidnapping wasn't dreadful enough.

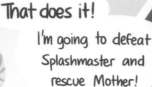

That does it!

I'm going to defeat Splashmaster and rescue Mother!

On your own?! Insanity!

Oh, gosh, no!

I've found the legendary hero, Cucumber! He's going with me.

R-Right, but

I see!

Well, that's wonderful! A pleasure to meet you, Cucumber.

It gives me hope to see the young hero who will soon rid us of this evil once and for all.

Um...

About that...

What?!

100 times, you say?

How horrible!

But I know there must be a way to defeat him for good!

Right, Cucumber?

Huh?!

Uh...

Right, Your Majesty?

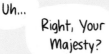

Hmm...

Now that we know, it would be irresponsible for us to allow this cycle to continue.

For the sake of Dreamside's future, we **must** believe there is a way...

even if things seem a bit hopeless at the moment.

Exactly!

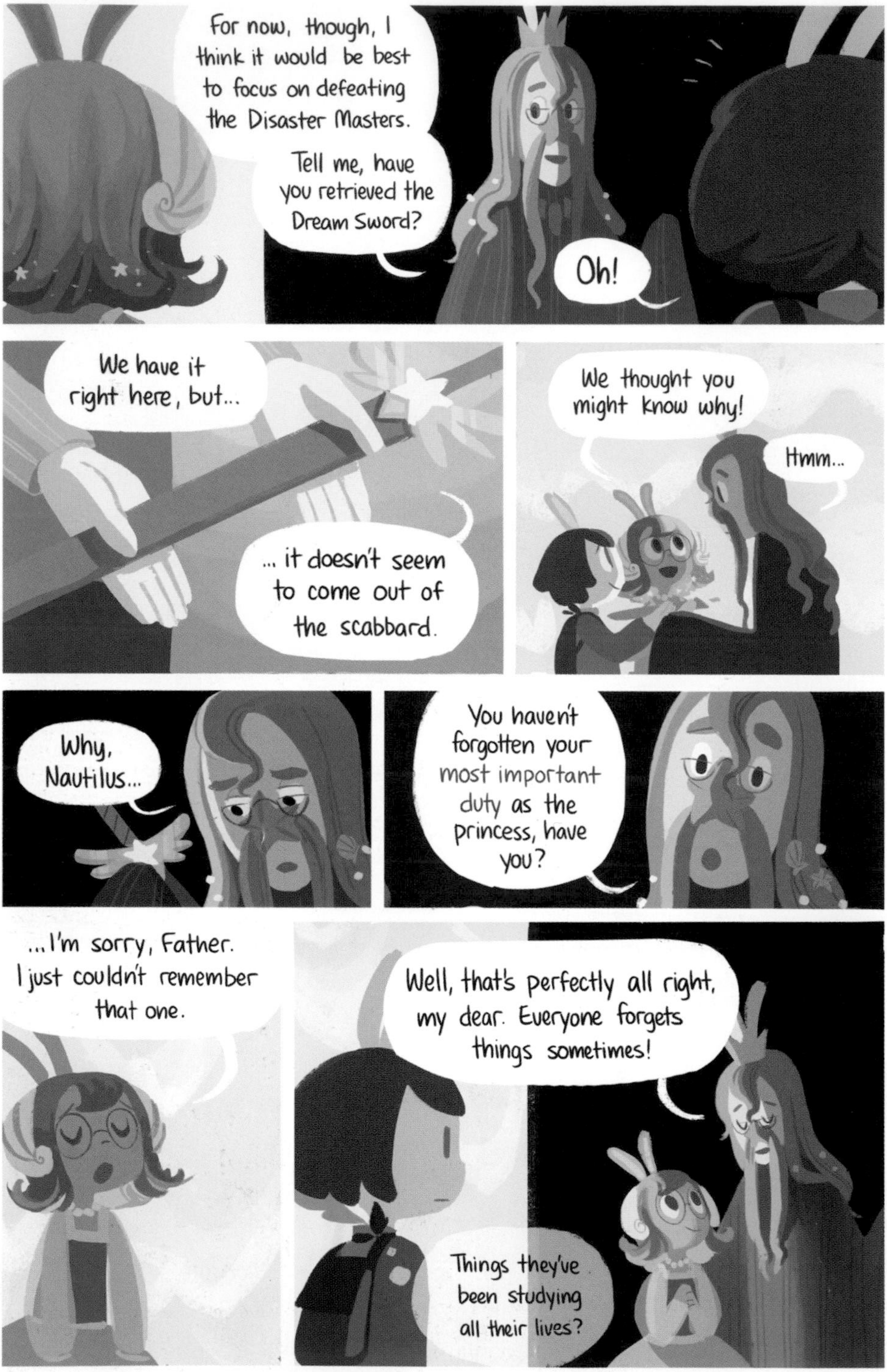
For now, though, I think it would be best to focus on defeating the Disaster Masters.
Tell me, have you retrieved the Dream Sword?
Oh!
We have it right here, but...
... it doesn't seem to come out of the scabbard.
We thought you might know why!
Hmm...
Why, Nautilus...
You haven't forgotten your most important duty as the princess, have you?
...I'm sorry, Father. I just couldn't remember that one.
Well, that's perfectly all right, my dear. Everyone forgets things sometimes!
Things they've been studying all their lives?

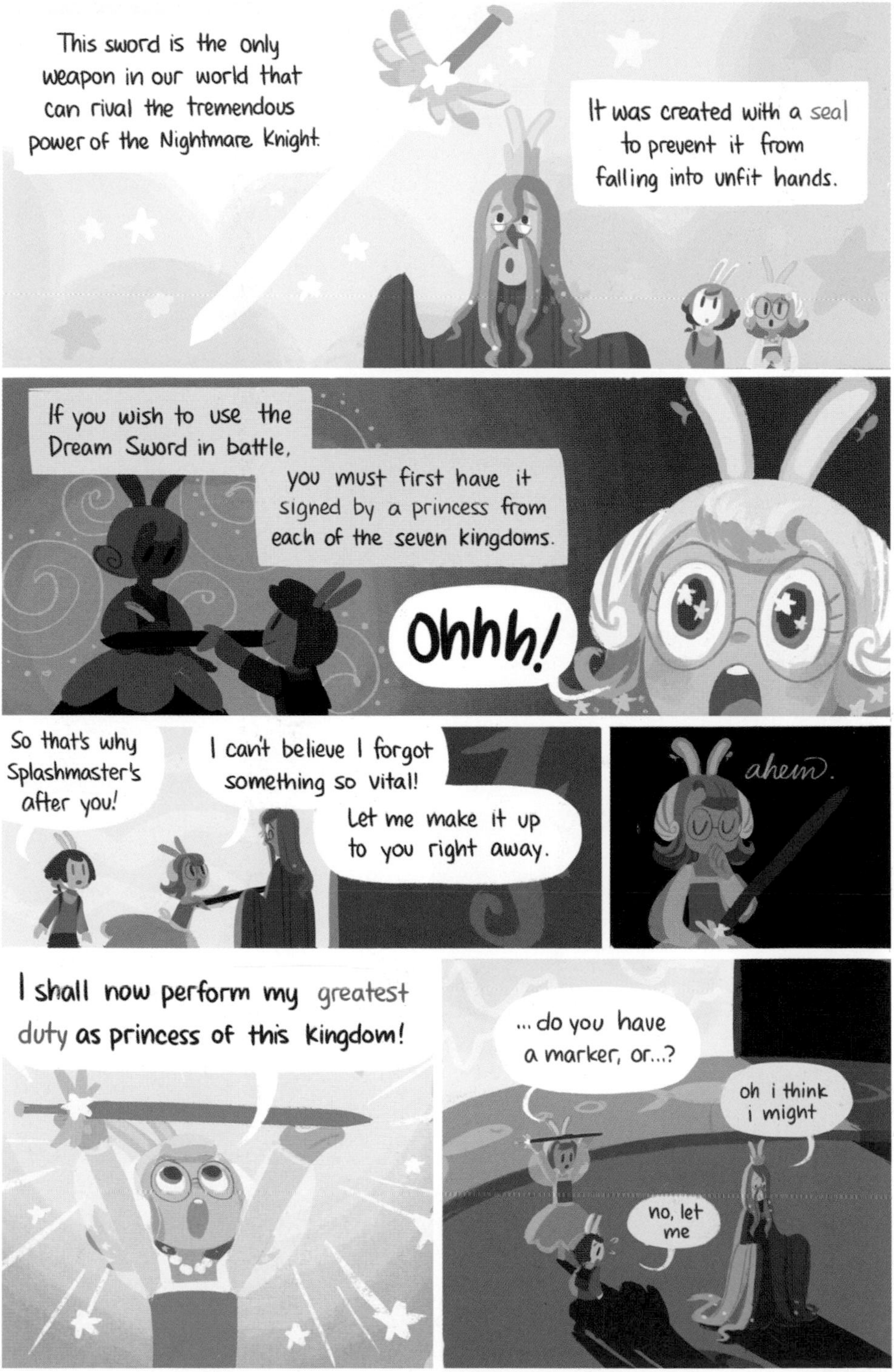
This sword is the only weapon in our world that can rival the tremendous power of the Nightmare Knight.
It was created with a seal to prevent it from falling into unfit hands.
If you wish to use the Dream Sword in battle,
you must first have it signed by a princess from each of the seven kingdoms.
Ohhh!
So that's why Splashmaster's after you!
I can't believe I forgot something so vital!
Let me make it up to you right away.
ahem.
I shall now perform my greatest duty as princess of this kingdom!
...do you have a marker, or...?
oh i think i might
no, let me

There!

Only six more to go!

Nautilus

"Only"...

That's all well and good,

but surely our brave hero will need a weapon to use against Splashmaster in the meantime.

Our armory should be able to supply you with a sword befitting—

Oh, uh!

I... can't really use a sword, Your Majesty.

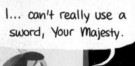

You can't?

Actually, my sister's the one who's excited to do all this hero stuff.

Oh!

Then... why are you here?

I-I wish I could tell you that.

Take a look, children!

The Extremely Specific and Pretty Much Completely Worthless Capsule Spell Machine!

the what

Allow me to demonstrate!

Simply turn this crank...

...and out comes a cute plastic capsule!

Oh, I can't take the suspense! Open it!

You try it, Cucumber!

O-Okay...

PUSH

"This capsule grants you the power to place a... comically oversized bathtub drain on any surface."

Oh.

WOWWW

Two of the same! Incredible!

My boy, with fortune like this,

you're well on your way to joining the Puffington's council one day!

Th- Thank you.

And now...

...it's my turn!

clank!

POP!

"This capsule grants you the power to order a pizza from anywhere...

...but only when nobody is in the mood for pizza."

I can't think of a single situation where I'd need to use something so pointless.

That's **amazing,** Father!

Isn't it, though?!

HA HA

Well, I suppose that's all
the help I can give you.

Splashmaster's made his
lair in Shipwreck Shelter,
just beyond here.

This battle may not
be an easy one,
but I have faith
that the two of
you can do it.

So do I!

Are you ready,
Cucumber?

W-We wouldn't turn
back if I said no,
would we?

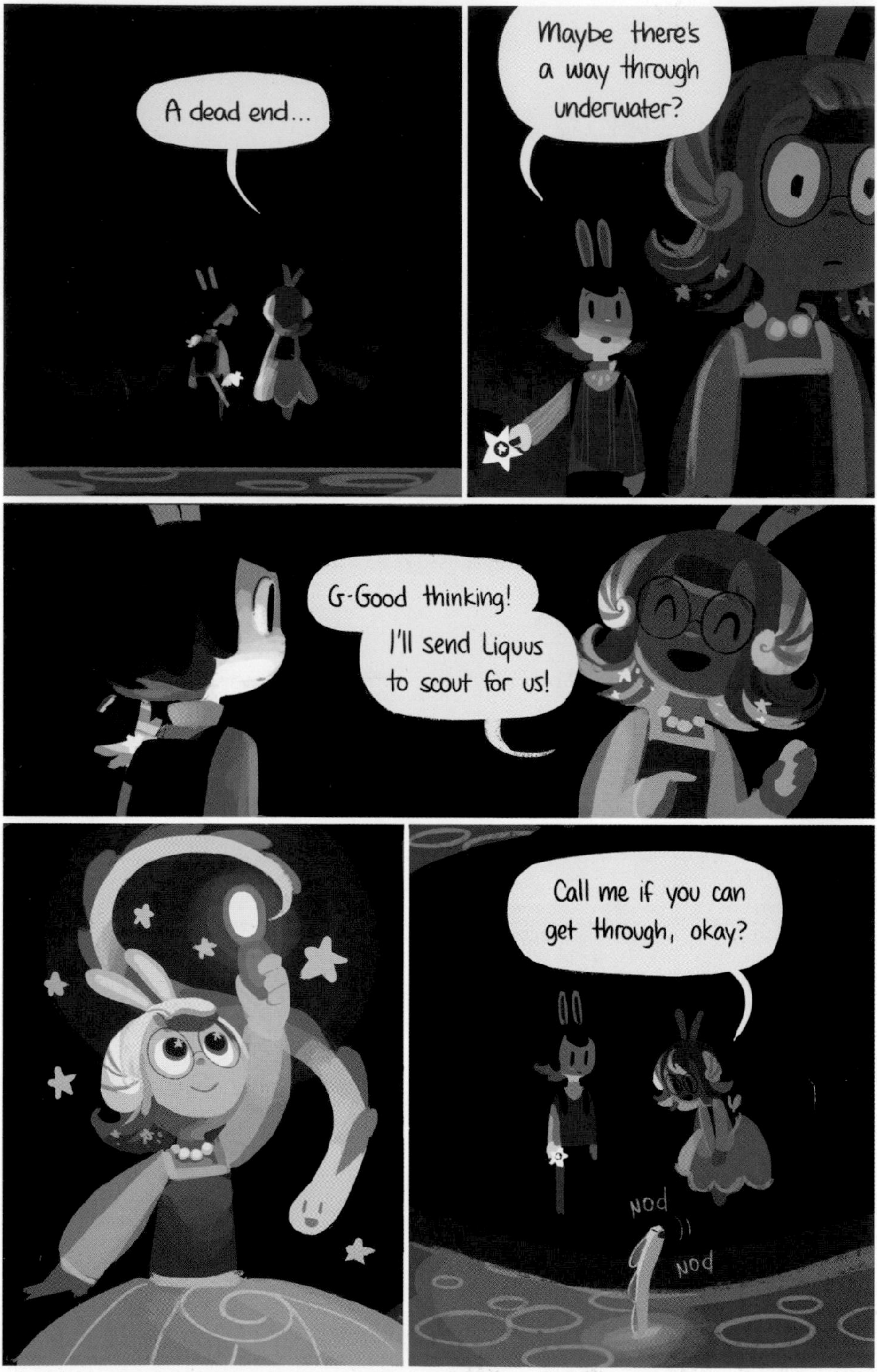
A dead end...
Maybe there's a way through underwater?
G-Good thinking!
I'll send Liquus to scout for us!
Call me if you can get through, okay?
NOD
NOD

Stay safe!

He's such a good boy.

Now all we have to do is wait for—

AAAAAAA

splish!

Hey, bros.

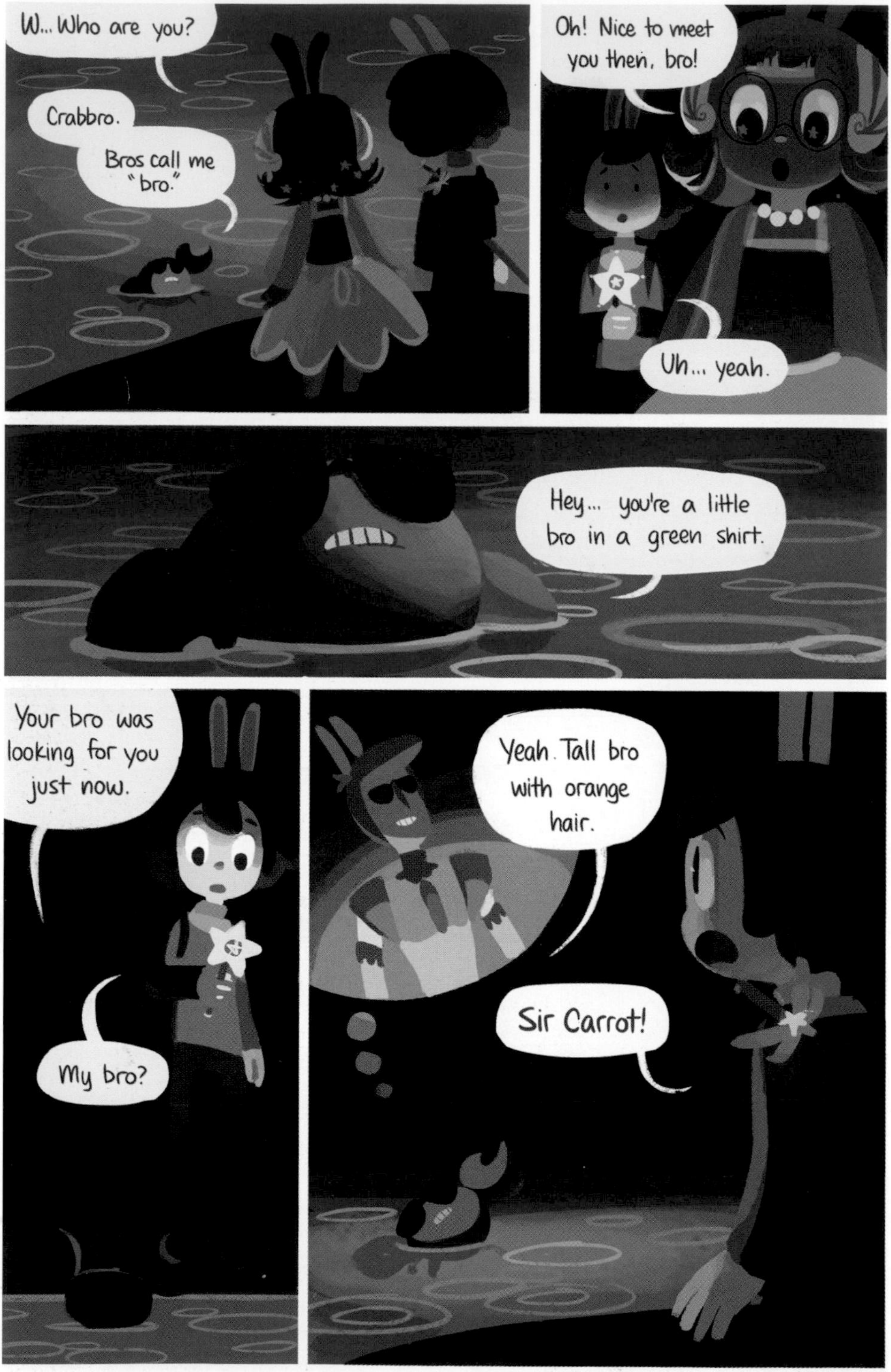

W... Who are you?
Crabbro.
Bros call me "bro."
Oh! Nice to meet you then, bro!
Uh... yeah.
Hey... you're a little bro in a green shirt.
Your bro was looking for you just now.
My bro?
Yeah. Tall bro with orange hair.
Sir Carrot!

...Okay. But here's a bro tip.

That squid's place? All water in there.

Not a lot of room for you bros to run around.

I guess we'll have to be careful not to fall in, then.

Y-Yes...

Well, thanks for the tip, um... bro.

Anytime. Good luck, bros.

bloop

Uh-oh...

What's the matter?

I, um... The truth is, I—

AAAAA

DINGA DINGA DING

Does that mean he found a way through?

Y...

Yes! There's an underwater tunnel.

If we swim through that, we'll be in Splashmaster's cave.

Great!

Then let's—

...Nautilus?

I-

I can't—

I can't swim!

Huh?!

Please don't look at me like that, Cucumber. We all have our weaknesses!

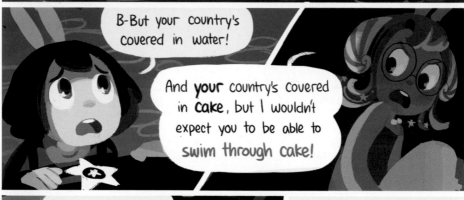

B-But your country's covered in water!

And **your** country's covered in **cake**, but I wouldn't expect you to be able to swim through cake!

what

It was a miracle I washed ashore when Splashmaster dropped me, but this is different!

I couldn't possibly hold my breath long enough to make it through!

Oh! Well, if that's all you're worried about, then it's okay.

I have a spell for this!

You do?

III

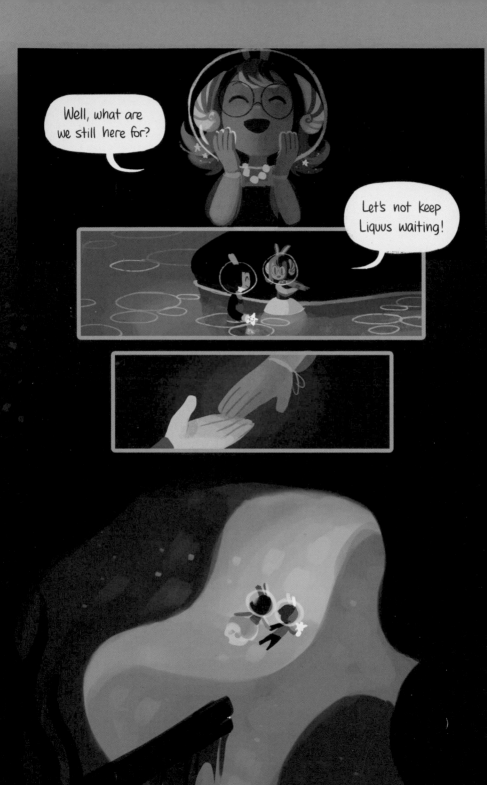

Splash!
Yayyyyy!
That wasn't so bad, was it?
Not at all! Thank you, Cucumber.
And thank you too, Liquus.
Are we almost there?

HUH?

Nooo!

Whatever you do, PLEEEEASE don't throw a huge barrel at my brother!

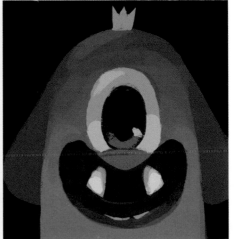

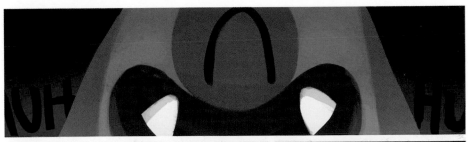

TINY BUNNYMAN THROW LIKE **BABY!**

Ugh, stop! You sound like my dad!

HUH HU HUH H

Ohhh! What shall we do?

noooooon

snap!

OWWW!!

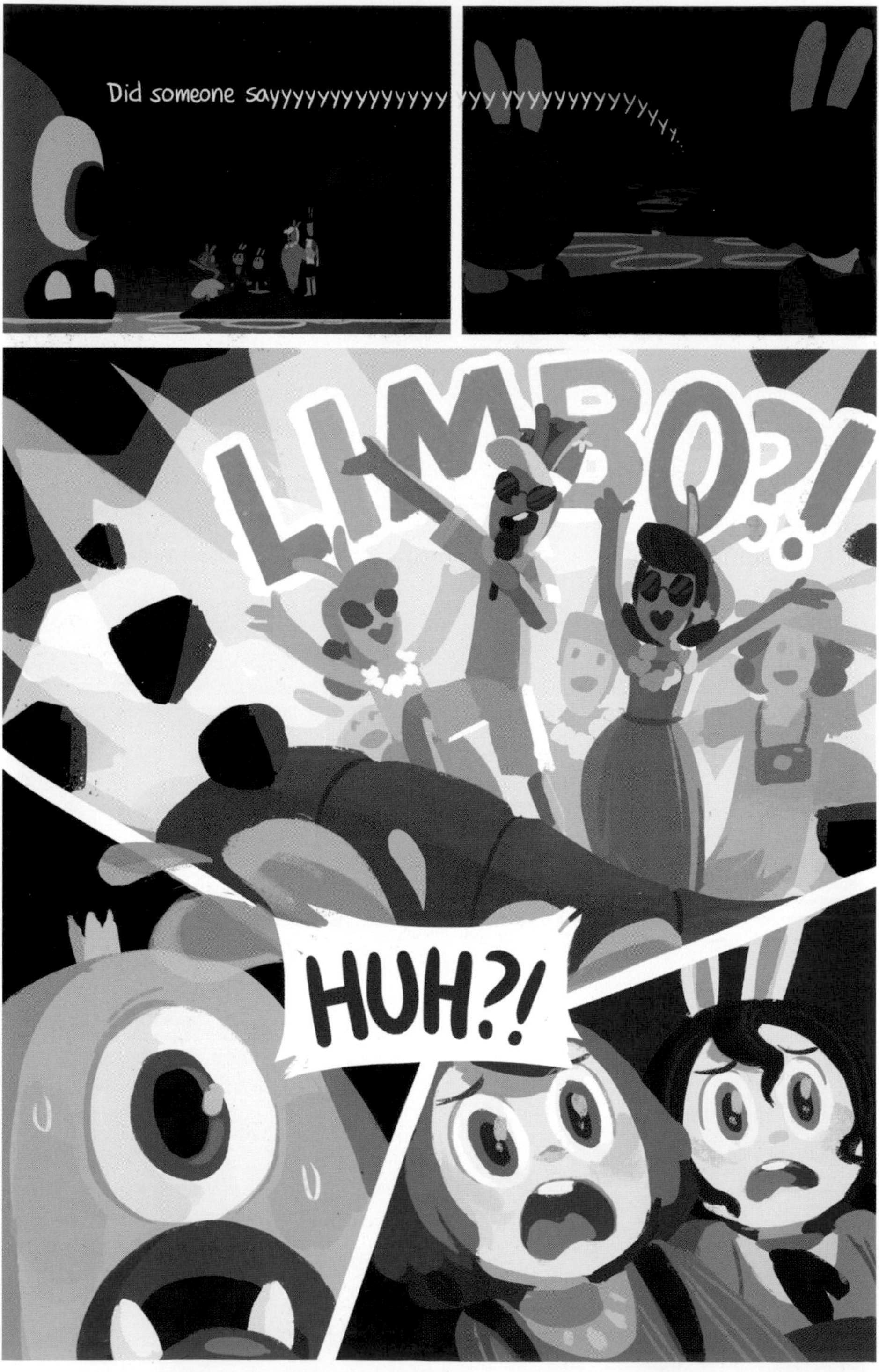

Did someone sayyyyyyyyyyyyyyyyyyyyyyyyyyyyyyyyyy...
LIMBO?!
HUH?!

Wh—

WHAT IS

14th ANNUAL LIMBO-THON

That's right — with this one-of-a-kind Limbo Dimension Generator...

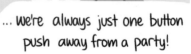

... we're always just one button push away from a party!

But keep in mind that it's a prototype, okay? Real delicate.

So don't go making a ruckus if you lose!

I don't **intend** to lose!

All right, all right, let's get this party **started!**

It's the ultimate battle for limbo supremacy!

Who will claim the crown?!

YAYYYYYYYYYY

Yeahh!

Wooo!

Best of luck!

Y- You can do it!

Knock him dead, what's-your-face!

BUT ME NEVER LIMBO BEFORE.

Hmph! Amateur!

What do you say, Princess? Care to show him how it's done?

Watch and learn!

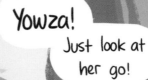

Yowza! Just look at her go!

That's the kind of skill you'd expect from the Ripple kingdom's very own **limbo princess!**

But it's not too late for you to nab that crown, Splashmaster!

How low can **YOU** go?!

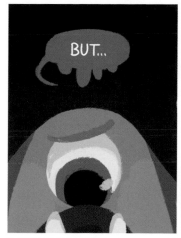
BUT...

BUT THIS NO FAIR.

What?

Surely you aren't expecting us to raise the limbo pole for you?

BUT IT TOO SMALL!

Lim-bo! Lim-bo! Lim-bo! Lim-bo!

No cheating, Splashmaster!

Are you a limbo king or a limbo **commoner?!**

LIM-BO! LIM LIM O! LIM-B O!

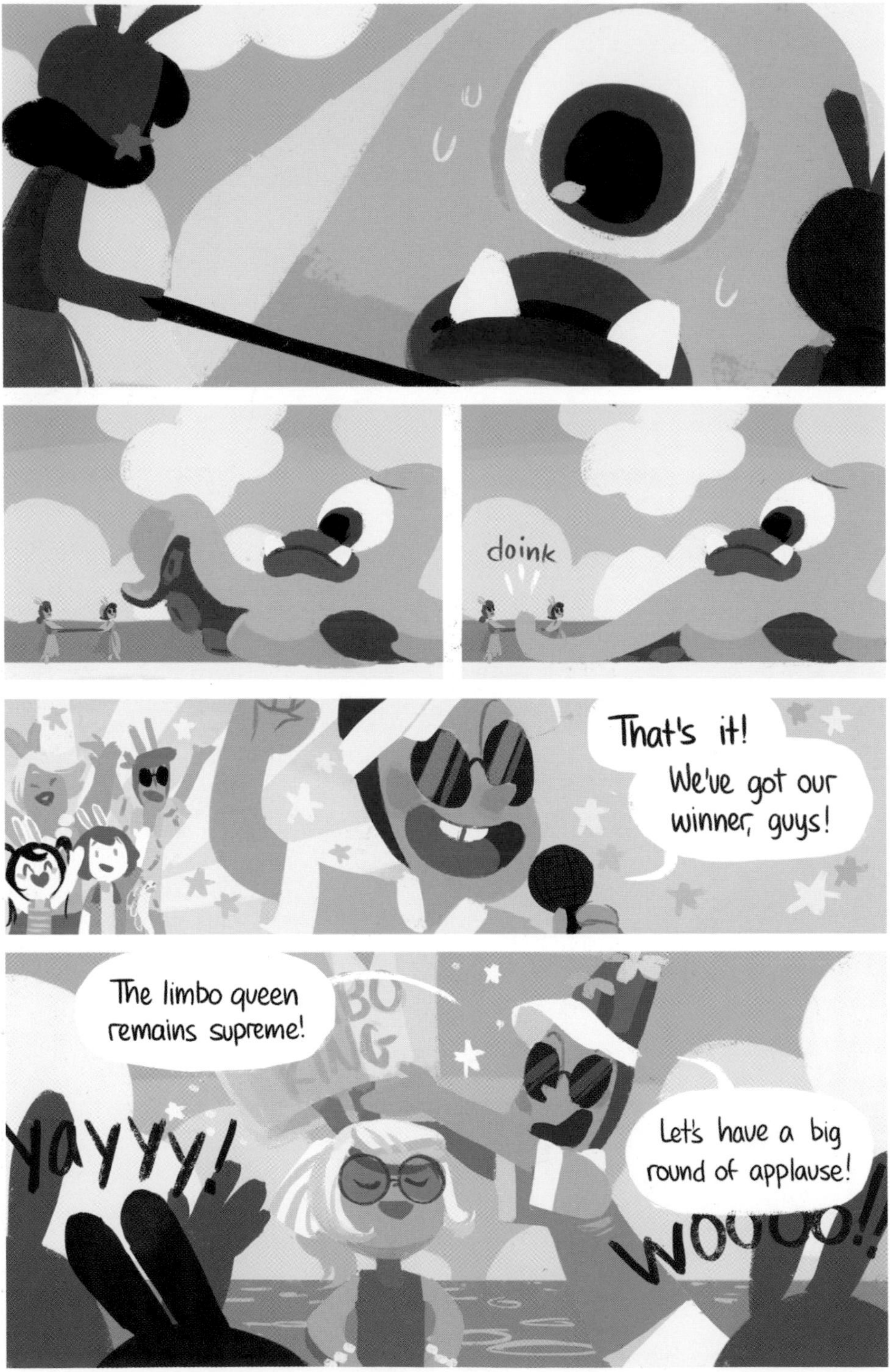
doink
That's it!
We've got our winner, guys!
The limbo queen remains supreme!
YAYYY!
Let's have a big round of applause!
WOOOO!!

Uh-oh!
SPLASH!

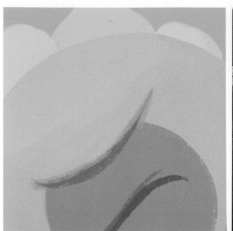

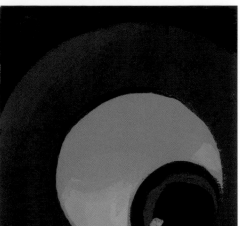

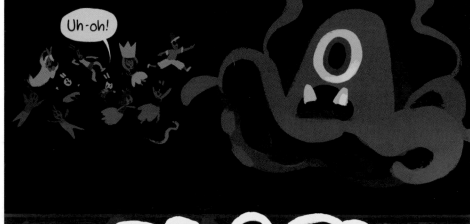

AAAAA

AAAAA!!

AAAAA!!

Stay calm, everyone!

Stay—

OOF!!

EEEEEE

Why's everybody leaving? They're about to miss the good part.

NOOO!!

HEELP!!

138

ZAP!

...For real? Where'd you learn how to—

please just help me pull

glub glub glub glub glub glub

drip

139

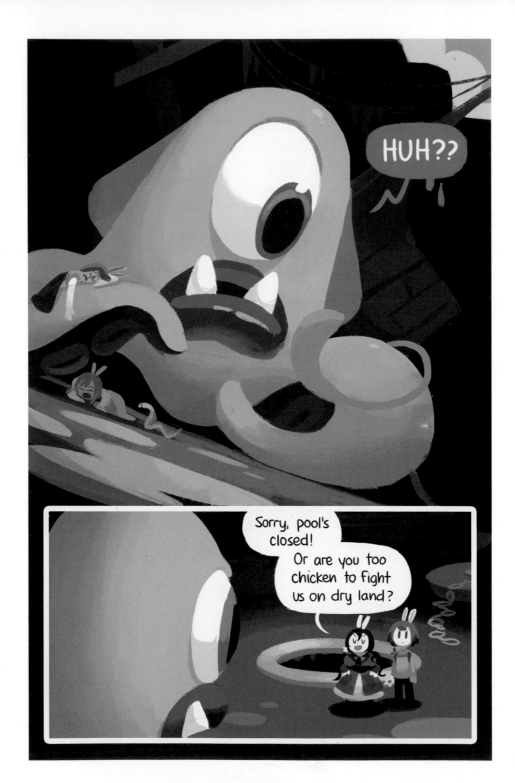

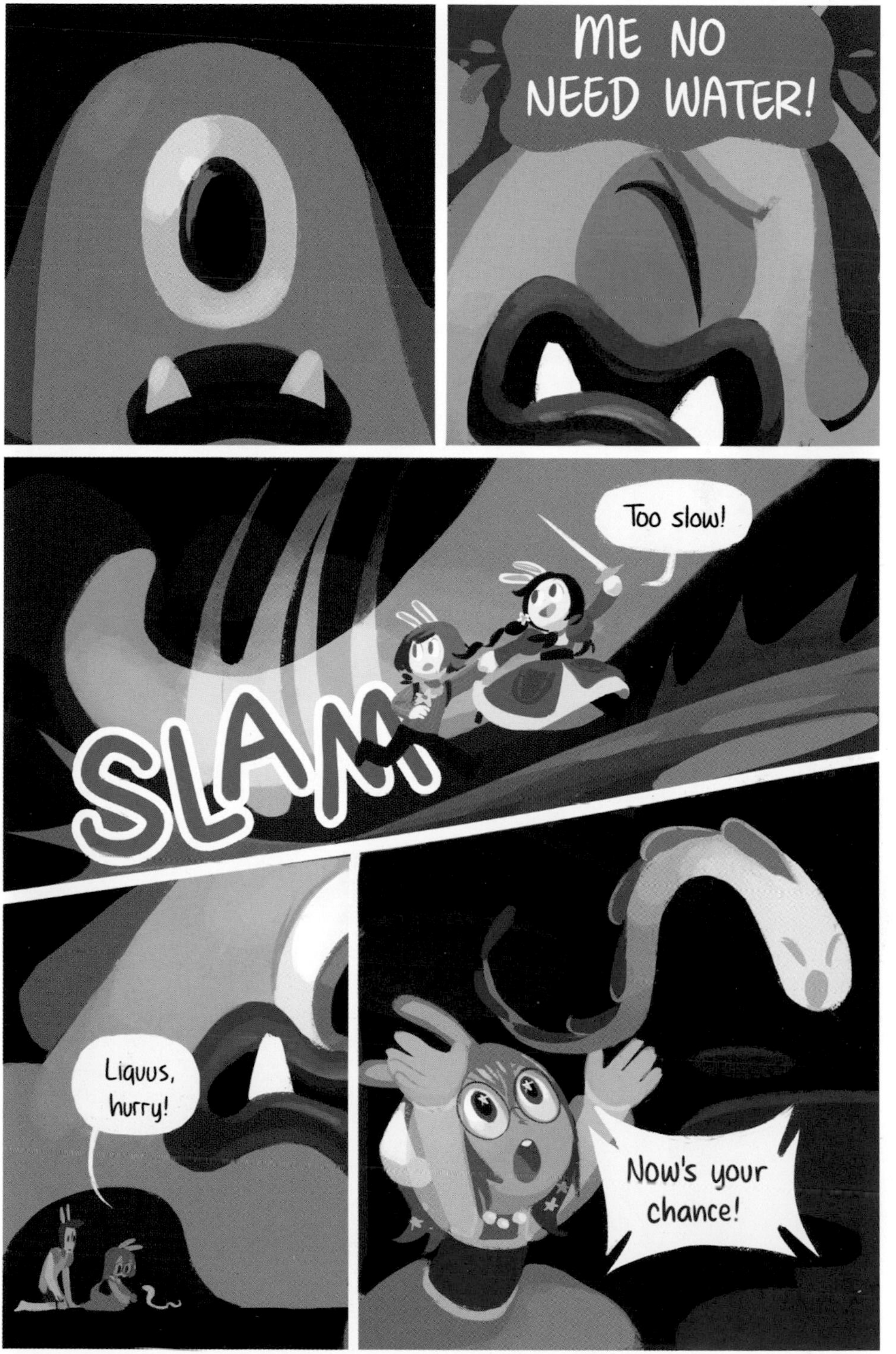
ME NO NEED WATER!
Too slow!
SLAM!
Liquus, hurry!
Now's your chance!

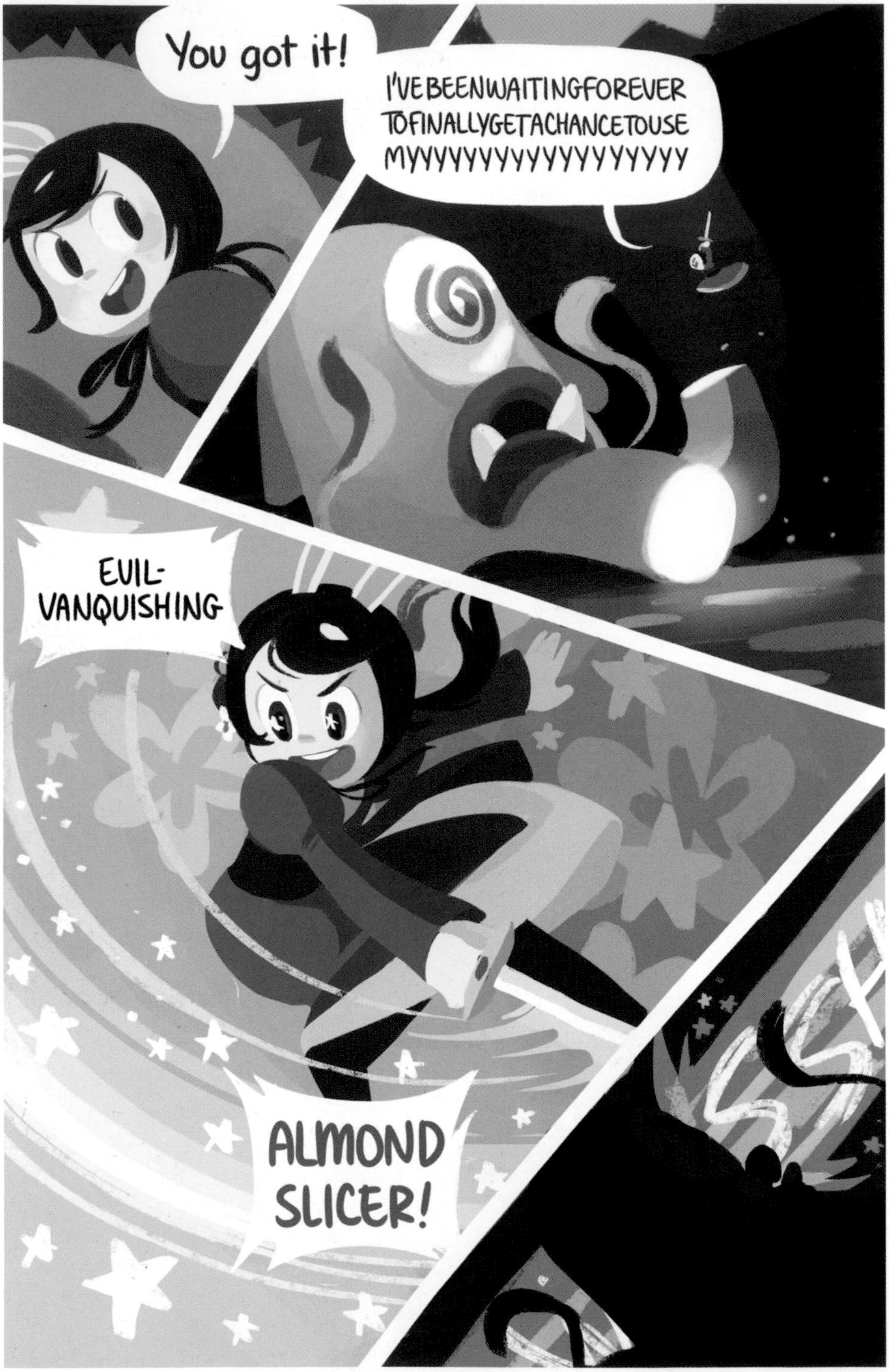

You got it!
I'VEBEENWAITINGFOREVER TOFINALLYGETACHANCETOUSE MYYYYYYYYYYYYYYYYYY
EVIL-VANQUISHING
ALMOND SLICER!

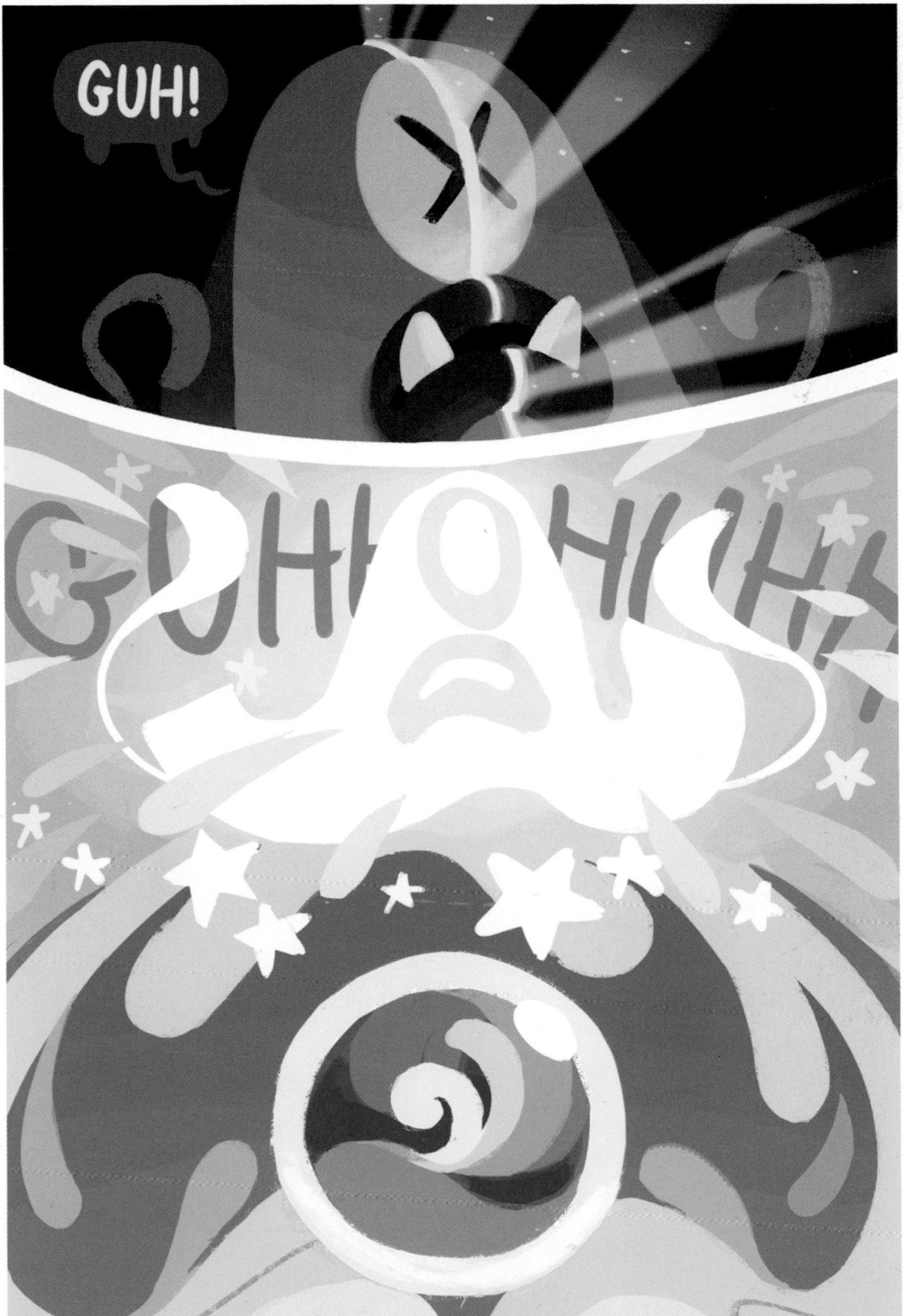
GUH!
GUHHHHHH

Is this really the Nightmare Knight's 100th resurrection?

His **HUH**?!

...So, Chardonnay couldn't keep that little detail to herself, could she?

I don't know what I'm going to do with that girl.

Why keep it a secret?

Oh, use your head, dear.

If I tell a hero the foe he's up against can't be defeated, **ever**, how do you think he'll react?

He'll lose his nerve, like **YOU** have!

didn't really have any to start with...

So we're the 100th guys to do this?

And after us will be others...

O Wise Dream Oracle,

isn't there **any** way to end the cycle?

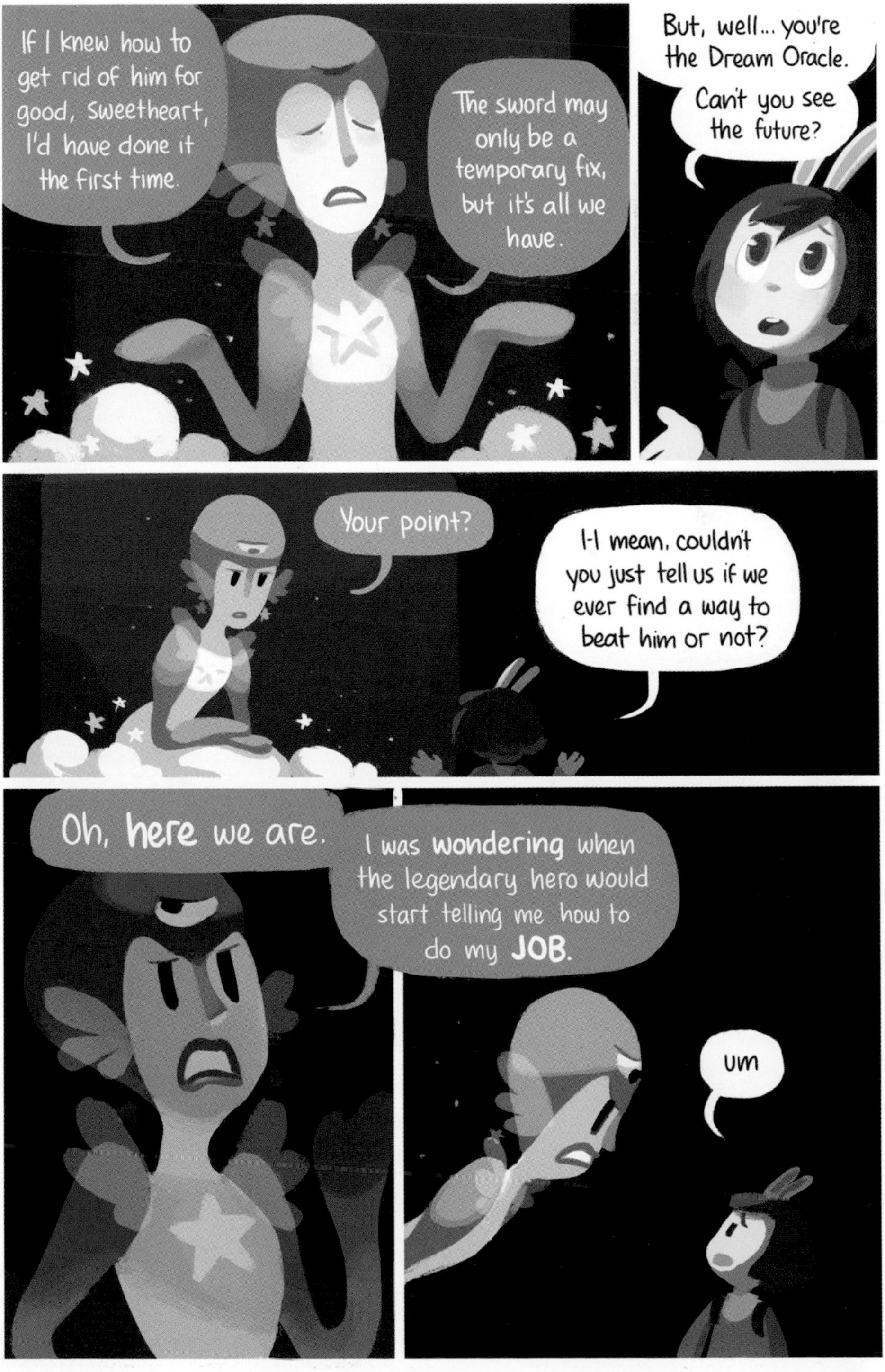
If I knew how to get rid of him for good, sweetheart, I'd have done it the first time.
The sword may only be a temporary fix, but it's all we have.
But, well... you're the Dream Oracle.
Can't you see the future?
Your point?
I-I mean, couldn't you just tell us if we ever find a way to beat him or not?
Oh, **here** we are.
I was **wondering** when the legendary hero would start telling me how to do my **JOB**.
um

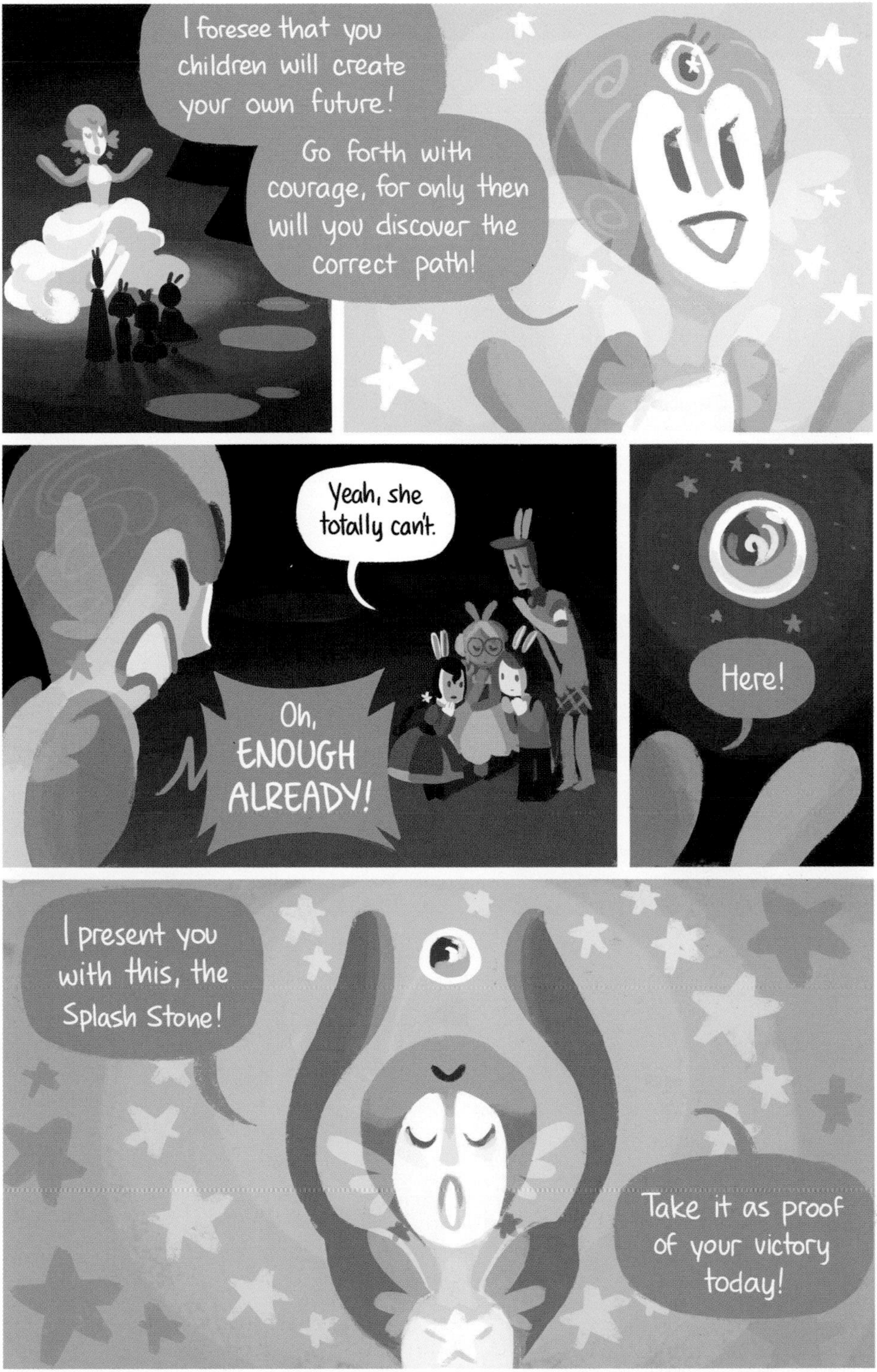
I foresee that you children will create your own future!
Go forth with courage, for only then will you discover the correct path!
Yeah, she totally can't.
Oh, ENOUGH ALREADY!
Here!
I present you with this, the Splash Stone!
Take it as proof of your victory today!

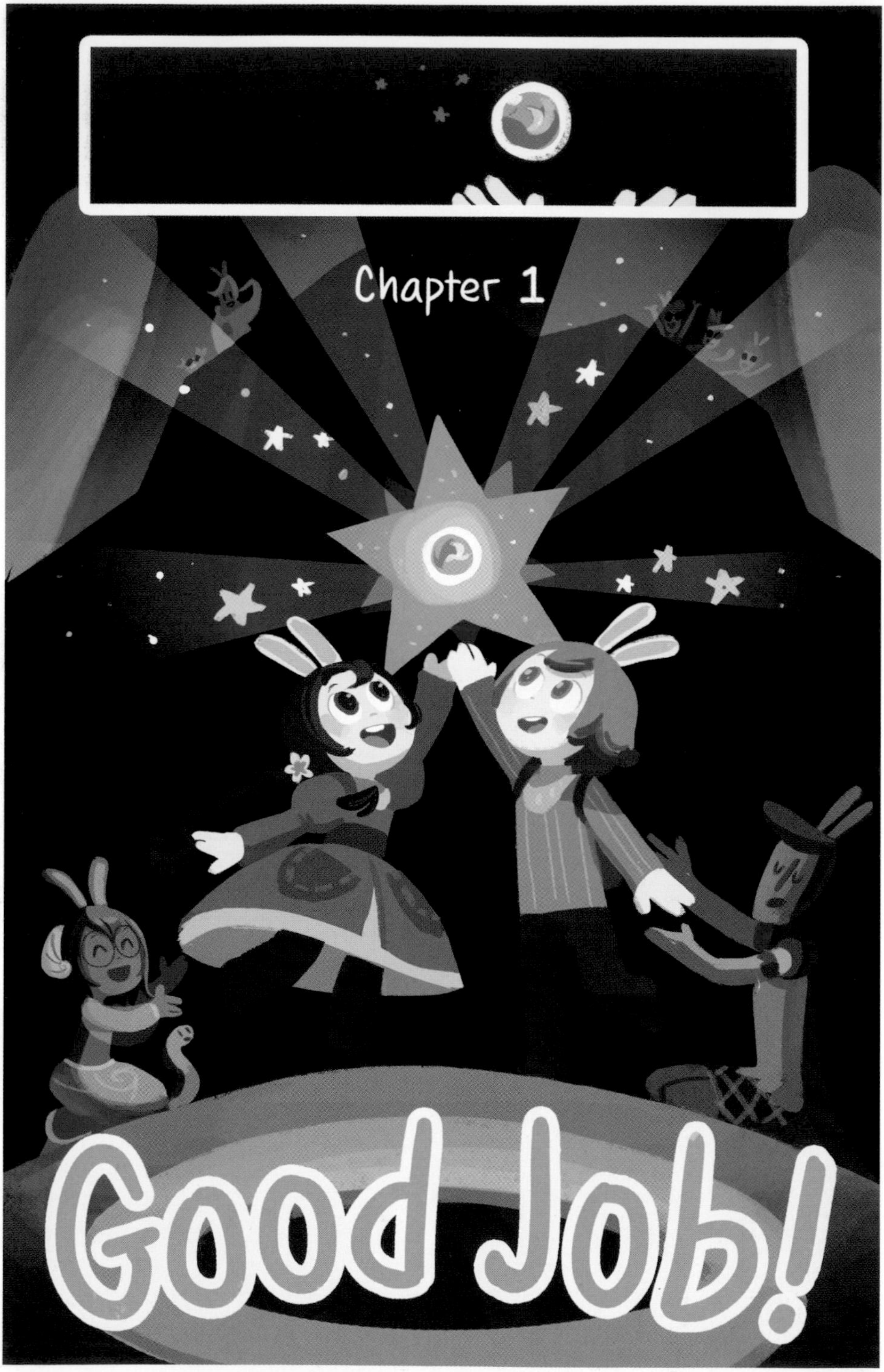
Chapter 1
Good Job!

Thanks to the power of teamwork
(and the power of limbo), the heroes
managed to defeat Splashmaster.

Now, with the first leg of their journey
behind them, they set their sights
on the Melody Kingdom.

But in light of a new revelation,
the future of Dreamside is
still uncertain.

And elsewhere, evil forces are already
plotting their next move...

Splashmaster
has fallen.

What?!
IMPOSSIBLE!

Not ... really.

He never **has** been the most
capable of my servants.

It was only a
matter of time.

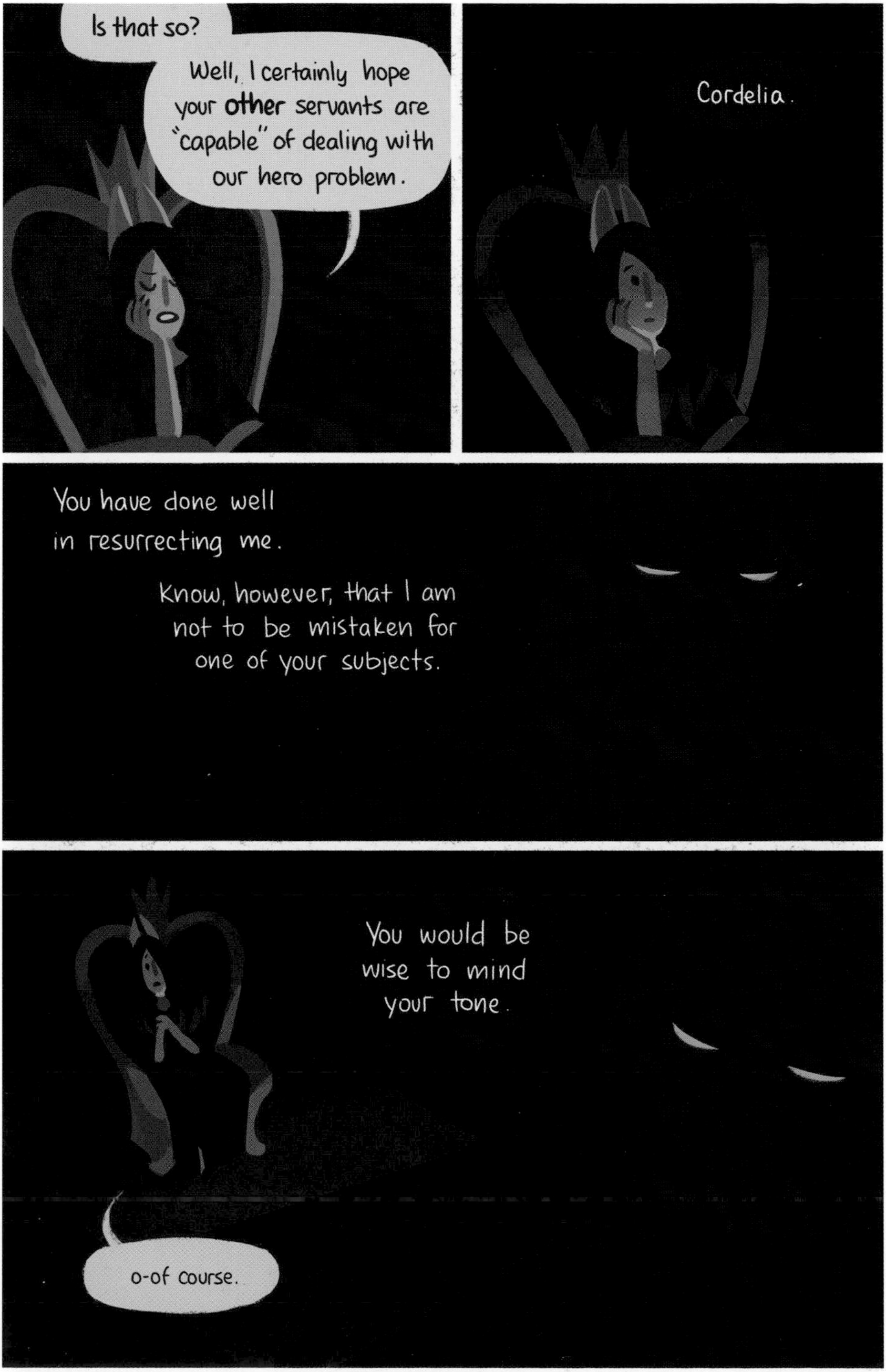

Is that so?

Well, I certainly hope your **other** servants are "capable" of dealing with our hero problem.

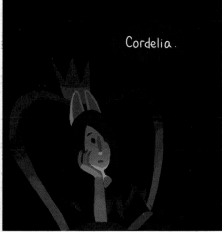

Cordelia.

You have done well in resurrecting me.

Know, however, that I am not to be mistaken for one of your subjects.

You would be wise to mind your tone.

o-of course.

The hero and his companions are headed for the Melody Kingdom.

Their journey will end there.

phew

But...

Peridot! Come here!

Whaaat?

Hm hm hm...
Excellent.

You may have
defeated Splashmaster,
Hero, but our battle
is only just beginning.

The Doughnut Kingdom
is already mine...

...and soon, **all** of
Dreamside will **kneel**
before can we get

rid of that?!

It's really starting to
creep me out!

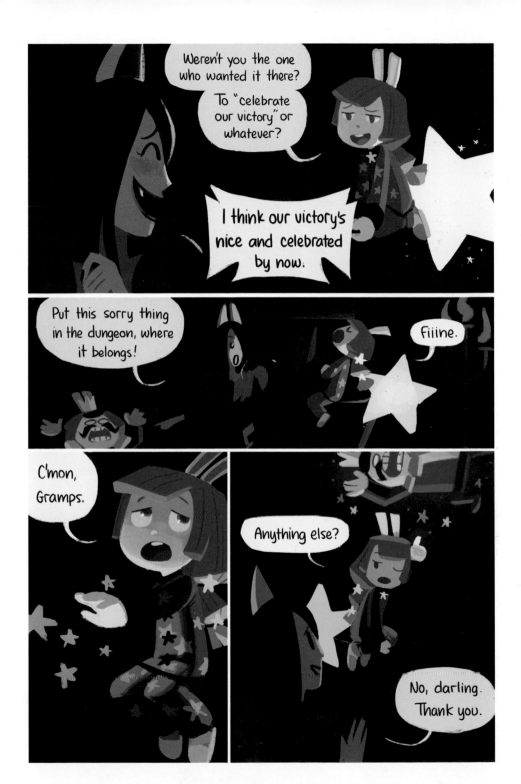

159

Right
down...

Eh?

You're still here?!
The door's unlocked, y'know! We don't actually **need** you for anything.

I dunno, it's kind of cozy down here. Maybe I'm gettin' old.

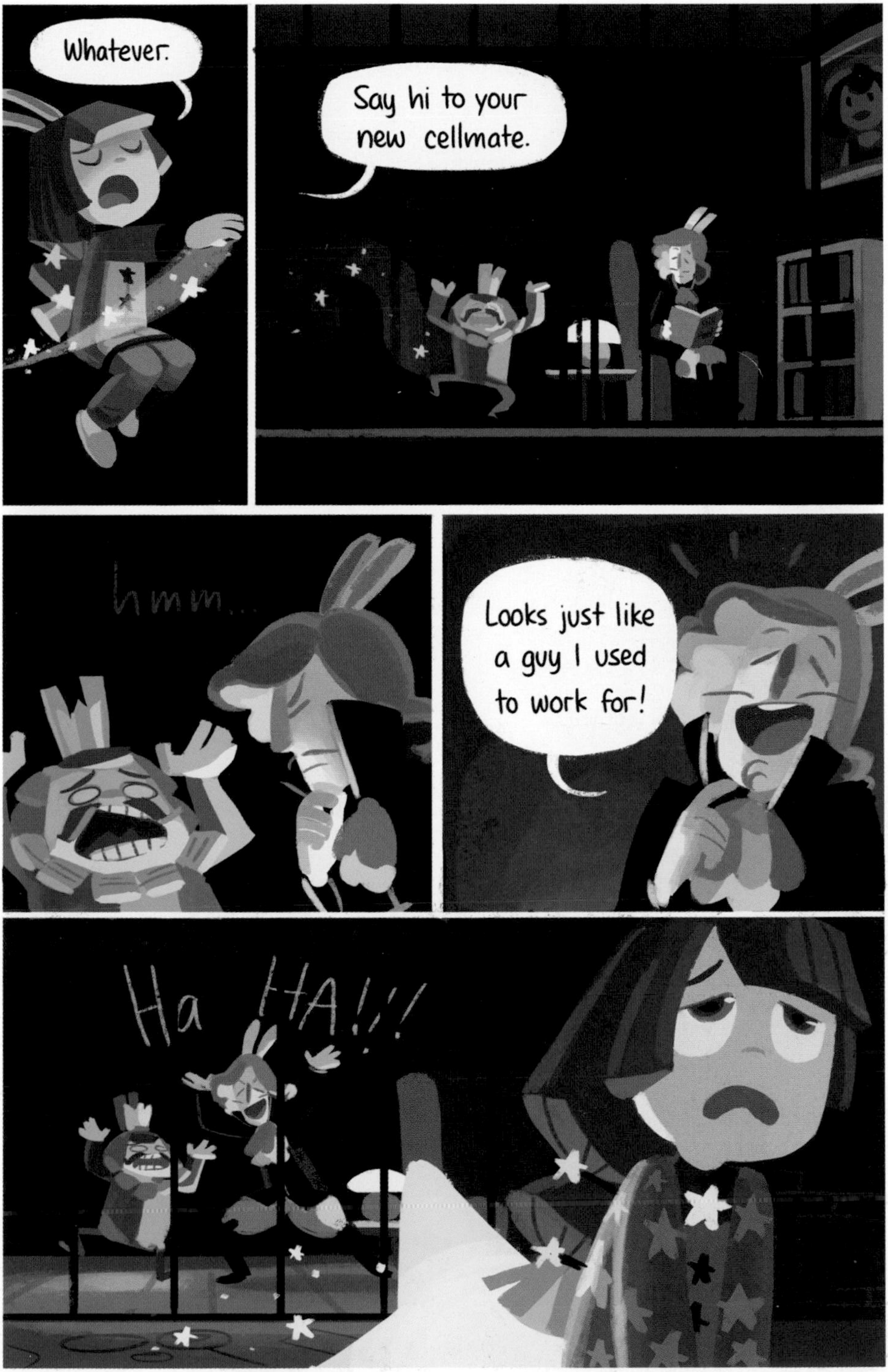
Whatever.
Say hi to your new cellmate.
hmm...
Looks just like a guy I used to work for!
Ha HA!!!

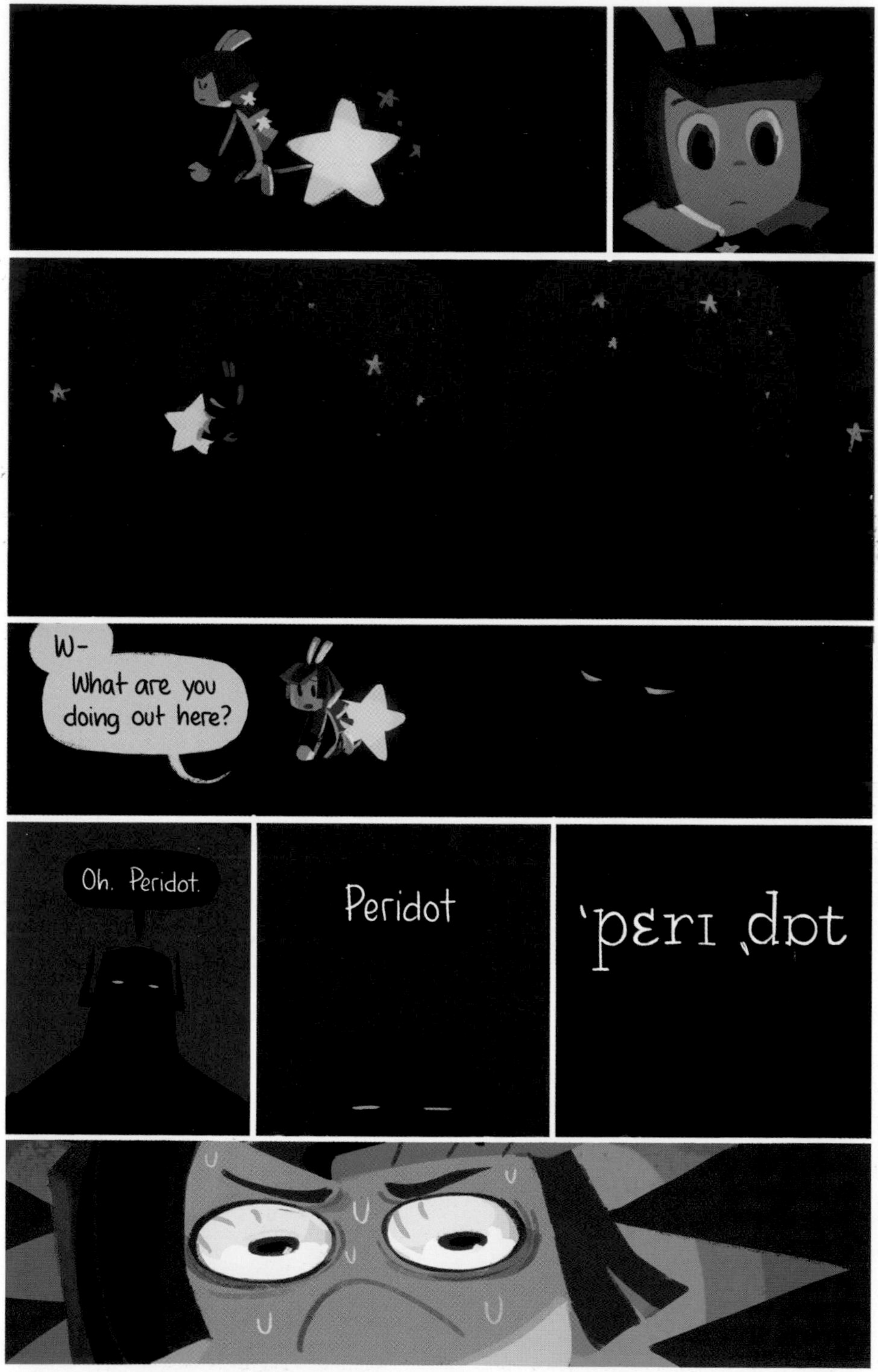
W-
What are you doing out here?
Oh. Peridot.
Peridot
ˈpɛrɪˌdɒt

Okay, I know you're all scary and invincible and stuff,

so I'm gonna let it slide **this time**,

but for future reference? It's "Peri - DOH."

Silent "T"! Got it?!

...I hadn't realized it was so important.

OF **COURSE** it's important!!

How would you like it if I said **YOUR** name wrong,

Mr. **Nightmare Knit?!**

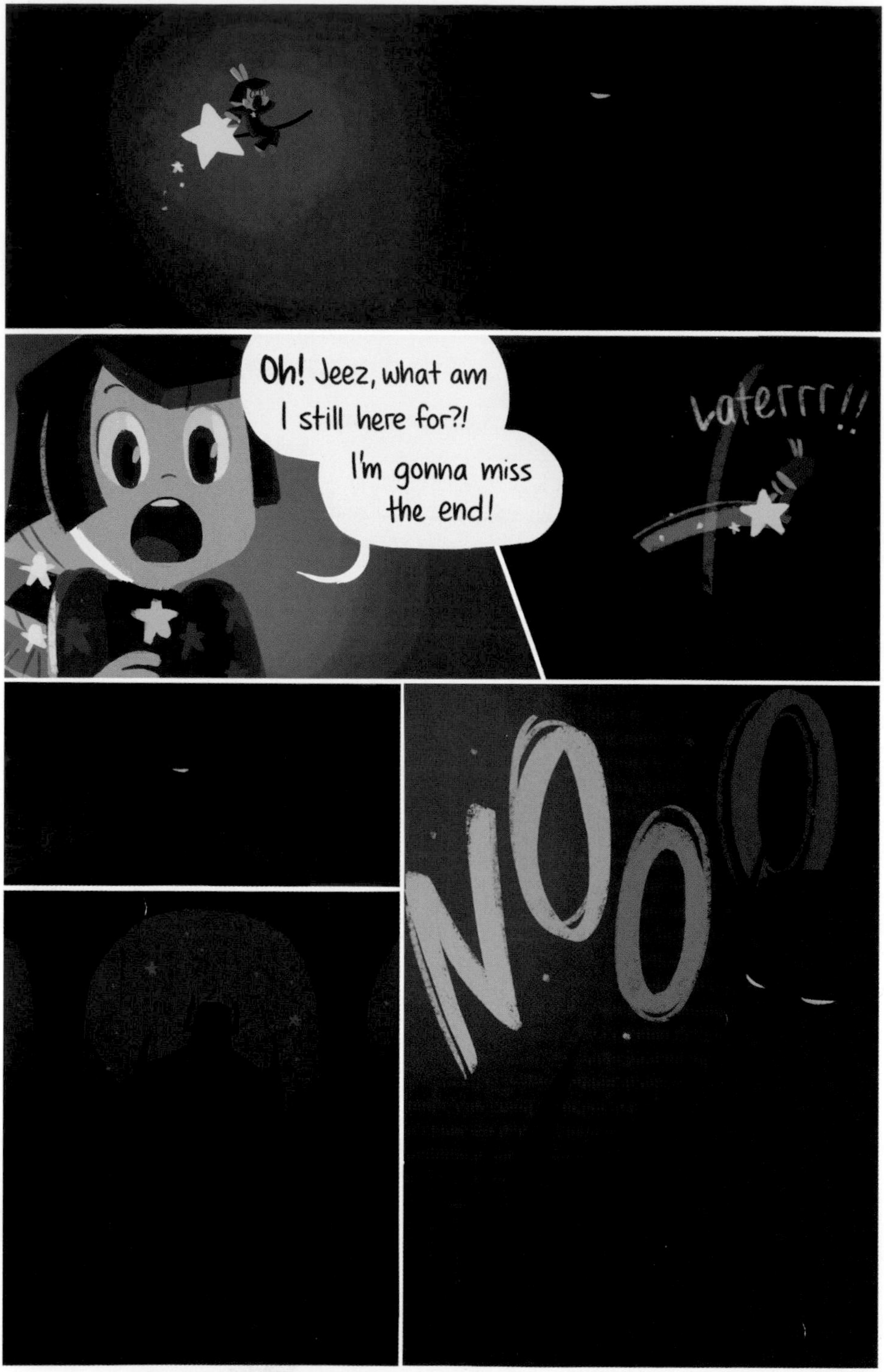
Oh! Jeez, what am I still here for?! I'm gonna miss the end!
laterrr!!
NOOO

Arrêeeete!

Quiet down, Princess! You want the whole castle to hear, or what?

The whole **COUNTRY** will 'ear if you don't **give that back!**

Oh! You mean...

...THIS old thing?!

Gee, I don't know... Something about the design just **bugs me.**

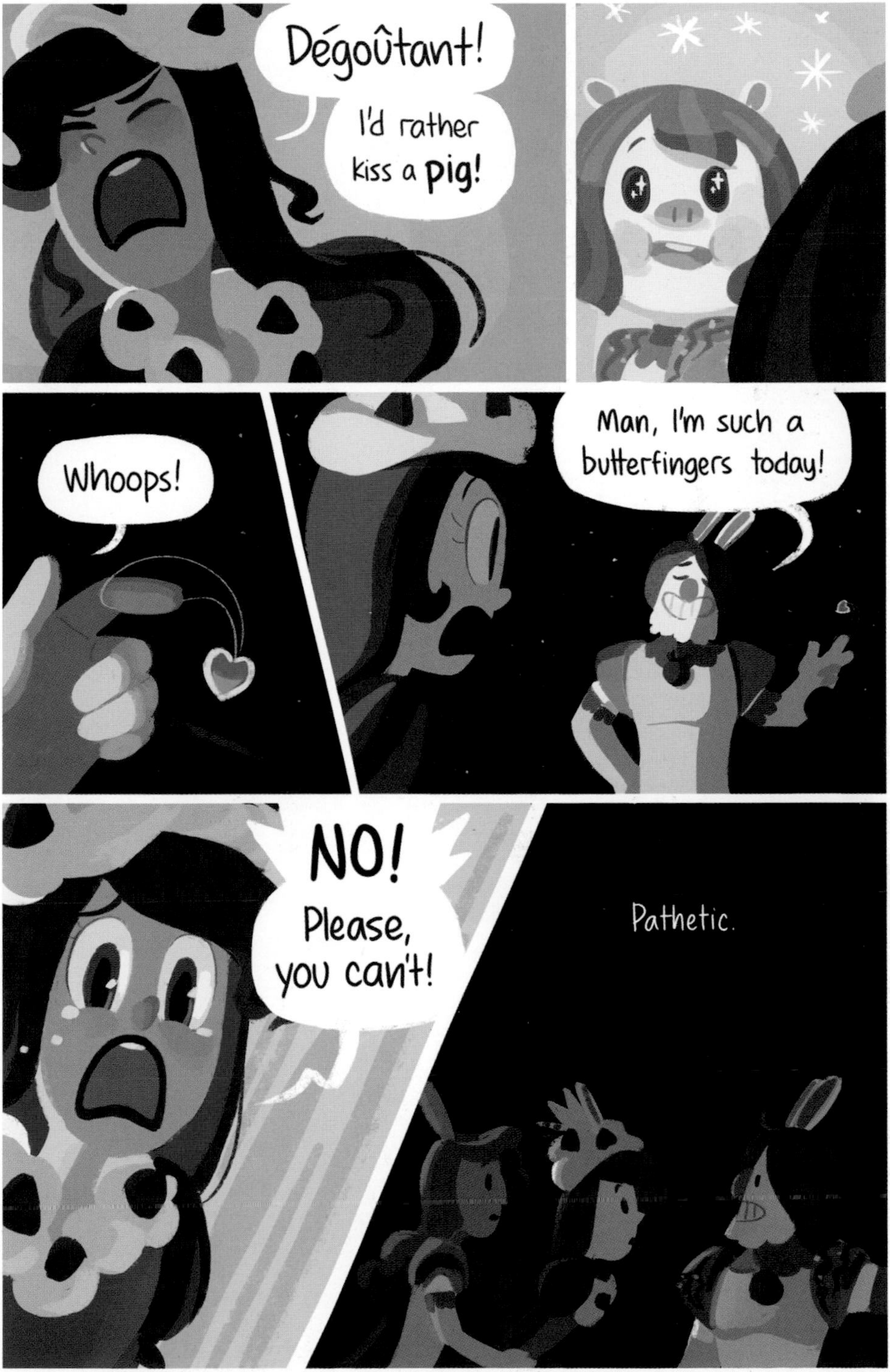

Dégoûtant!
I'd rather kiss a pig!
Whoops!
Man, I'm such a butterfingers today!
NO!
Please, you can't!
Pathetic.

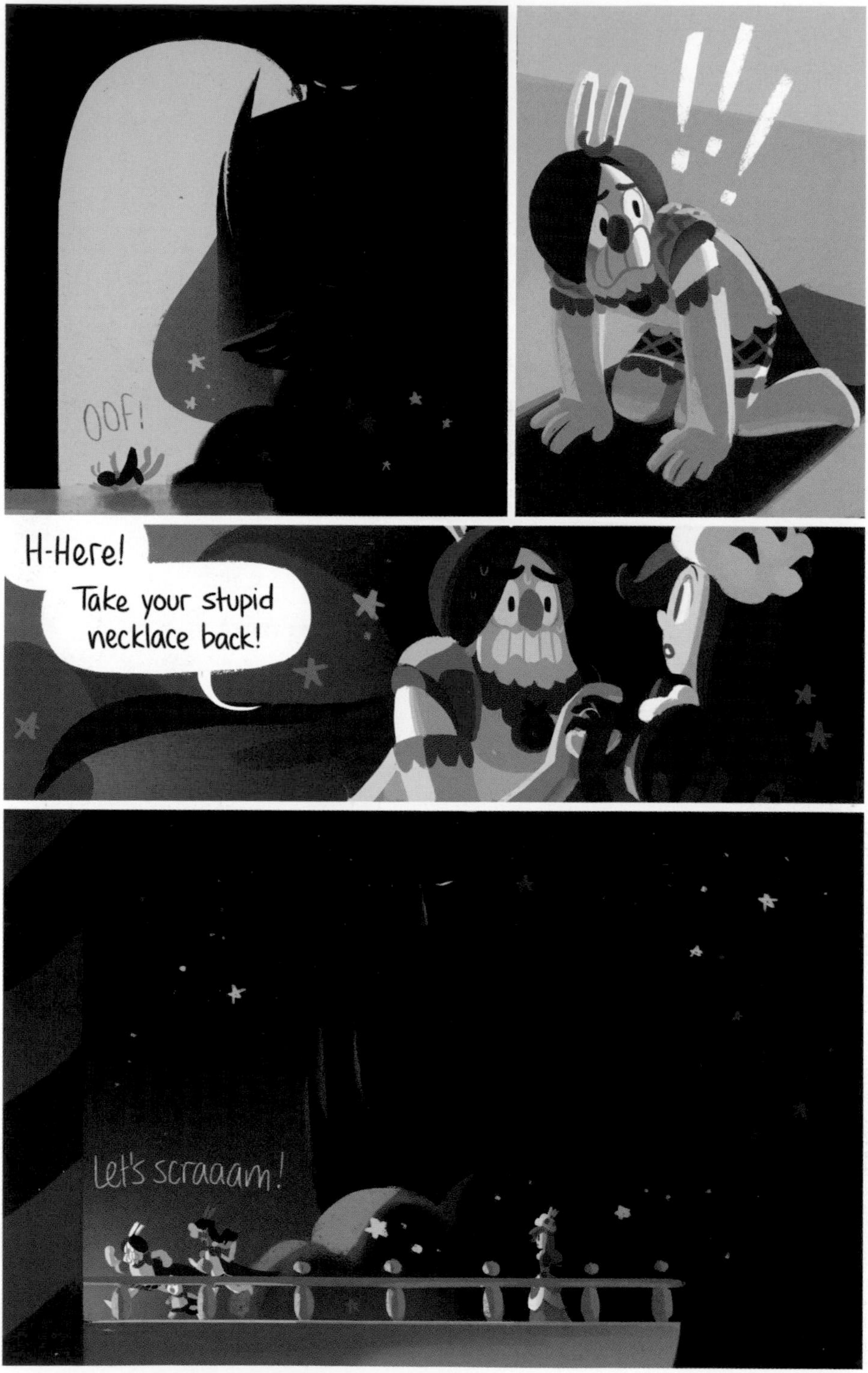
OOF!
!!!
H-Here!
Take your stupid necklace back!
Let's scraaam!

And so, the time has come for us to say goodbye.

You've done phenomenal work, children!

We are in your debt.

Please, Your Majesties, think nothing of it!

Yeah! It's just part of the job.

Thanks for, um, everything, Your Majesty.

And thank you too, Nautilus!

I should be thanking you! I, um...

Um.

I bet I'd still be stranded on the beach if you hadn't been there.

Oh no!

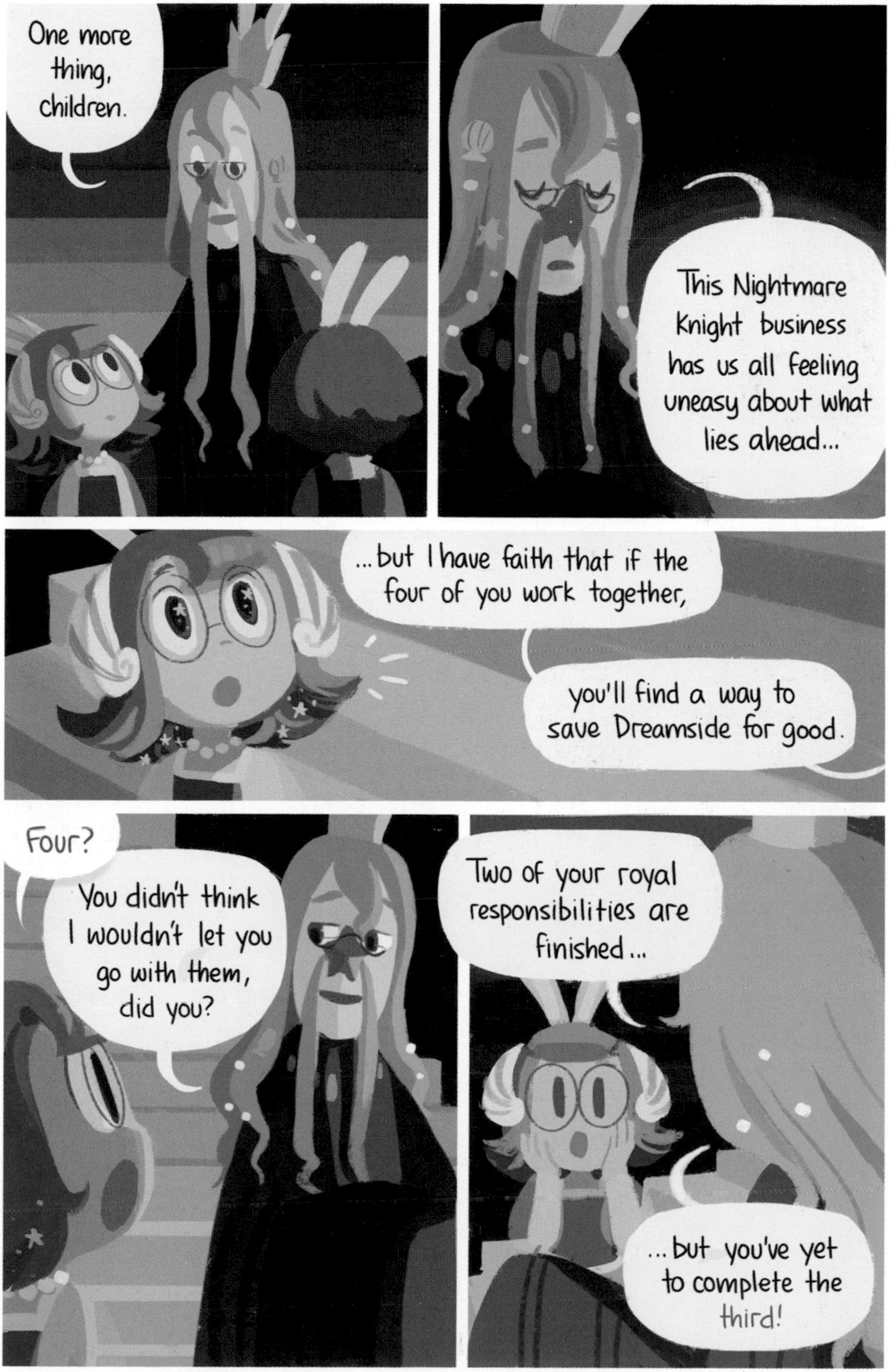
One more thing, children.
This Nightmare Knight business has us all feeling uneasy about what lies ahead...
...but I have faith that if the four of you work together,
you'll find a way to save Dreamside for good.
Four?
You didn't think I wouldn't let you go with them, did you?
Two of your royal responsibilities are finished...
...but you've yet to complete the third!

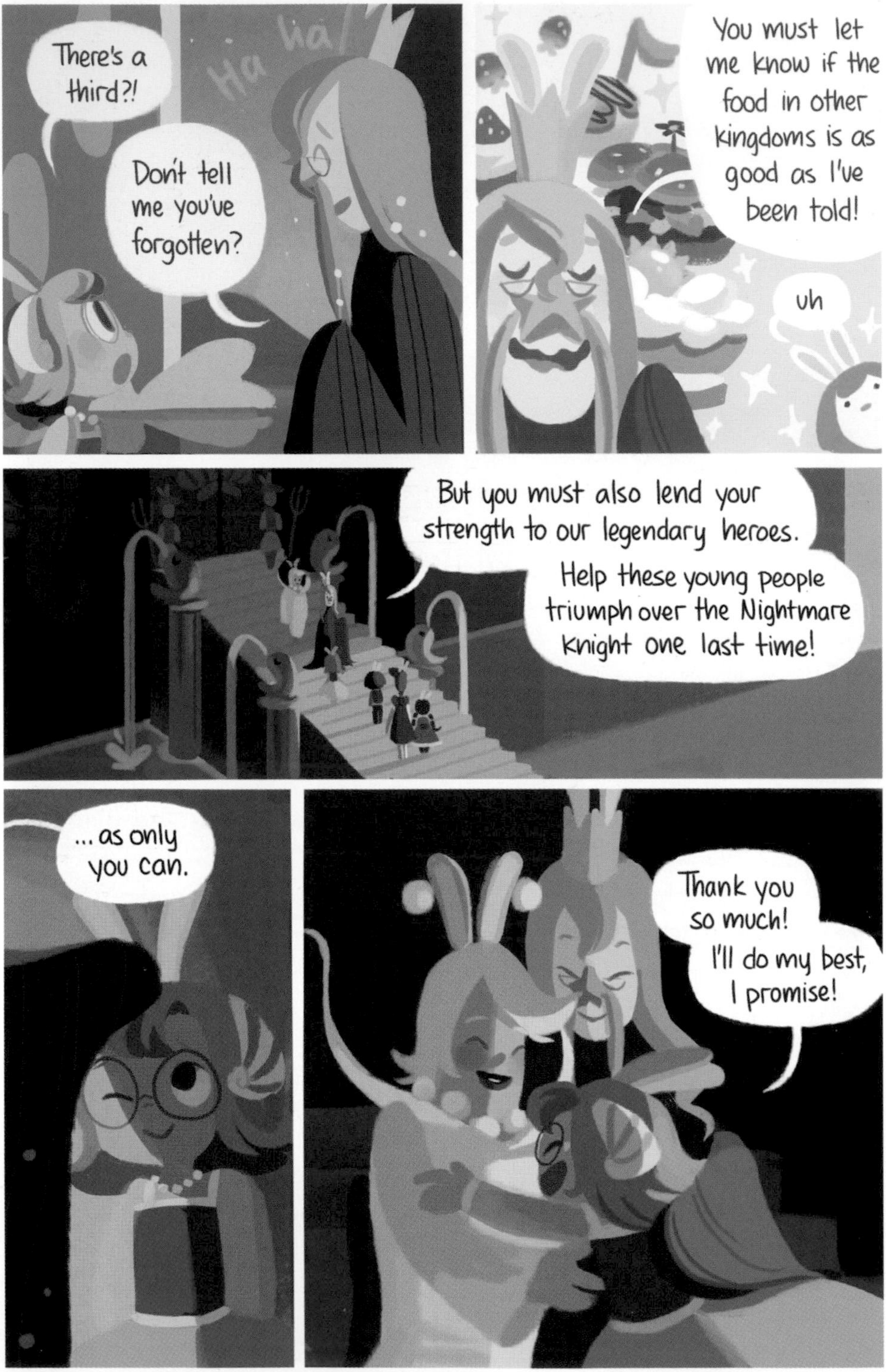
There's a third?!
Ha ha
Don't tell me you've forgotten?
You must let me know if the food in other kingdoms is as good as I've been told!
uh
But you must also lend your strength to our legendary heroes.
Help these young people triumph over the Nightmare Knight one last time!
... as only you can.
Thank you so much!
I'll do my best, I promise!

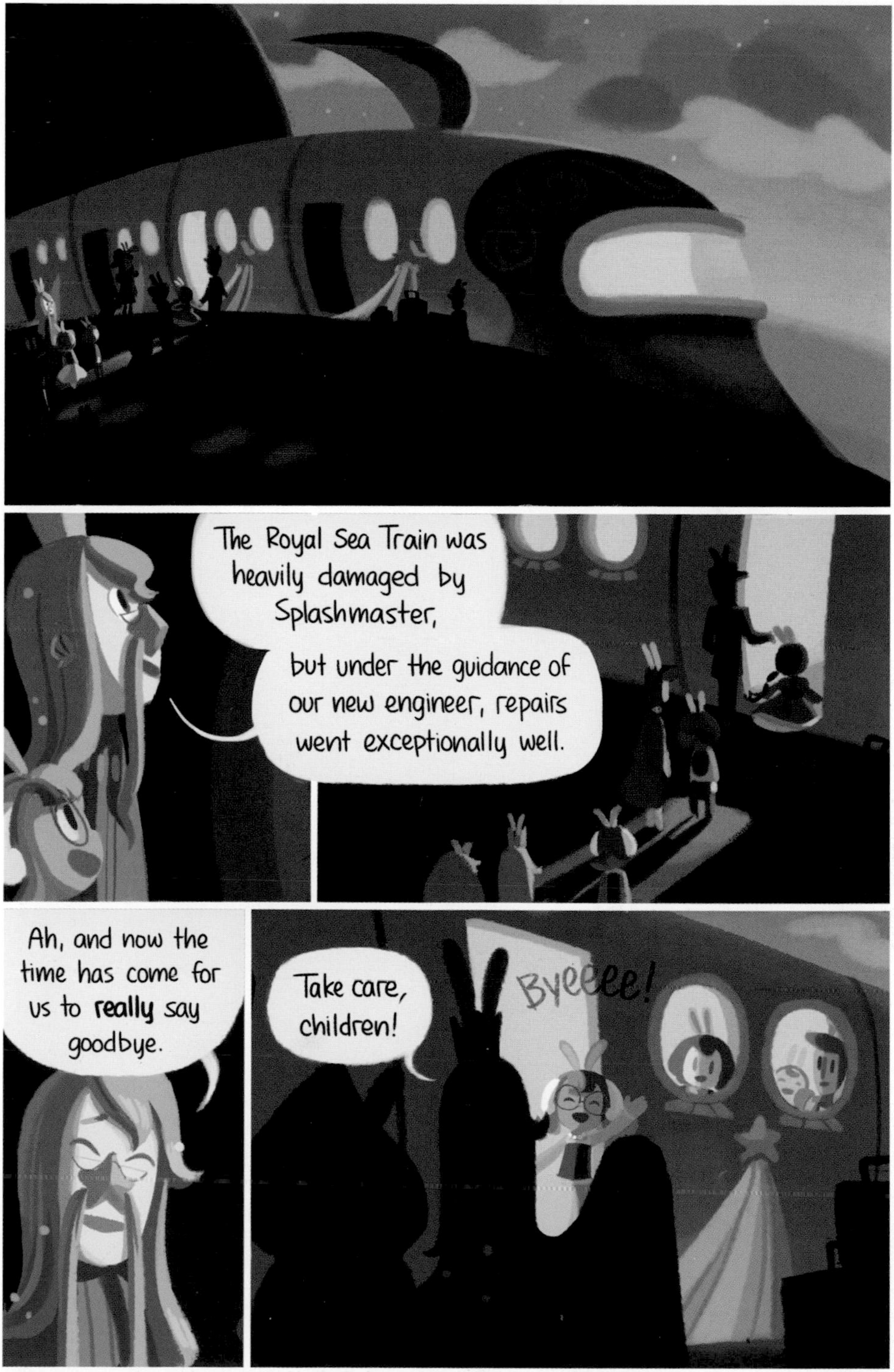
The Royal Sea Train was heavily damaged by Splashmaster,
but under the guidance of our new engineer, repairs went exceptionally well.
Ah, and now the time has come for us to **really** say goodbye.
Take care, children!
Byeeeee!

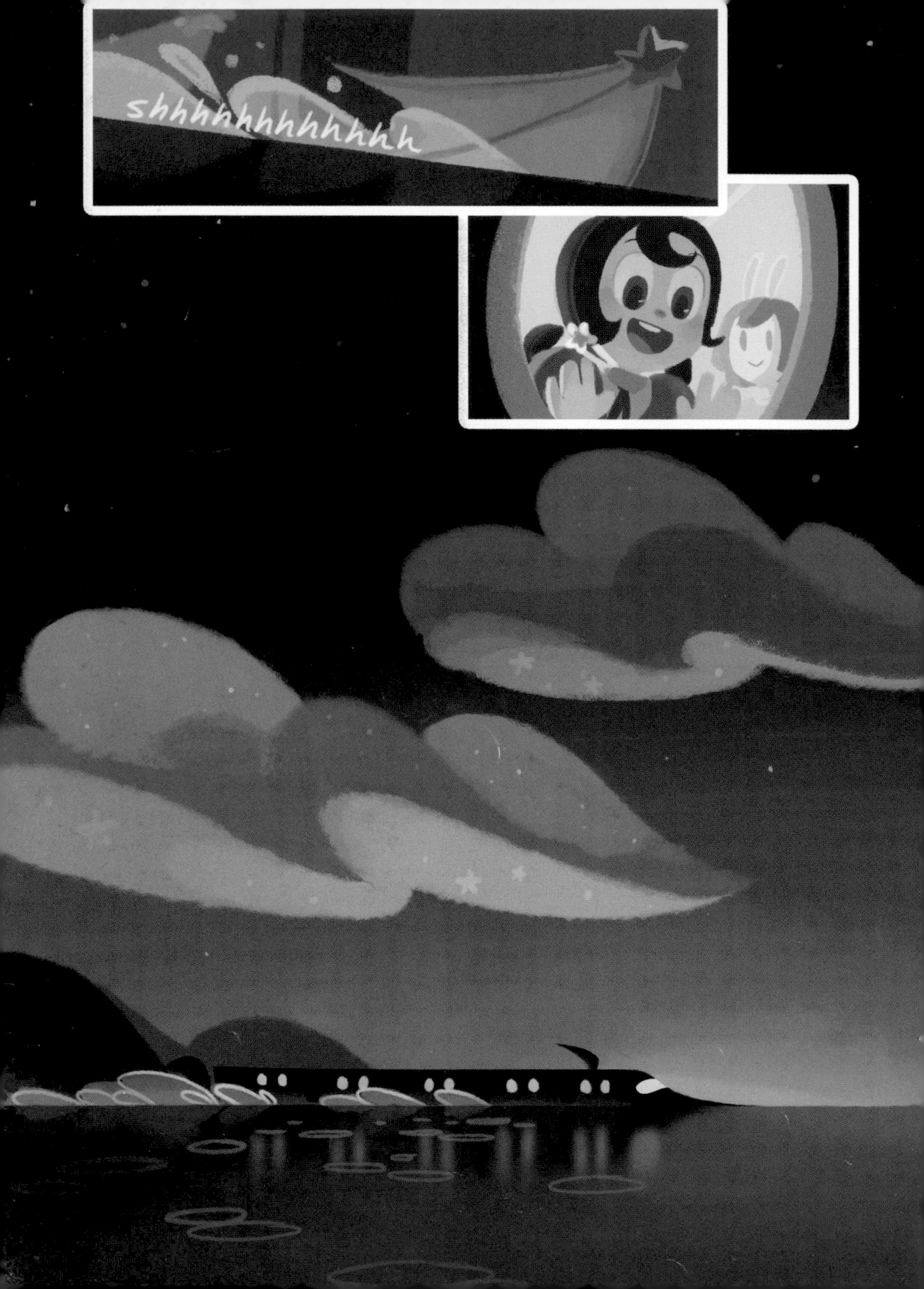
shhhhhhhhhhhhh

My companions and I have set out for the Melody Kingdom, where we shall seek the aid of the fair Princess Piano. Rumor has it that the princess' songs are the most beautiful in all of Dreamside, but I laugh at such rumors! What sound in this world is more angelic than the voice of Princess Parfait?

18th, ♥ ♪ ☺ ☆

Dearest Diary,

Mother and Father allowed me to leave home today. This is a journey of great importance, and the fate of our world hangs in the balance...

but I'm **SO EXCITED!** ☺

I can't wait to see the Melody Kingdom! I wonder how Princess Piano is doing.

UGH! I can't believe the bad guy's been brought back to life 100 times! where's the fun in this epic quest thing if 99 other dorks beat me to it already??
I guess I just have to be the first hero to do it right, huh? I bet the ~~knt~~ Nightmare ~~Night~~ Knight isn't even that tough if he's lost so many times!

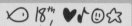 18th, ♥⟋☺☆

I still don't think I'm a hero, but if it means people in the future won't have to worry about the Nightmare Knight anymore, I think I want to do what I can to keep him from coming back. Maybe one day, there will be someone like me who can go to school if they want to!

...I kind of wish I knew what to do, though...

C'mooooon!

Are we **theeeere yeeeet?!**

Not for a few more hours!

And—hey, stop that!

The Sea Train truly is a marvel, Your Highness.

Isn't it?

It's a shame we'll have to wait another hour for breakfast, though.

Indeed. I must say, I'm quite famished.

Knock Knock

♪ Snack caaart! ♪

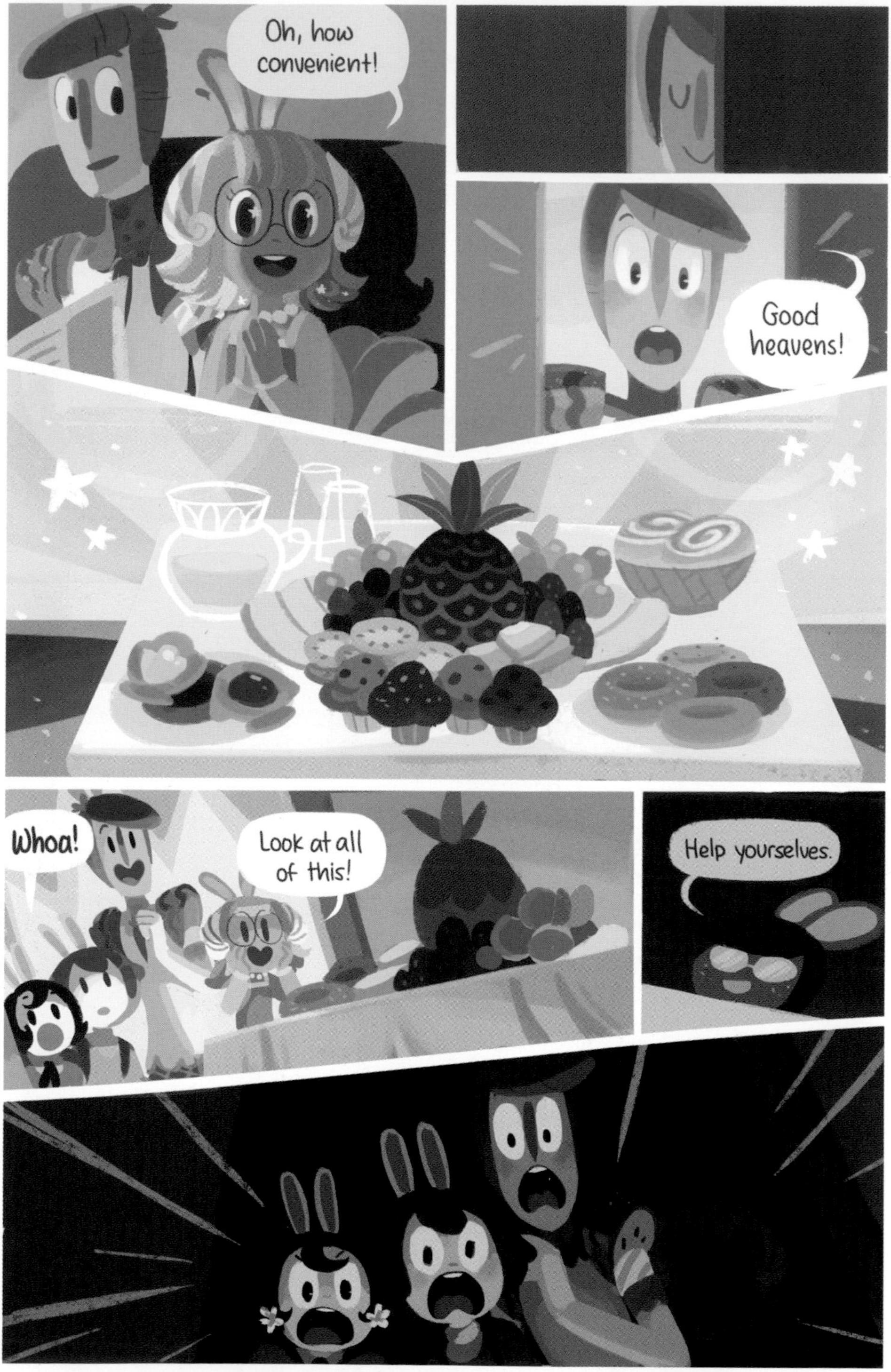
Oh, how convenient!
Good heavens!
Whoa!
Look at all of this!
Help yourselves.

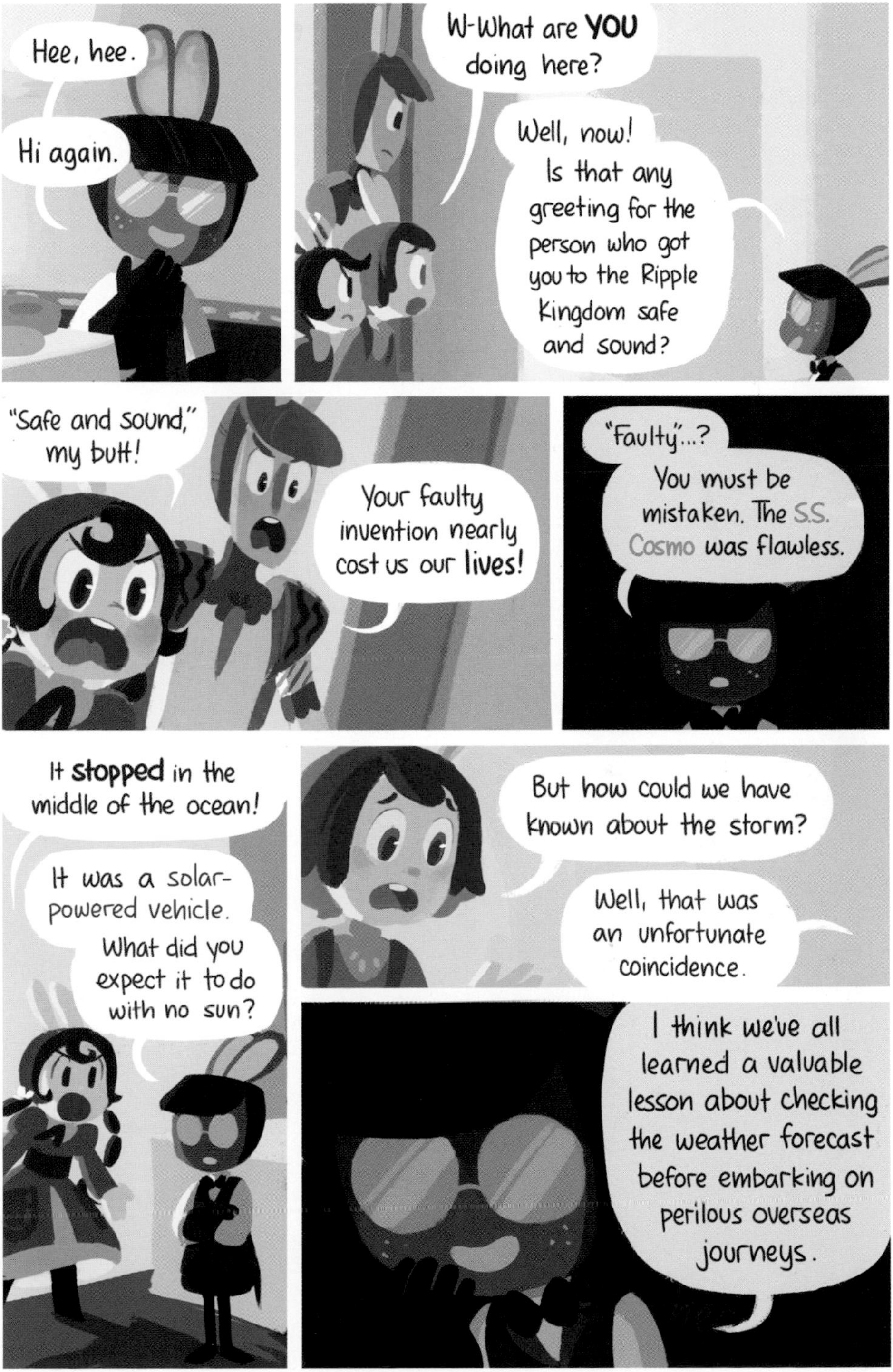
Hee, hee.
Hi again.
W-What are YOU doing here?
Well, now! Is that any greeting for the person who got you to the Ripple Kingdom safe and sound?
"Safe and sound," my butt!
Your faulty invention nearly cost us our lives!
"Faulty"...?
You must be mistaken. The S.S. Cosmo was flawless.
It stopped in the middle of the ocean!
It was a solar-powered vehicle.
What did you expect it to do with no sun?
But how could we have known about the storm?
Well, that was an unfortunate coincidence.
I think we've all learned a valuable lesson about checking the weather forecast before embarking on perilous overseas journeys.

I'll teach **YOU A LESSON!**

Almond!

You know...

That giant squid monster destroying my ship was as heartbreaking for me as I'm sure it must have been for you.

I-I don't think heartbreak is the issue here.

But since the

test

was such a success,

I don't mind that I've lost a good invention in the process.

J-Just what—

Have a muffin!

You've earned it.

You still haven't told us.

What are you doing here?

Hee.

Why **wouldn't** I be on this train, Cucumber?

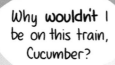

I'm **DRIVING IT!!**

NO

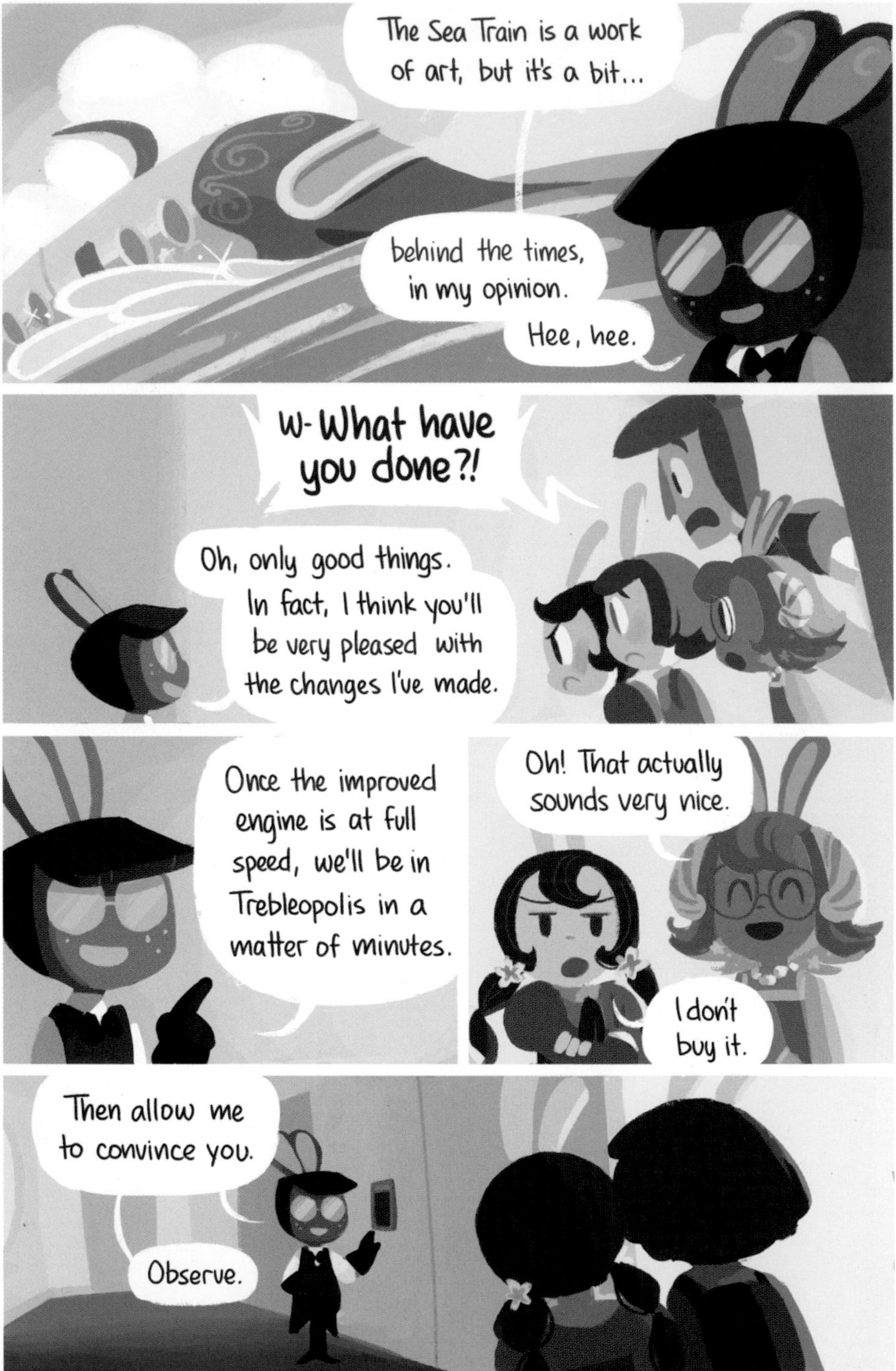
The Sea Train is a work of art, but it's a bit...
behind the times, in my opinion.
Hee, hee.
W-What have you done?!
Oh, only good things.
In fact, I think you'll be very pleased with the changes I've made.
Once the improved engine is at full speed, we'll be in Trebleopolis in a matter of minutes.
Oh! That actually sounds very nice.
I don't buy it.
Then allow me to convince you.
Observe.

Computer! Speed up the train, please!

...

beep!

COMMAND RECOGNIZED:

9:32 AM

"Blow up the train, plea... I can do that for you

"BLOW UP THE TRAIN"

ACTIVATING DETONATOR

Oh.

Oops.

WHAT

Y-You put a **bomb** on the train?!

Maybe.

Are you CRAZY?!

I've been called that.

Well!

As fun as this reunion has been, I really should be going.

I wish there were enough room for all of you on this emergency escape platform, but, well.

Oops.

COSMO!!

You'll just need to find that bomb yourselves! But that should be no trouble for you, right?

Good luck, friends!

Wait! UGH!!

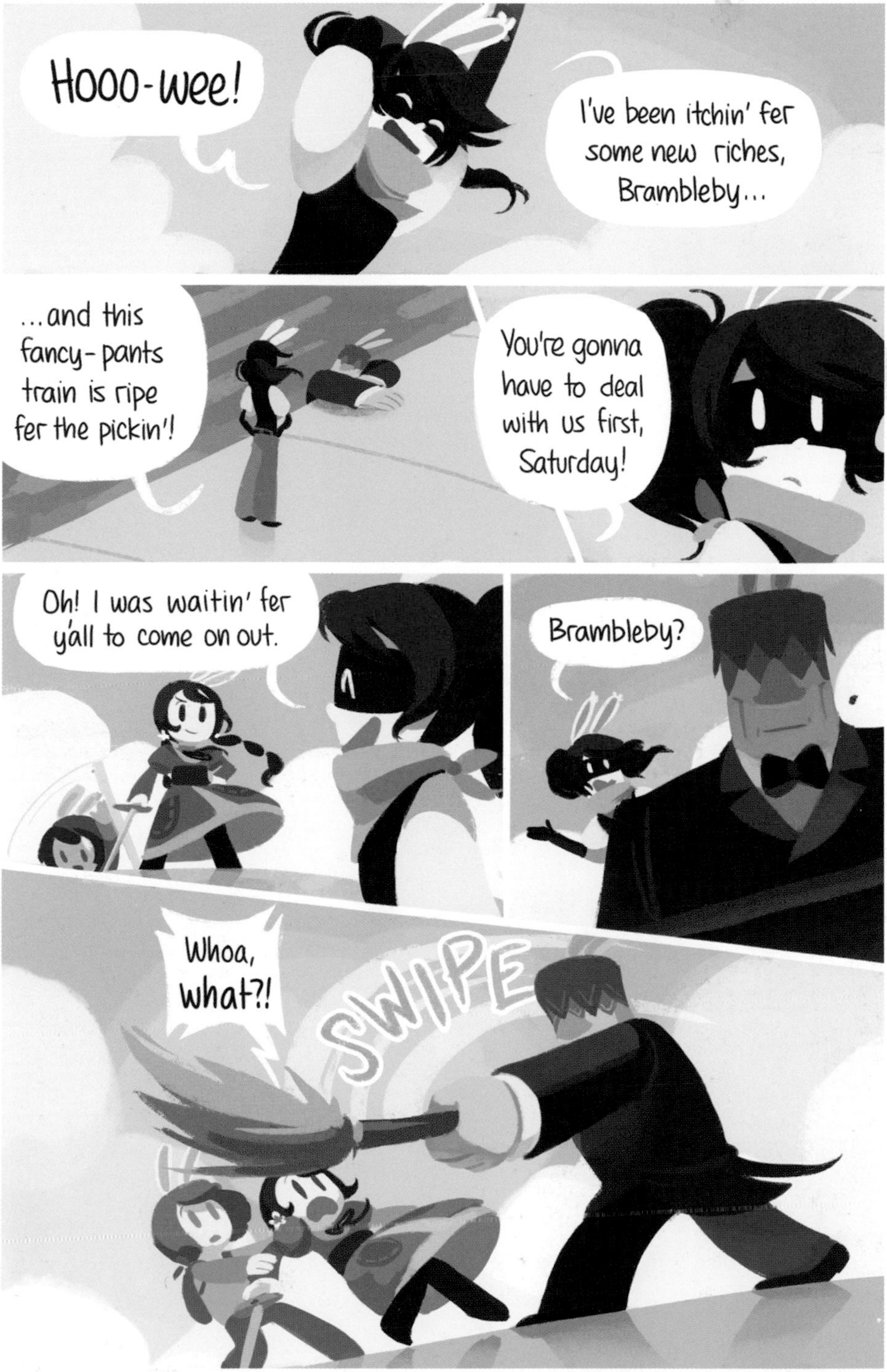
Hooo-wee!
I've been itchin' fer some new riches, Brambleby...
...and this fancy-pants train is ripe fer the pickin'!
You're gonna have to deal with us first, Saturday!
Oh! I was waitin' fer y'all to come on out.
Brambleby?
Whoa, what?!
SWIPE

I gotta run. Y'all have fun, now!

slam!

Just us, huh?

Didn't really think you were the fighting type.

Only if Saturday orders it.

...You know, it's a lot harder to talk to you without signs on the walls.

flip flip flip flip

I couldn't find my whiteboard.

Oh.

190

We've no time to waste, Your Highness!

We **must** find that explosive!

Let's leave no stone unturned!

Grummmm mmmmble

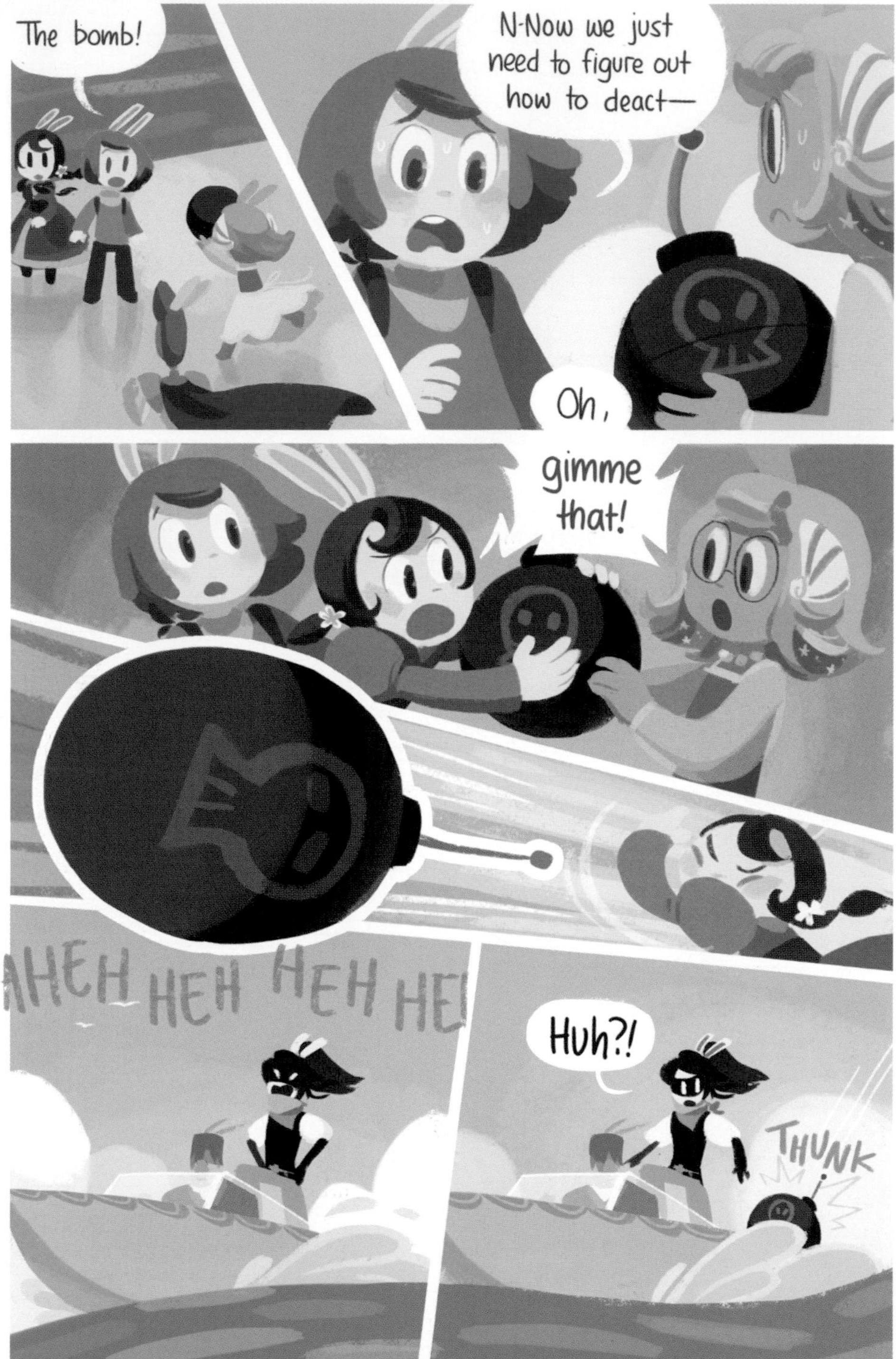
The bomb!
N-Now we just need to figure out how to deact—
Oh,
gimme that!
HEH HEH HEH HE
Huh?!
THUNK

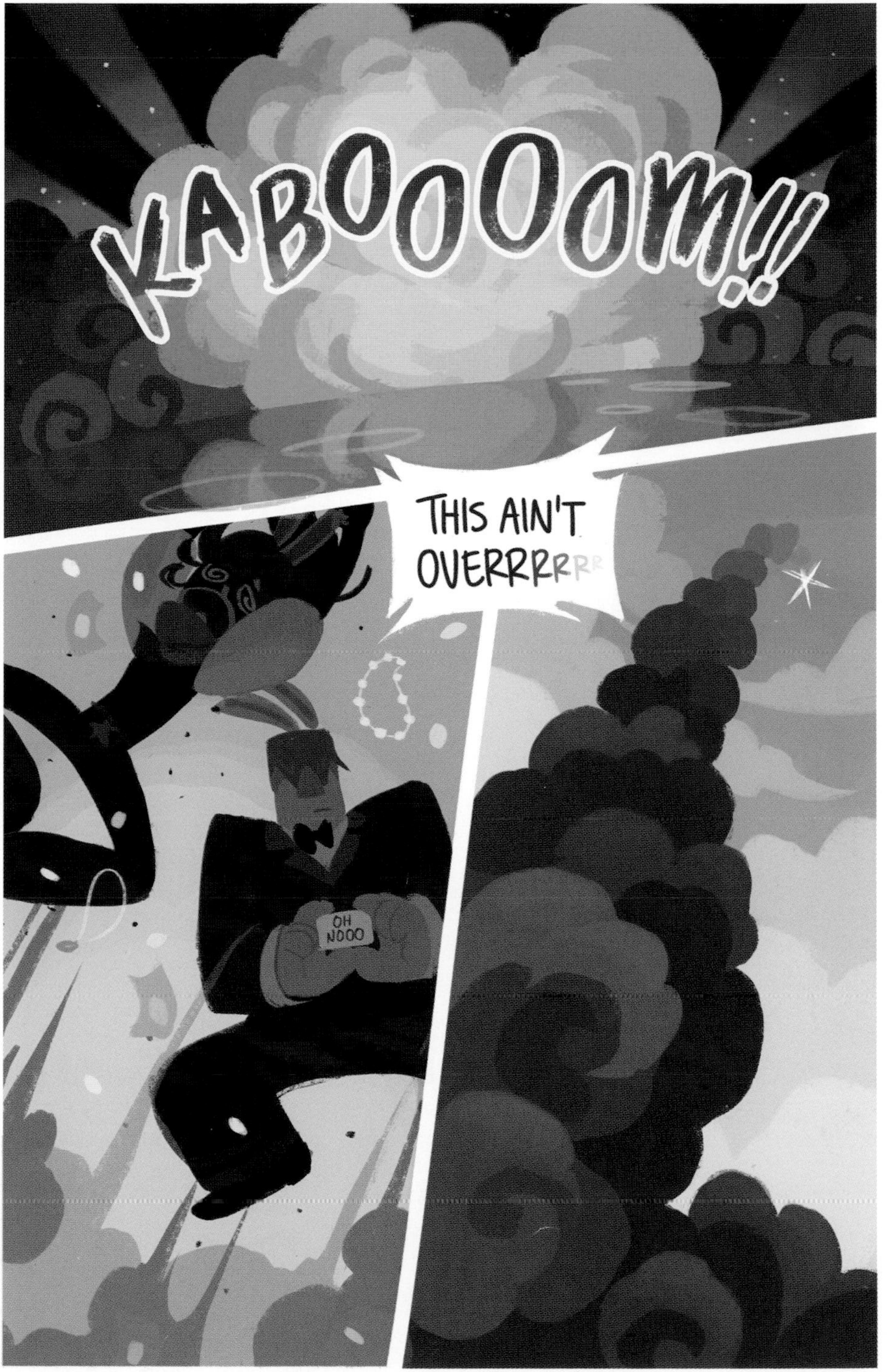
KABOOOOM!!
THIS AIN'T OVERRRRRR
OH NOOO

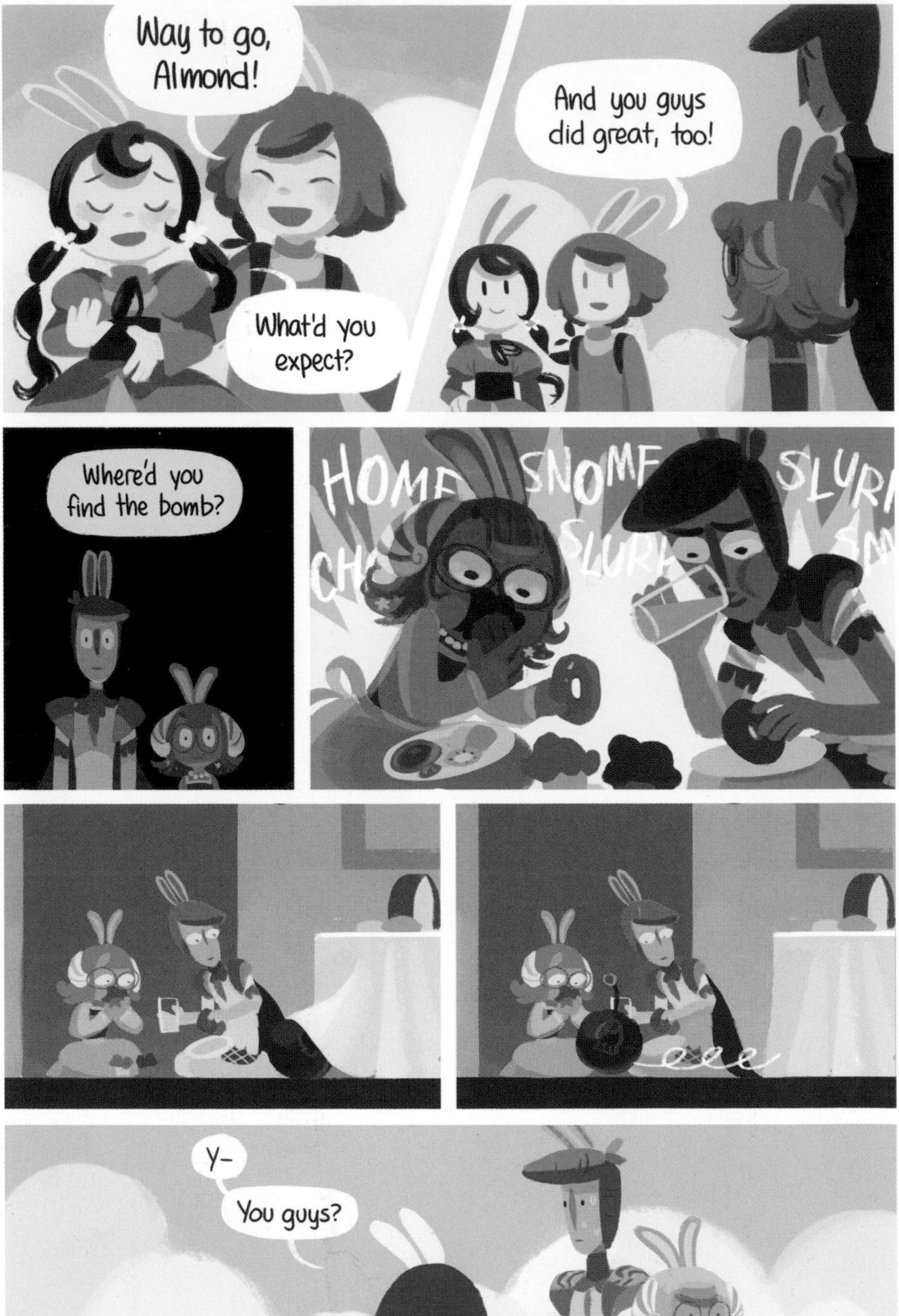
Way to go, Almond!
What'd you expect?
And you guys did great, too!
Where'd you find the bomb?
HOME
SNOMF
SLUR
CH
SLURP
Y-
You guys?

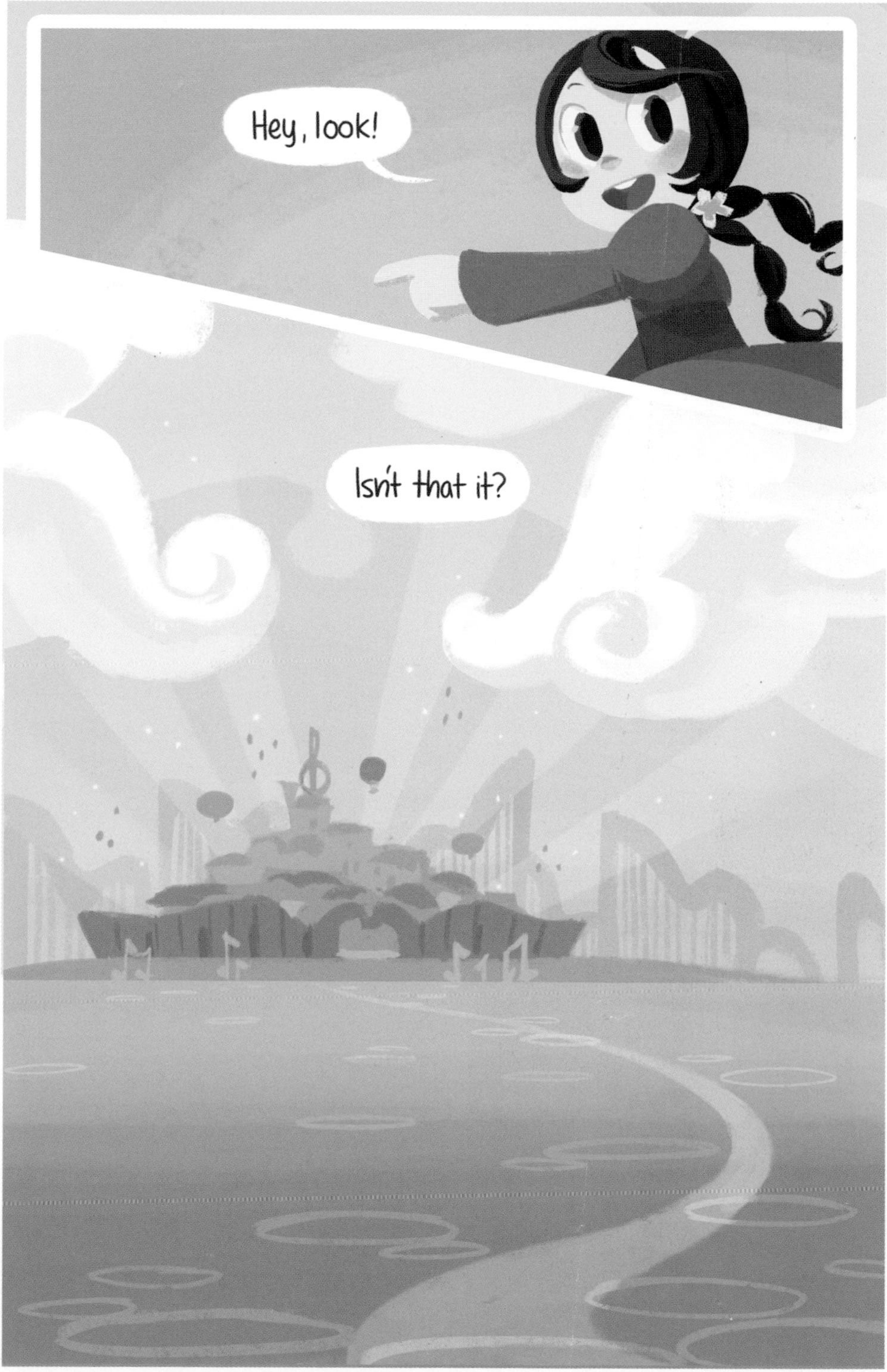
Hey, look!
Isn't that it?

To be continued in...

Reader questions for...
Almond $ Cucumber!

"Q" Almond, that final attack was the ☆**coolest!**☆

I know, right?!

It's just like Punisher Pumice's Pretty Pumice Power Punisher! I spent **months** practicing at home!

Y-You can still see the evidence in our backyard.

I still feel like it was missing something, though.

Like what?

A good one-liner, you know?

If you say the right thing just before you finish the bad guy off, it makes your attack sooo much cooler!

Pumice does it all the time!

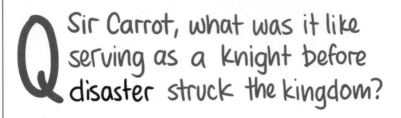

Q Sir Carrot, what was it like serving as a knight before disaster struck the kingdom?

Before the Nightmare Knight's resurrection, the Doughnut Kingdom was a land of peace and prosperity.

Guess you didn't have a lot to do then, huh?

On the contrary, I had many daily responsibilities!

Nothing quite matches the thrill of rescuing stray pets and massaging His Majesty's feet!

He really means that, doesn't he.

I think so.

Reader questions for...
Bacon!
Q why
Huh? Why what?
If you're asking why lollipops always get those hard edges that cut your tongue when you lick them too long, I dunno...
... but I asked Sir Tomato once, and he got really mad—
NUH-UH!!
I haven't gotten to answer a single question yet, and there's NO WAY I'm losing my spot AGAIN!
DO IT OVER!!

Reader questions for...
Peridot & Cordelia!

That's better!

Q Peridot, do you have any siblings?
NO.

Q Hey, Peridot, what do you really think of our "heroes"?
She's dumb!

I-I mean THEY'RE dumb!!

UGGGHHH, why am I getting all the dumb questions?!
There, there.

Q Peridot, why did you learn magic?
So I could boss people around? Duh. Why does **anybody** learn magic?
WH—

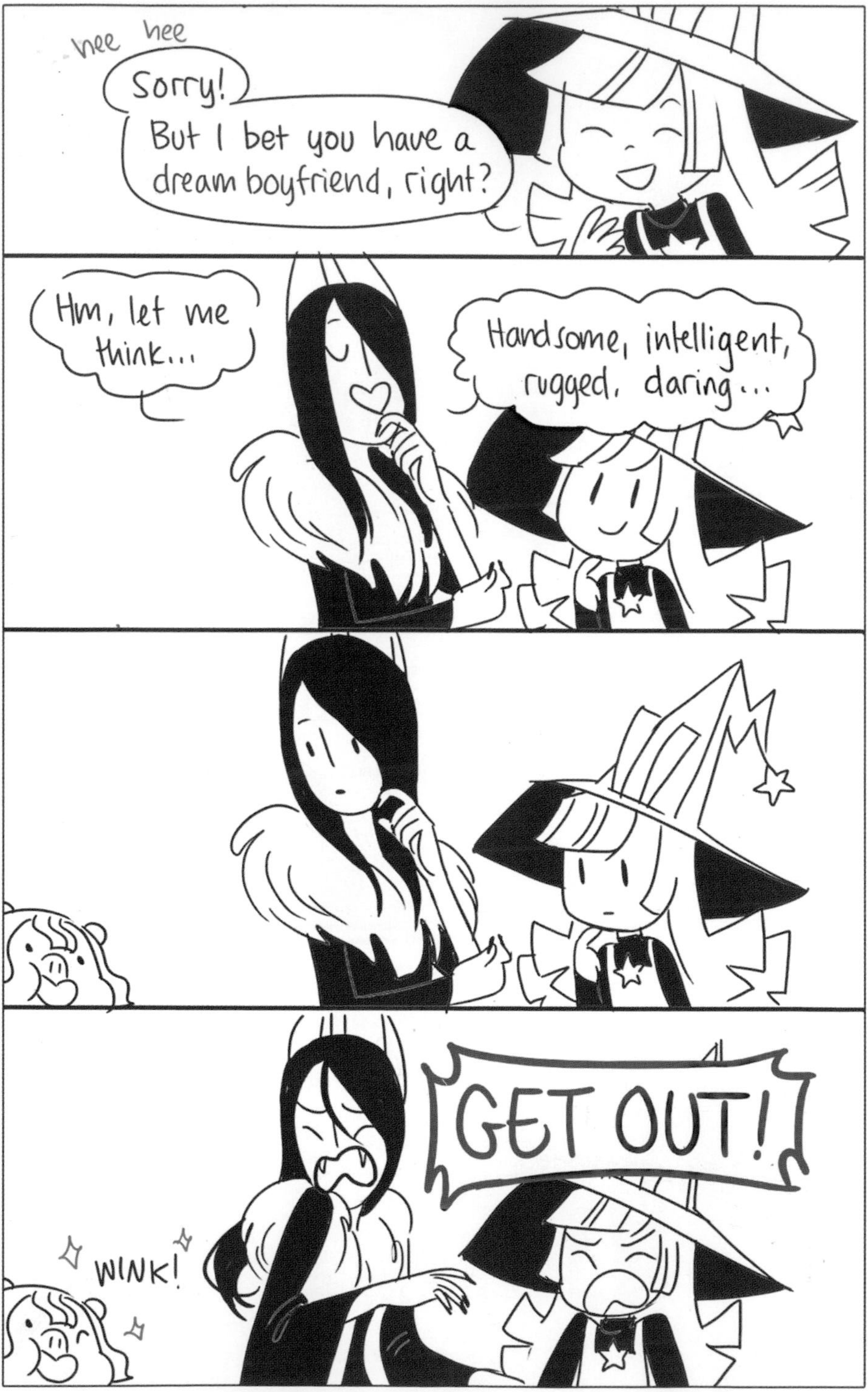
hee hee
Sorry!
But I bet you have a dream boyfriend, right?
Hm, let me think...
Handsome, intelligent, rugged, daring...
GET OUT!
WINK!

Princess Nautilus

Atk ★
Def ★★★★
Sp ★★★★

🧴 R.I.S.
🐟 fishy earrings
👓 rose-tinted glasses

Every heroic quest needs some positive energy, and the Ripple Kingdom princess has more than enough to spare. No trial is too daunting, no enemy too great, no, uh...

How did the rest of that go? I forget.

Splashmaster

Atk ★★★★★+
Def ★★
Sp ★

BUNY SMASH

While he may be the first, and therefore the weakest, of the Nightmare Knight's seven henchmen, Splashmaster's physical strength is nothing to sneeze at. It's just too bad he doesn't have the smarts to match.

Chardonnay

Atk ⭐
Def ⭐
Sp ⭐

☕ the Oracle's coffee
👕 the Oracle's laundry
💟 an unbreakable spirit

The Dream Oracle's hapless devotee and personal assistant. Chardonnay wants nothing more than to be helpful, and she won't give up no matter what! But has she ever considered that her job might be getting in the way...?

King Kelp

Atk ⭐
Def ⭐
Sp ⭐⭐⭐⭐⭐

🔨 octo-stick
📘 history book
💊 spell capsule

Ruler, father, scholar, and goofball. Upon meeting him, one wonders if Queen Conch is the only grounded member of the family.

But, hey, at least they have fun.

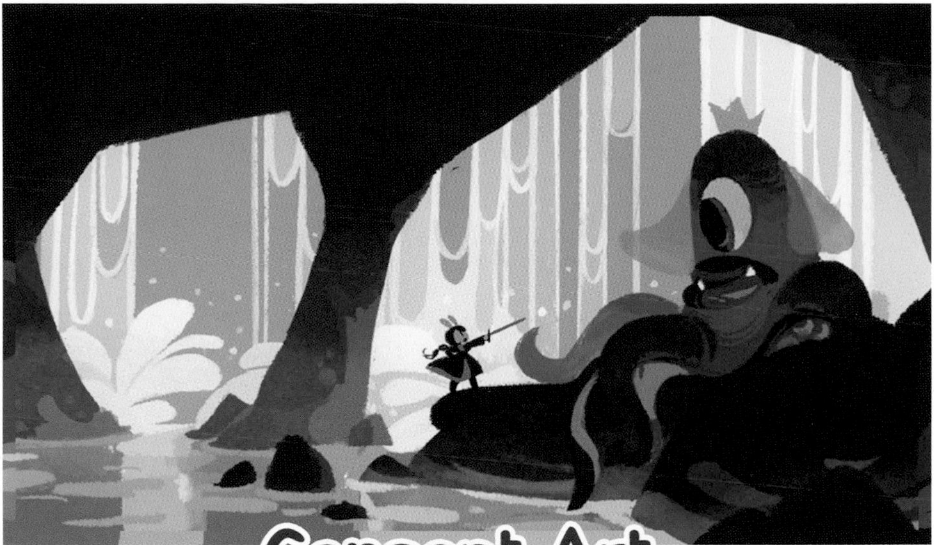

Concept Art

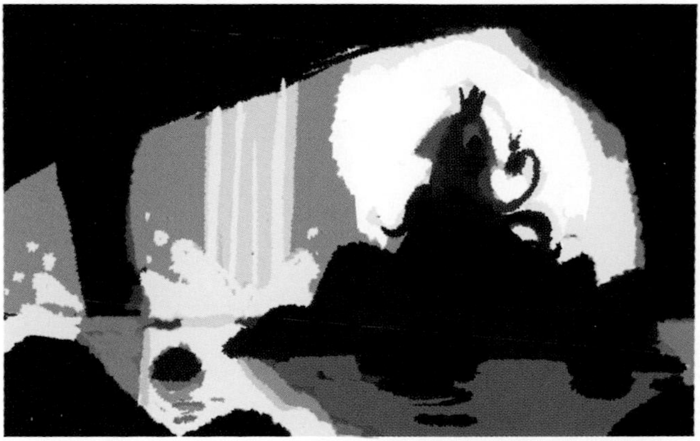

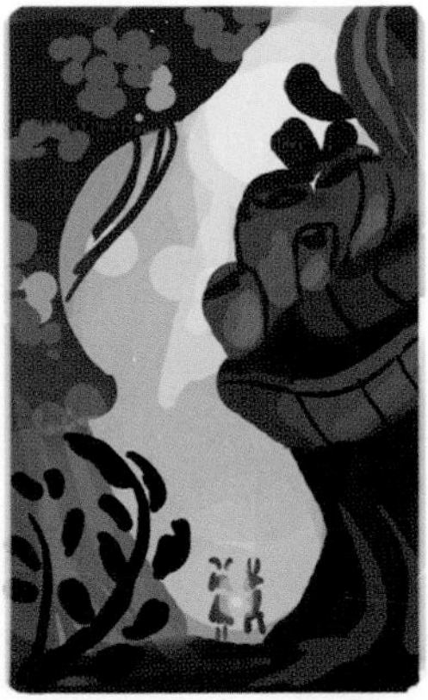

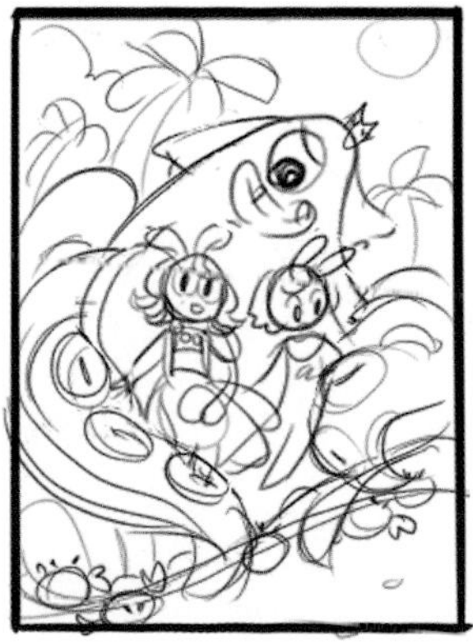

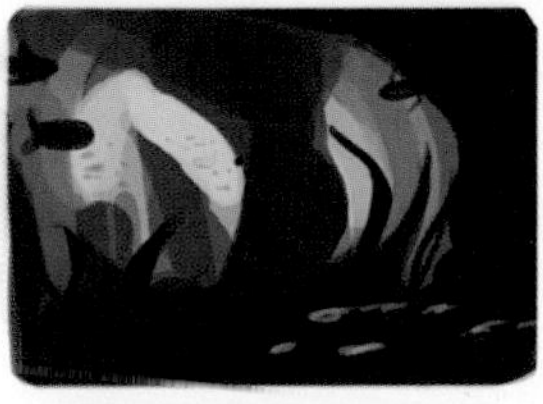

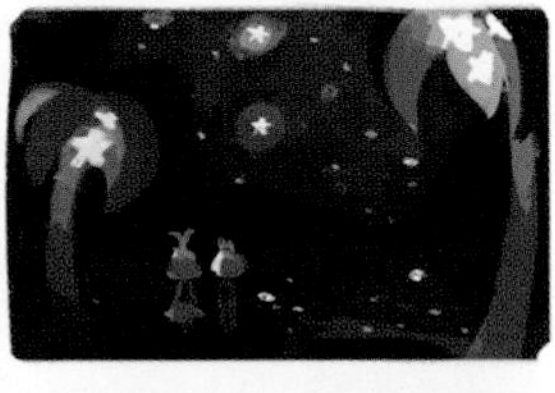

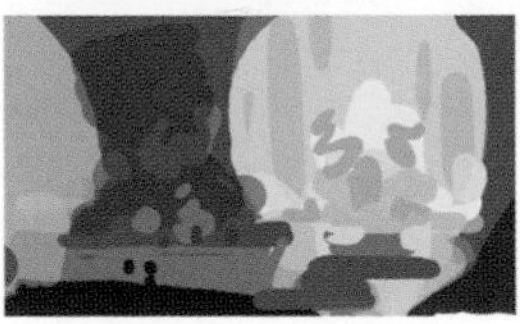

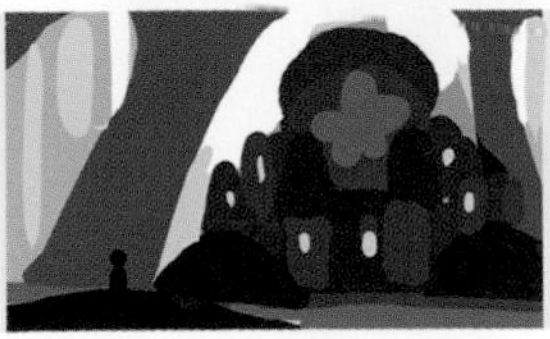

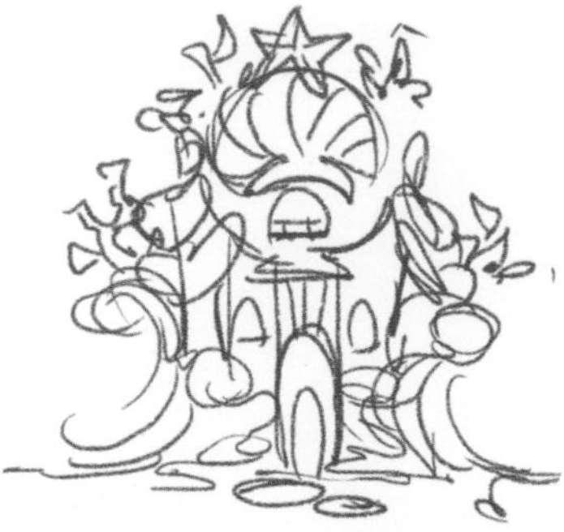
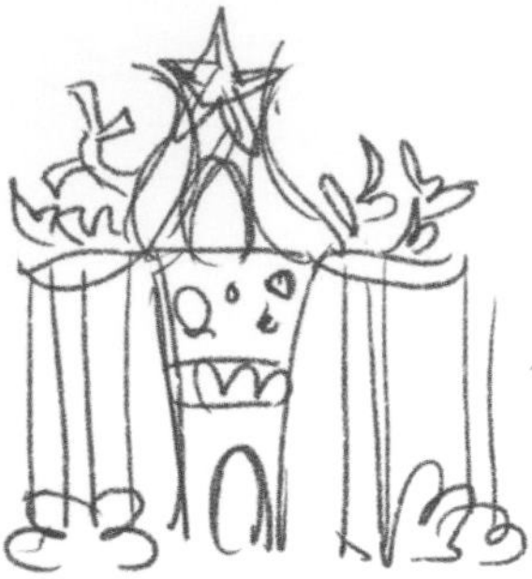
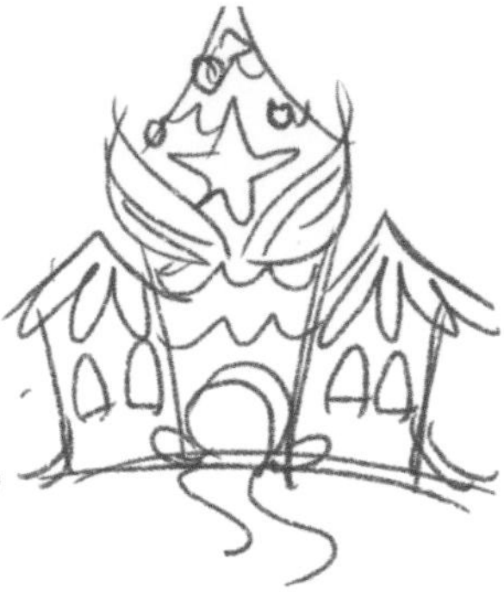
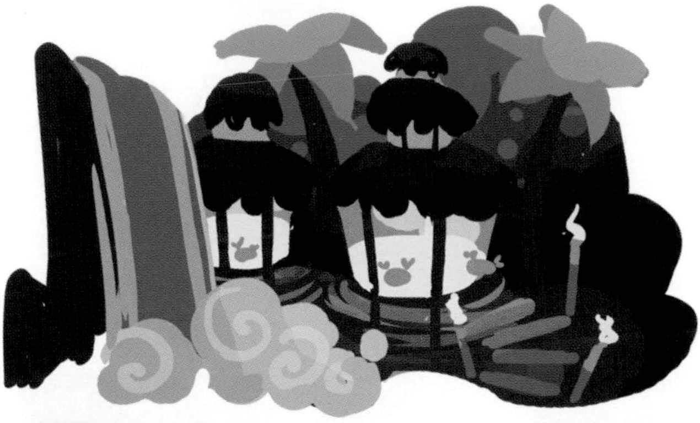
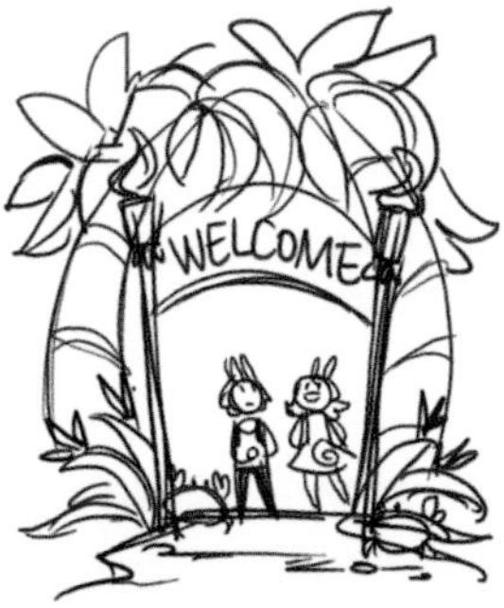
WELCOME
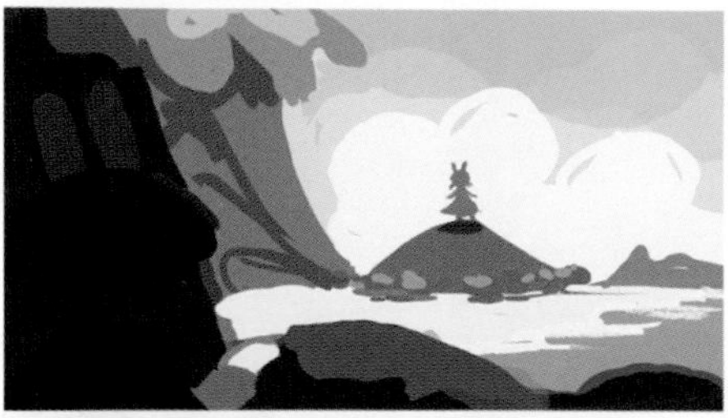
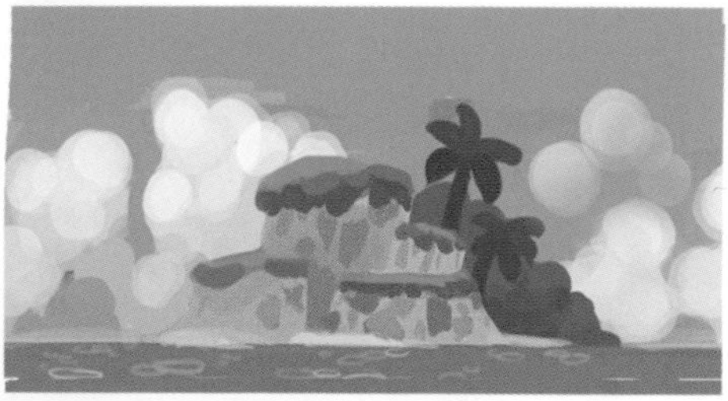
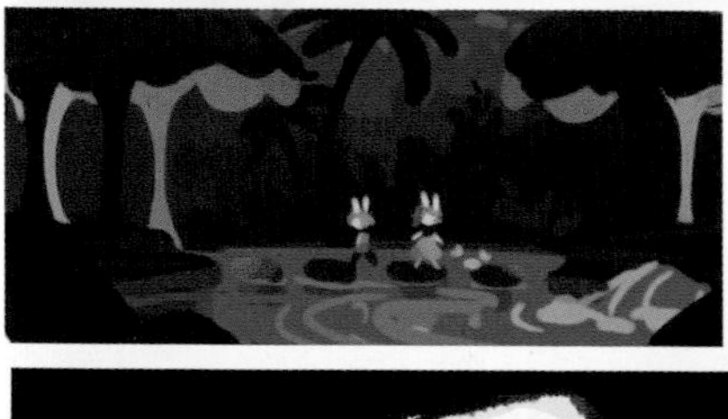
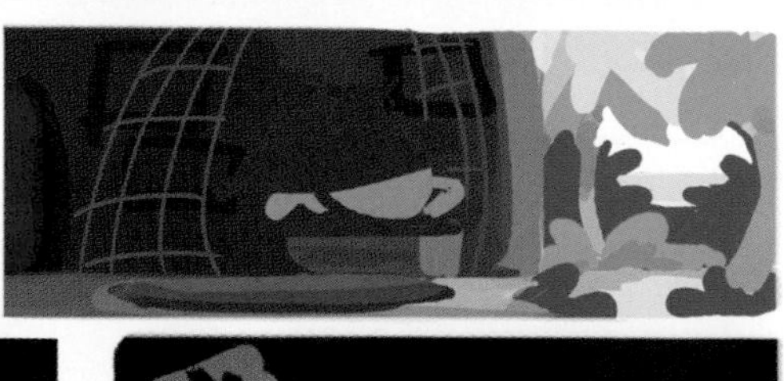
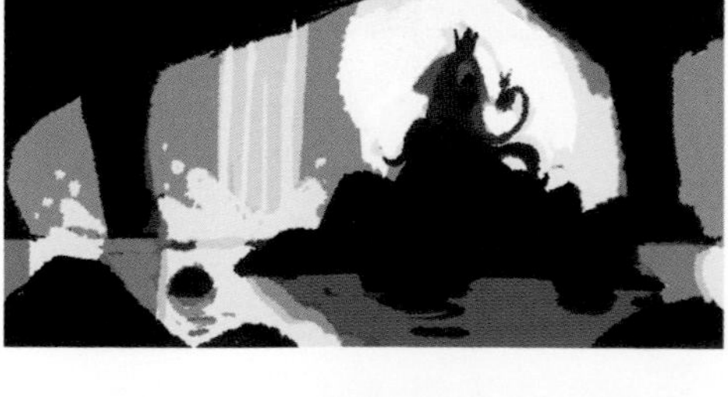
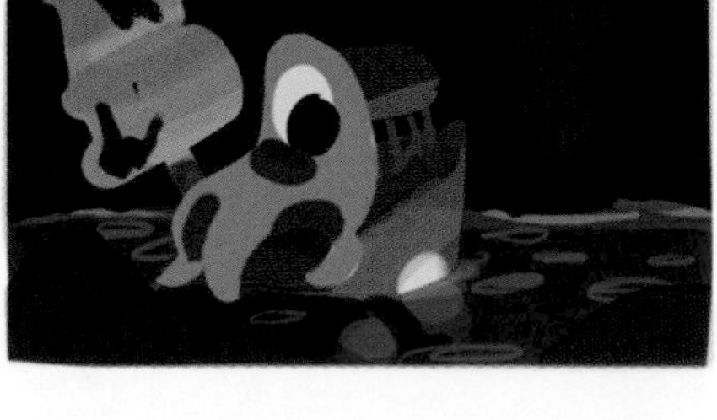

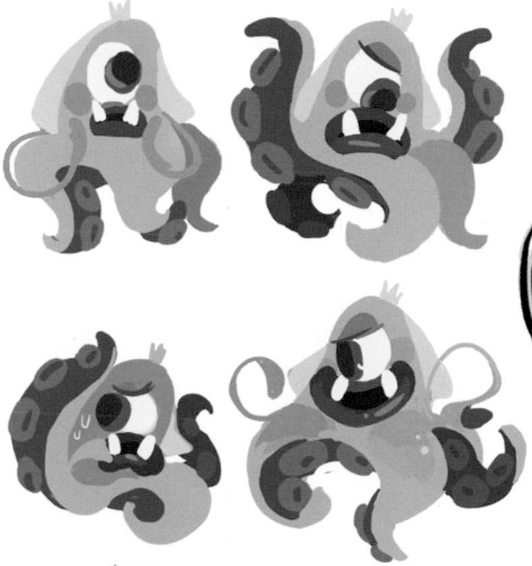

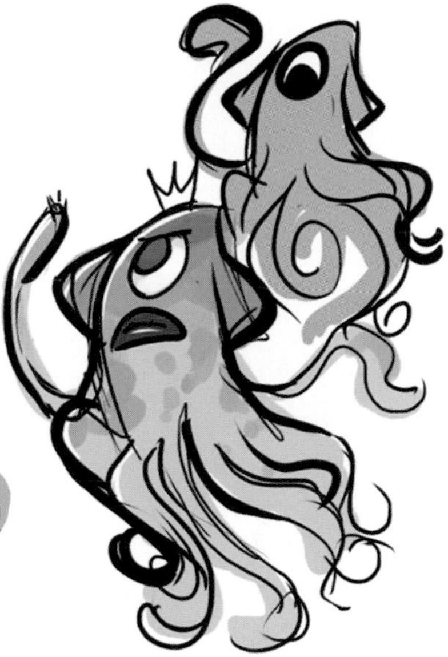

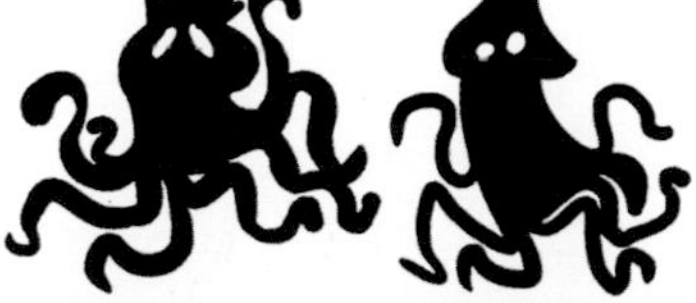

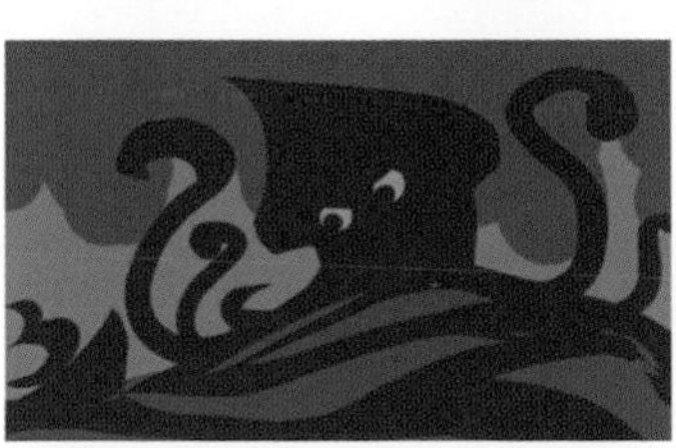

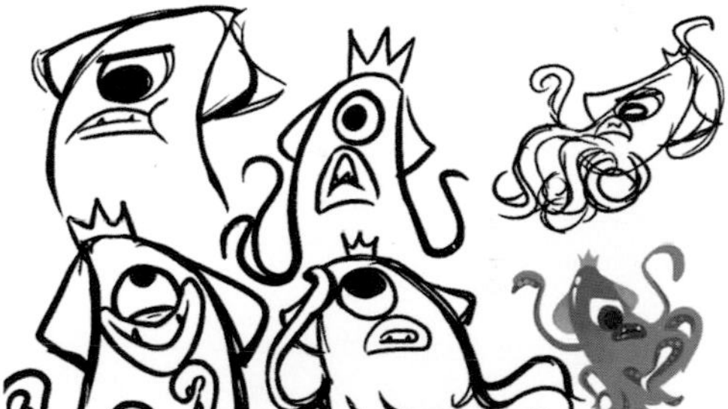

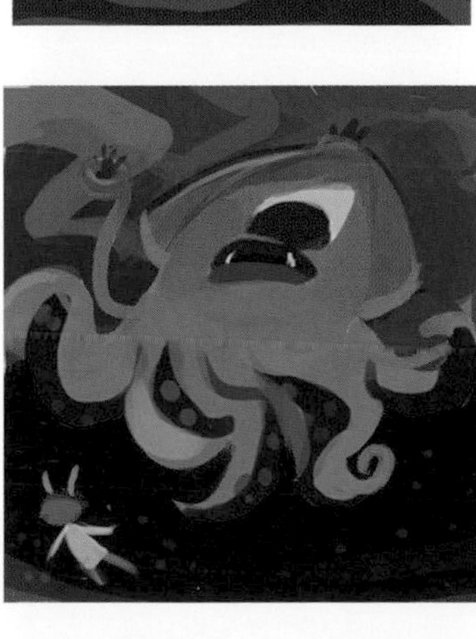

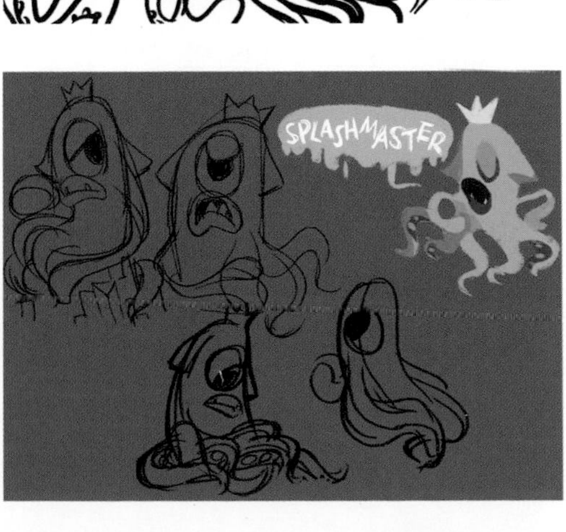
SPLASHMASTER

welcome to the
Ripple kingdom!

Greetings!

You may think you've seen everything
the Ripple Kingdom has to offer, but
you haven't had a proper tour yet.
If you're thinking about a vacation,
please allow me to be your guide!

Pack a swimsuit!

Make it cute, see?

Pack a camera!

For capturin' memories
and whatnot, see?

Pack sunscreen!

...Do bunny people
need this?

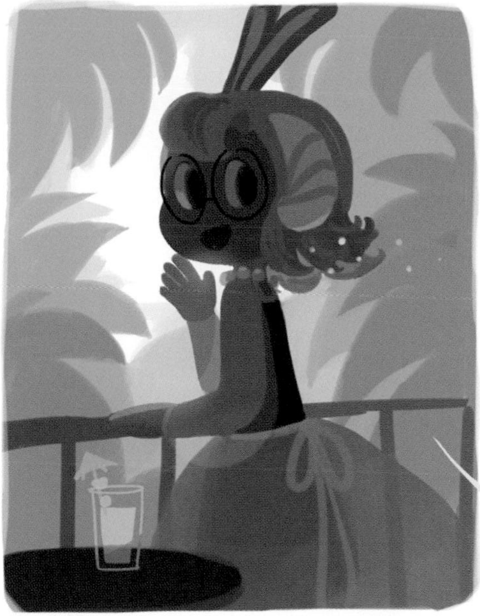

Think it's impossible for just anyone to get a room at the ultra-exclusive, extra-extravagant

Crabster Resort?

...Well, yeah, it kind of is. With its five-star service and gorgeous accommodations, it's no wonder every VIP in Dreamside stays there.

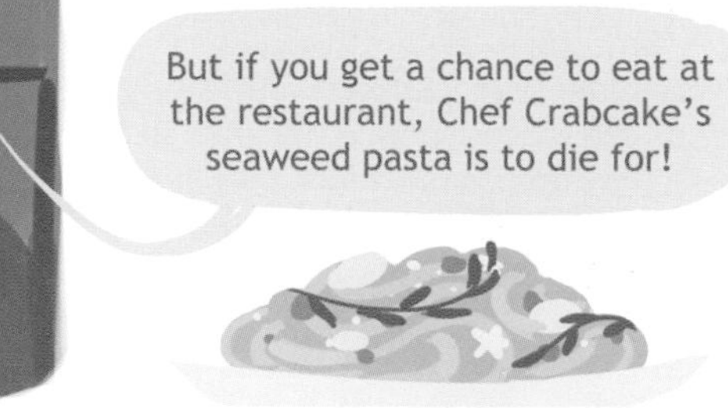
But if you get a chance to eat at the restaurant, Chef Crabcake's seaweed pasta is to die for!

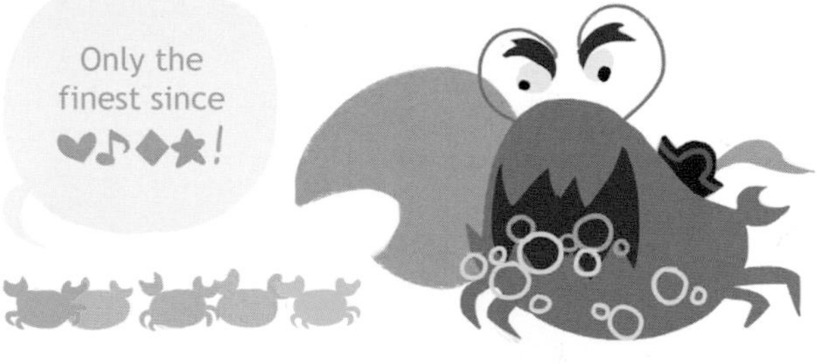
Only the finest since ♥♪◆★!

By the way...

Bubblebeard, who founded the resort twenty years ago, is an ex-pirate captain...which might explain why he runs such a tight ship.

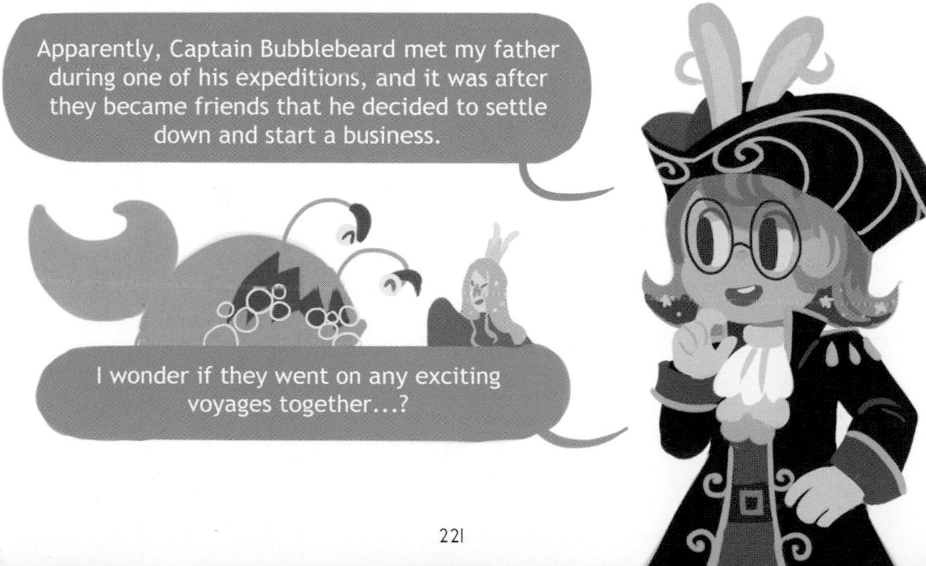
Apparently, Captain Bubblebeard met my father during one of his expeditions, and it was after they became friends that he decided to settle down and start a business.
I wonder if they went on any exciting voyages together...?

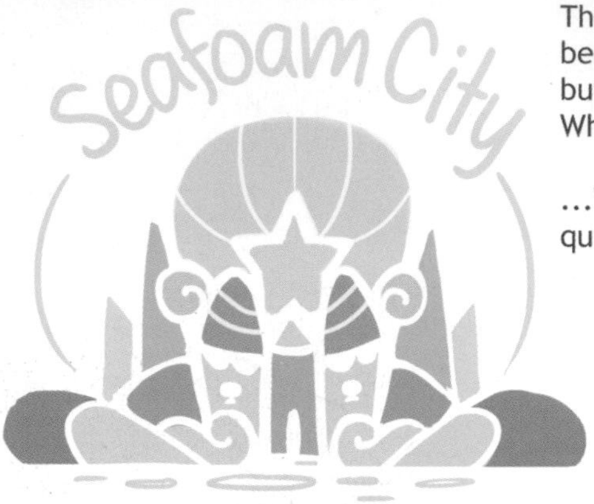
Seafoam City

The Ripple Kingdom's capital may have been wrecked by Splashmaster recently, but it's usually a beautiful, lively place. Why not see for yourself?

...What's that? How did it get repaired so quickly, you ask?

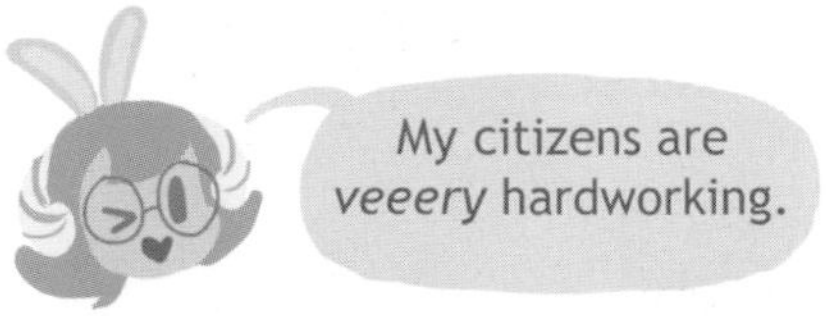
My citizens are *veeery* hardworking.

Did you know that Seafoam City is home to one of the largest magic libraries in the world? While it's not quite on par with Puffington's Academy, it still draws scholars from all over.

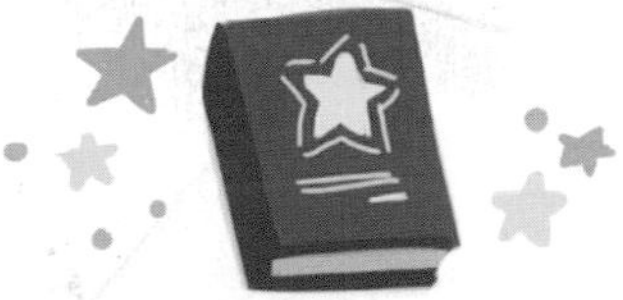

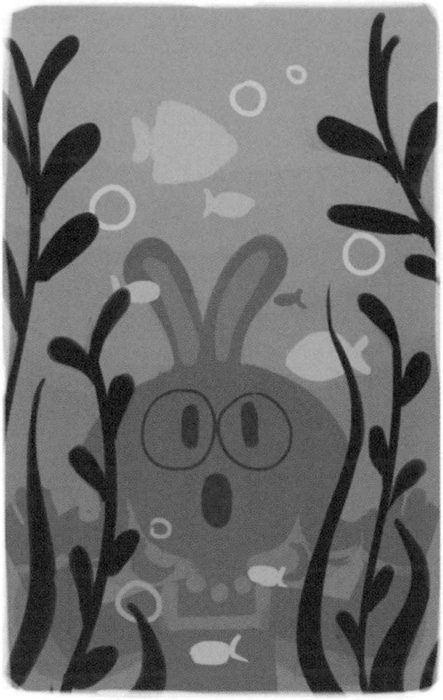

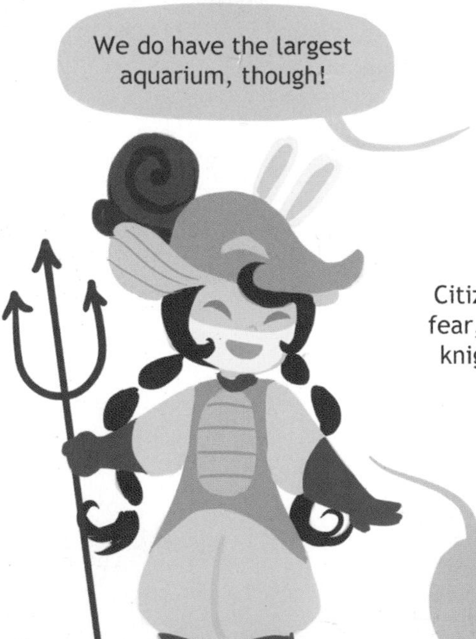
We do have the largest aquarium, though!

Citizens and tourists alike have nothing to fear, as King Kelp's fiercely loyal sea horse knights uphold peace on the city streets!

(...Okay, so maybe they weren't much help against Splashmaster, but they usually do a pretty good job. You should have seen them escorting people to safety!)

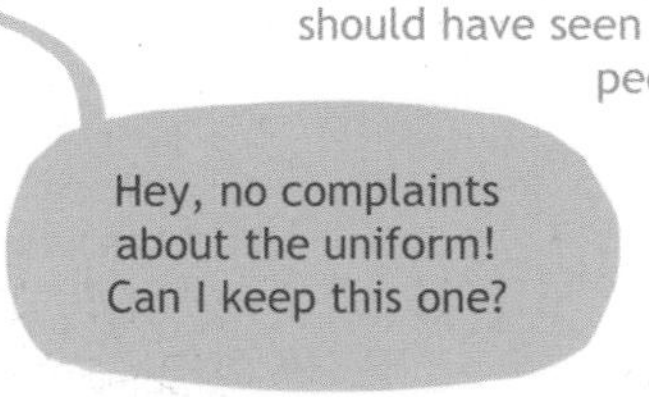
Hey, no complaints about the uniform! Can I keep this one?

Before you head home, be sure to stop by...

Seastar Lagoon

This stargazing spot, loved by romantic poets and philosophers for millennia, is one of Dreamside's top tourist attractions.

You already know this, but any wish made on a shooting star reflected in the lagoon's magical waters will be granted instantly. The chances of it happening are pretty low, but still...what would you wish for?

"Me ol' ship, good as new!"

"The safety of our darling Nautilus and her friends."

"Peace for every bro."

And my wish is for you to return to our kingdom very soon!

See you $again!$

Crrrrrk

crrk

crrrck

crrck

CRASH!!

OUF!

Well, hey!
Would you look
at that.

Cabbage? Is
zat you?

One and
only.

Mais, where **is**
zis place?!

What 'as
'appened
to us?!

Whoa-ho,
Chief!
Calmez-vous!

We're in the
dungeon.

Cordelia tossed us
in here after she
took over Caketown.

QUOI?!

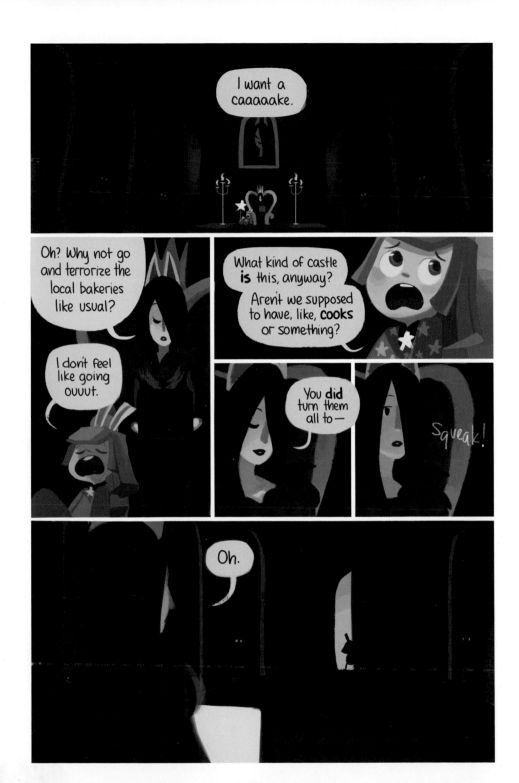

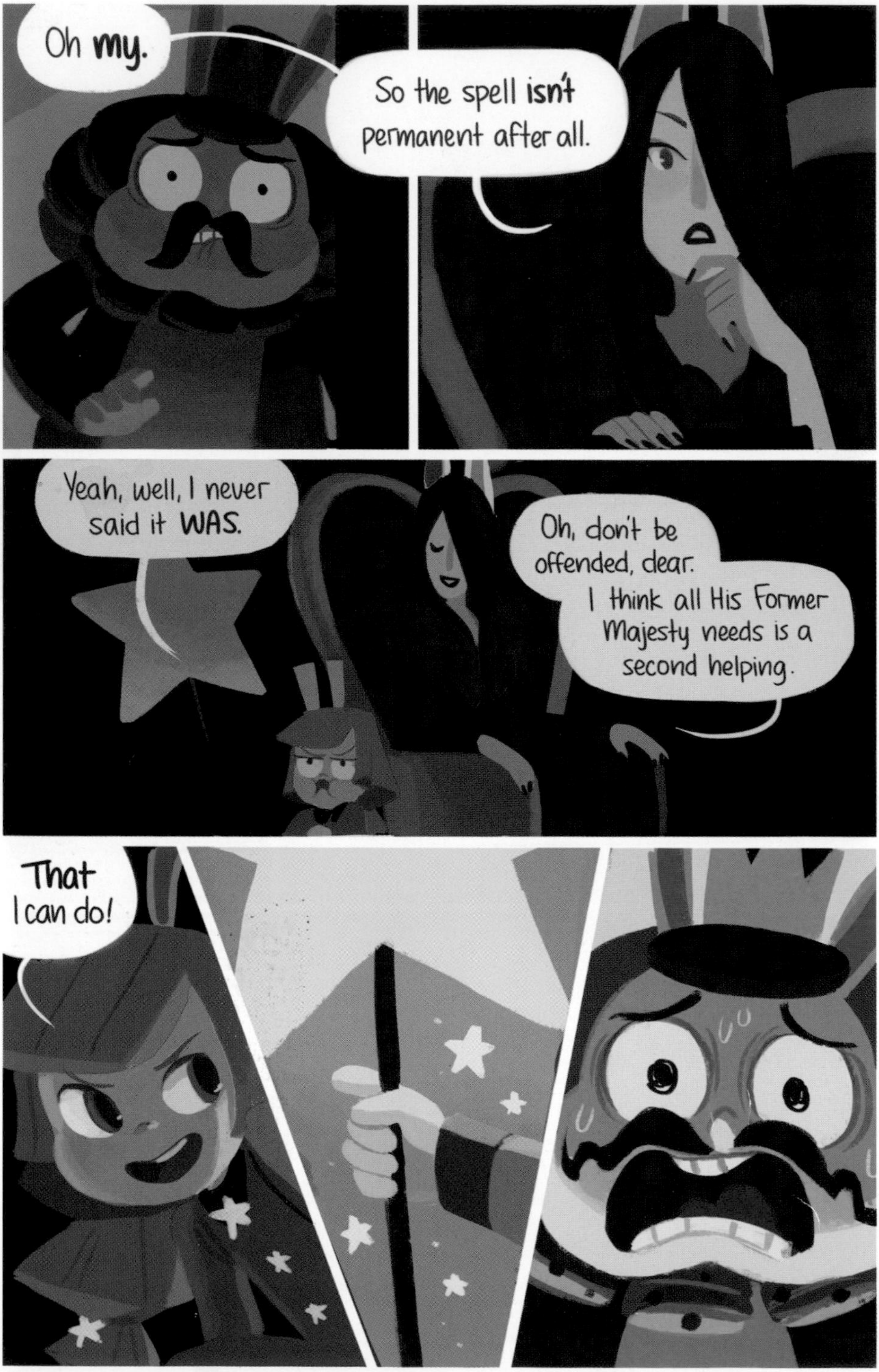
Oh my.
So the spell isn't permanent after all.
Yeah, well, I never said it WAS.
Oh, don't be offended, dear.
I think all His Former Majesty needs is a second helping.
That I can do!

Thank you for reading!

Seafoam City

Seastar Lagoon

The Ripple Kingdom

Shipwreck
Shelter

Coral Canyon

Bubblebeard
Beach

LIMBO

Crabster Resort

First Second

New York

Copyright © 2018 by Gigi D.G.

Published by First Second
First Second is an imprint of Roaring Brook Press, a division of
Holtzbrinck Publishing Holdings Limited Partnership
175 Fifth Avenue, New York, New York 10010

Library of Congress Control Number: 2017941161

Hardcover ISBN: 978-1-25015-982-3
Paperback ISBN: 978-1-62672-833-2

Our books may be purchased in bulk for promotional, educational,
or business use. Please contact your local bookseller or the Macmillan
Corporate and Premium Sales Department at (800) 221-7945 ext. 5442
or by e-mail at MacmillanSpecialMarkets@macmillan.com.

First edition 2018
Book design by Rob Steen

Cucumber Quest is created entirely in Photoshop.

Printed in China by RR Donnelley Asia Printing Solutions Ltd., Dongguan City, Guangdong Province.

Hardcover: 10 9 8 7 6 5 4 3 2 1
Paperback: 10 9 8 7 6 5 4 3 2 1